Men Cry

Alone

Also by Philip Paris

The Italian Chapel

Orkney's Italian Chapel: The True Story of an Icon

Nylon Kid of the North

Trouble Shooting for Printers

Men Cry

Alone

To Bryan

Best Wishes

Philip Paris

Philip Paris

Published 2012 by FeedARead Publishing

Photography and cover design by William Palmer.

Acknowledgements

My grateful thanks to all those who helped me in this journey of mine to gain an understanding of domestic abuse and dementia: the UK charities for abused men – ManKind Initiative, Abused Men In Scotland, Esteem; the various professionals in law, social work, police, psychiatric medical care and nursing home care, the church, the Rape and Abuse Line plus the men who told me their stories of abuse from previous partners. My thanks to Iain, Phyllis and Gale for proofreading text, and to those who provided quotes for the jacket – Erin Pizzey, Mark Brooks, Susan Brown and Alzheimer Scotland. And my everlasting gratitude to my wife Catherine for her love, support and encouragement.

One in four women and one in six men
will suffer domestic abuse.

Home Office, British Crime Survey 2010/11

Chapter One

Alfred had been a barber for nearly sixty years. He had cut some men's hair for the whole of that time and had marked the passage of their lives from the top of their head; watched them change into young men wanting a style to attract the girls, then later needing something suitable for a bridegroom; seen them become proud fathers and, with their crowns increasingly bare, even prouder grandfathers. Longstanding customers — friends in a strange way — came often to the little shop, even if there was in reality nothing left to trim.

But in all those decades he had never been asked to do something like this, and as he trudged along the street he thought his heart would break. Alfred felt the weariness of every one of his seventy-seven years more than he had ever done. He prayed silently for the strength to get through the task ahead with courage, and not to let down Ben, who faced great suffering with extraordinary bravery.

Poor wee mite. Why did these horrible things happen to such nice families?

Ben's father, David, was a regular and had first brought his son to the shop when he was only four. The boy had been so excited that the old barber was still smiling when he had returned home to Enid in the evening. Now Ben was expected to live for just a few weeks; one of those terrible disorders of the blood.

It was early December and Alfred clutched the lapels of his coat tightly in an attempt to keep out the fingers of icy wind that were feeling their way through the canary yellow scarf, which his wife had tied around his neck before he had left. The business was closed for the day. There was no way he could chat to customers, recounting the stories and jokes that he was famous for locally. Not today. As he walked up to the house, he wondered if he could ever again make someone laugh.

The front door was opened by David; a good man, only thirty-two. Alfred remembered him as a child being brought in by his own father. They shook hands, hanging on for a while, drawing strength and comfort from physical contact with another person.

'Thank you for coming, Mr Alfred.'

David had called him this as a youngster, a combination of friendliness plus respect and the name had stuck, even in adulthood. Now his son used the same form of address.

'Ben's upstairs with Jessica.'

'How is she?'

Alfred had met his wife only once. Women rarely entered the domain of his traditional gentlemen's shop, which clung to a bygone era of masculinity with no thought or concern for political correctness.

'She's holding on, but I think ... when it's all over ...'

'I know lad. I know,' he said, patting him on the shoulder as he walked into the hallway.

Never having been in the house before, he let the other man lead the way. He thought David was also 'holding on' and suspected he would crumble when their only child was gone. The couple had tried so hard to have a baby that it made the illness seem all the more cruel and unfair.

Ben was in bed, Jessica sitting beside him. They were surrounded by tractors. There were pictures of them all over the duvet cover, as well as soft and hard toy tractors of every size and colour and a large picture on one wall, showing a 1955 Ferguson.

'Hello, Mr Alfred.'

He was so thin.

'Hello, Little Ben.'

Alfred often joked with him that there was a man called Big Ben, who lived in the clock tower in London and used a gigantic hammer to strike the famous bell that told everyone in the entire world the correct time.

'How are you today?'

'I'm okay. Mummy says I can have ice cream for lunch.'

'Ice cream! Wow. I had ice cream once. It was in 1958. There was only one flavour in those days ... Brussel sprout.'

The boy grinned.

'It wasn't Brussel sprout.'

'Oh, maybe it wasn't.'

'You can stay for lunch if you want,' he said, his voice high and squeaky, weak.

Alfred began to suspect he was making an enormous effort for this visit. But it had been Ben who had wanted him to come, insisted on it until his parents had relented and made the unusual request.

'Well, let's cut that hair first, shall we?'

Jessica stood up.

'I'll leave you men to it,' she said, laying a hand gently on the old man's arm before leaving the room.

David propped up his son with pillows, while Alfred took off his cap, scarf and coat then brought out his scissors, comb and gown, the latter having been washed thoroughly by Enid the previous evening. He tucked in the gown around Ben, spreading out the material on the bed so that his head looked as though it was sticking out of a sea of perfectly still, deep blue water. He made a great fuss of cutting his hair, though there wasn't much.

'Did you know I've sharpened my scissors especially for this occasion?'

'Goodness, they've not been sharpened since I was a small lad,' said David, who was standing by the window. 'You're

3

honoured indeed, son.'

'Now that's got to be an exaggeration. I'm sure I did them about twenty years ago ... or perhaps it was a bit longer, when the King was on the throne.'

Ben remained quiet so the two men kept up the banter. They managed to make him smile at times, particularly when Alfred did his impersonation of Shirley Temple singing 'On the Good Ship Lollipop'. It was better than listening to the clicking of scissors in silence.

'There. How does that look, sir?'

From the bedside table Alfred had picked up a small mirror that he guessed had been left for this very purpose. The boy examined himself, as he had seen his father and other men do. In different circumstances it would have been a comical mime.

'Thank you, Mr Alfred. Now I'll be smart when I meet God.'

It was too much. David turned his back to face out of the window, while tears rolled down Alfred's cheeks and fell on to the image of a tiny green tractor. He tried not to let his voice crack when he spoke.

'Well ... you remind God that I'll be seeing Him soon, and I'll want to know what Little Ben has been up to.'

Ben didn't notice he was crying. He was tiring, sinking back into the soft comfort of the pillows.

'Will you cut hair in heaven?'

This time the barber couldn't answer. He put down the mirror and carefully removed the gown. Then he sat on the bed and with great tenderness stroked the boy's hair with his hand, the indentation of the scissors still visible on the thumb, until Ben had fallen asleep.

When Alfred walked through the front door Enid put her arms around him and hugged tightly. They had both been dreading this task of his.

'Was it really awful, love?' she asked, full of concern.

They held each other for a long time before he answered. After fifty-six years of marriage, she understood more clearly from his silence how he had been affected than if he had burst out sobbing.

'I'm sure David and Jessica were both very grateful for all you've done.'

'Little Ben said he wanted to look smart when he met God. I couldn't hold back the tears.'

'Oh, Alfred.' Enid felt her own eyes moisten, although she had never met any of the family. 'Come into the kitchen and get warm. You're half-frozen. I'll make a pot of tea. Do you want something to eat?'

'I don't think I could.'

'You've not eaten all day,' she said, helping him take off his coat.

'Perhaps we'll have supper early,' he said, walking along the corridor.

He sat at the kitchen table and watched her moving around, putting water in the kettle, lighting the gas on the ring. Enid was a small woman, her greying hair tied tightly in a bun, a defiant protest against the convention of a 'perm and set'. When loose, it reached almost halfway down her back and he always maintained it was the best hair he had ever felt, though Alfred would never suggest cutting it himself.

He had loved this woman since they had first met at a barn dance in the local church hall, when he was a gangly lad of seventeen, all awkwardness and embarrassment, just beginning his apprenticeship. She had been a beauty and still was in his eyes. During all those years he had never desired or had feelings for any other woman, and he would do everything within his ability to care for her.

The couple relaxed as they chatted and drank their tea, comfortable in each other's company. They had brought up a daughter, Kate, and helped with two grandchildren. All of them were coming for lunch on Christmas day.

Alfred's life revolved around his family and the barber's shop. People often asked when he was going to retire, but he loved everything about it: meeting customers, making them laugh, hearing their tales. Enid had always supported this passion, sending him off in the morning with his packed lunch, wrapping him up on cold days, making sure the fire was lit for his return each afternoon. He didn't work late and took Thursdays off. The lifestyle suited them both and so he carried on while he could.

They shared a wicked sense of humour and even during the hardest times had always seen the funny side of life, laughing their way to come out the other side still smiling. Enid loved to hear him recount stories in the evenings about the various men who had called at the shop. Her husband never seemed to have an uneventful day.

As they walked into the living room a short while later, Alfred was saying:

'I can't decide whether to contact David or leave it for him to let me know of any news.'

'David?'

'David and Jessica, love ... whether to contact them about Ben.'

'Ben? What's wrong with him?'

'But you know. I went to see him this morning at home.'

'This morning? Why didn't you tell me you had gone to someone's house?'

She was becoming angry and he was becoming frightened.

'Don't, love. You remember how I told you about Ben dying.'

'Dying? You told me no such thing. Why are you making up such a dreadful lie? You're being cruel to me, and I'm not having it.'

'Don't upset yourself, love. You're just tired. Let's sit together by the fire.'

When she lashed out, Enid had no concern about hurting him or fear of harming herself, no recollection that she was a grandmother of seventy-five with an arthritic hip, or that she had loved this man since seeing him across the dance floor when she was only fifteen.

Alfred was a fraction too slow to react and her fist caught him just below his left eye. He staggered back for two steps and then tripped, his legs no longer agile enough to keep him balanced. His fall was broken by the settee, which he landed on before rolling on to the floor.

A similar incident had occurred the previous month when she had pushed him over. On that occasion he tried to get up straight away and Enid had laid into him with fists and feet. Half an hour later, she had no memory of the event and had fussed over him for the rest of the week. Alfred pretended to have fallen and made as light of his injuries as possible, but his world was crushed, and he had been forced to close the business for several days in a state of absolute shock. He had told no one of the real reason. What happened between a man and wife was between them and God.

This time he remained lying down, which put him out of range of her fists and gave him both hands free to fend off her kicks. The first blow was wild, hitting him on the arm. He ignored it, although knew there would be an ugly yellow bruise that would take ages to fade.

The next kick was aimed at his head and he was ready for it, catching her foot and taking out almost all of the momentum, so that the tip of her shoe caught his lip with only a glance. He tasted blood, but hung on grimly.

Now Enid was the one caught off guard. There wasn't any furniture near enough for her to reach to keep balanced, which made her even more livid. She screamed abuse; terrible words that he couldn't believe were being uttered by this gentle woman whom he cared so much about.

7

'Stop it!' he shouted. 'Stop it!'

She was beyond understanding and struggled wildly to free her foot with the unbridled energy of someone who was deranged, while he hung on with the strength given to him by love. People in the street walked past their gate and the family next door finished their apple pie while listening to the one o'clock news, with no knowledge of the tragic scene being played out close by.

The elderly couple struggled, cursed and pleaded. Alfred could easily have tipped her over, but she could have hurt herself in the fall, hit her head on the dresser behind. He couldn't risk it, so tried another tack.

'I love you. I love you.'

It was no use. There was nothing to connect with. At that moment Enid had no idea of the identity of the man she was trying to injure, or why she should want to do such a thing.

Then her shoe came off. They were both taken by surprise and looked at each other quite bewildered, uncertain of what to do. Alfred moved first, throwing the shoe above the settee where it fell out of sight and reach.

Somehow the action seemed to break the spell and his wife simply limped out of the room. Alfred got up quickly, so that if she suddenly came back he was either more ready to defend himself, or could try to pretend nothing had happened.

He was sitting in the armchair when Enid entered about twenty minutes later. She was wearing slippers. Later on, when he could do so without her noticing, he would put her shoes in their normal place by the front door.

A few months earlier, when he had first noticed her forgetfulness, Alfred had decided that the best course of action was to present a face of normality, both to her and the world outside. He felt certain this was the wisest thing. Even in his darkest moments, he couldn't bring himself to acknowledge the word 'dementia'.

'Are you alright, love?' she said. 'You look very pale.'

His legs felt like jelly and his cheek was tender to touch, but she appeared to have no after-effects from the fight, nor memory of what had occurred.

'Yes, love, just a bit tired. I think I'll lie down for a while.'

'You go up to bed and I'll bring you a hot water bottle,' she said full of concern. 'It's really turned very chilly.'

Chapter Two

Tom's hand shook as he tried to switch on his mobile. He was six feet tall, more than fourteen stone and even at thirty-six considered to be one of the toughest players on the local rugby pitch. But he had just fled in terror from his wife and locked himself in the bathroom. He could hear her outside, mocking him, tapping on the door with the blade of the carving knife with which she had chased him up the stairs.

As she was outside the bathroom that meant Amy was safe in her bedroom further along the corridor. If Tom had thought their seven-year old daughter was in danger he would have been out like a bullet, regardless of whether Gemma had a weapon. But the violence had always been directed solely towards him.

How have I been reduced to this? How can I be so weak?

He dialled 999 ... and hesitated. It was shame and humiliation that prevented his finger from pressing the green button. For more than two years he had kept the abuse secret, a private matter that was no one else's business. The black eyes and bruises had been easy to blame on the sport he loved and nobody suspected the real cause, he was sure of it. But a couple of months earlier the situation had taken a new, sinister, turn when Gemma had attacked him during the night with a cricket bat.

He had forgotten they even had the thing, but she had obviously been hunting around the house for a suitable implement to hit him with while he slept. She had gone for his legs. Fortunately, the wood had made contact with the thick muscle in his calf, rather than his shin, and after the first blow he had recovered sufficient wits to roll across the bed, out of reach. When he had wrestled the bat from her she had burst into tears, saying it was all because of a terrible nightmare and promised such an incident would never happen again. But then she often said this after an 'accident'.

Since that night Tom hadn't slept properly and felt so weary he was beginning to find it difficult to think straight during the daytime. Even if his wife got up to go to the toilet, he would lie for hours afterwards, making sure she really had gone back to sleep.

Tom was still looking at the mobile in his hand, the number on the display reading 999. He was no coward, but he wasn't bloody Rambo either. He knew nothing of martial arts or how to disarm someone safely so that neither person was likely to be hurt. The tapping had stopped. He listened intently then called out Gemma's name just loud enough for her to hear if she was the other side of the door. There was no reply. Had she gone to their daughter's room? It was too much of a risk.

He pressed the green button.

That decision would change his life forever.

'Do you require police, ambulance or fire brigade?' asked the man who answered.

'Police.'

Tom had never rung the emergency services before and didn't know quite what to expect. He was put through to another operator.

'Police emergency,' said a female voice. 'May I take your contact details?'

Tom gave the woman his address and telephone number.

'What is the problem?' she continued.

'My wife ...'

'Yes, sir.'

'She has tried to hurt me.'

'Are you hurt?'

11

'No.'

'What assistance do you need, sir?'

What should he say?

'My wife has chased after me. I'm locked in the bathroom and am worried about my daughter.'

'Are they both in the house?'

'Yes.'

'Has your daughter been hurt?

'No.'

'Does anyone in the house need medical help?'

'No.'

It sounded as if he was ringing for nothing.

'Is someone in the house in danger?'

'I believe so.'

'The police are en route and will be with you as soon as possible. Do you need any other assistance?'

'No, thank you.'

The line went dead. It was done. What had been going on was no longer a secret.

The building was strangely silent and he wondered if he should risk unlocking the door to check on Amy. But if the police were on their way perhaps they would arrive soon. He decided to hang on, but the wait was torment.

The doorbell didn't ring, but about fifteen minutes later Tom could hear voices downstairs. He realised Gemma must have heard him make the call. She had been outside the bathroom after all, listening, then had gone quietly downstairs to open the front door. That meant she was speaking to the police first.

Tom hurried to the kitchen, from where he could hear people talking, and burst into the room. It was the worst impression he could possibly have made. The two policemen, one about fifty and a young lad in his early twenties, turned instantly towards him, ready for trouble. Gemma was crying and gave a small shout of alarm before rushing to the other side of the table.

Why was she crying?

For a moment Tom simply didn't know what to say.

'Just calm down, sir. There's no need for any further violence. It never solves anything.'

It was the older of the two policemen speaking.

Violence?

Tom felt muddled, his mind working like treacle.

They think he was the aggressive one.

'It's not me. It's her. She's the one ... always beating me.'

It wasn't so much the expressions of disbelief that stung him to the core, but rather their look of disgust. Tom felt he was an honourable man, living by what many would consider to be an old-fashioned code of conduct, instilled into him by his rather severe father, and he could see how his statement appeared. He was bigger than either of the policemen and his wife was barely eight stone. On the surface, it was a ludicrous comment.

But they didn't know how she used a weapon that he had no defence against ... surprise. Creeping up to hit him on the head as he watched television, throwing something at him when he least expected it, attacking him while he slept. How could he explain such things to them in a believable way? He suspected, feared, that the men had already made up their minds.

Suddenly, Gemma rushed across the room and for an instant Tom thought she was going to assault him right there, in front of the police. It would almost have been a relief for such a thing to happen in front of witnesses.

'My darling.'

He hadn't realised Amy had come downstairs and was standing behind him in her pyjamas, bewildered at being confronted with the strange scene in the kitchen, made worse by just waking up. Gemma skirted around Tom, grabbed their daughter and pulled her towards the other end of the kitchen.

'Daddy?'

Before she could utter another word, Gemma smothered the

girl so fiercely in a hug that she couldn't speak.

'Don't worry, darling. You're safe now. Daddy won't hurt you.'

Him hurt her?

'Me hurt her?' said Tom, expressing his thoughts verbally. 'Me?'

He was becoming angry. It was exactly what Gemma had expected ... what she wanted. The two policemen moved on either side of him.

'It's not me! It's her!'

Tom was shouting now. Everything he did was making the situation worse for himself.

'Come along, sir. Let's talk about all of this calmly at the station.'

'You're taking me away? It should be her.'

Part of Tom thought this couldn't really be happening. He was in his own house and about to be forcibly removed for doing nothing more than raising his voice, while he had been kicked, slapped and scratched, or hit with pans or thrown objects and had never told anyone before this evening.

Gemma was kneeling on the floor, holding Amy, who was squirming to be free. No one else could see her face except Tom and for a moment their eyes locked. She gave a small smile of triumph.

This had been planned all along. How could he have been such a fool?

The seriousness of the situation hit him with such impact that it seemed as though his body was collapsing in upon himself so that he felt dizzy and weak, with barely the strength to stay upright. The police thought he was a danger to his wife and child. He worshipped his little girl and he still loved Gemma. They had had some tremendous times together and if it wasn't for her strange temper, her need to punish and control, he was sure they could have a great life.

14

The young officer clasped a hand firmly on his arm. Tom looked at him pleadingly.

'It's not me,' he whispered in despair.

He knew they didn't believe a single word he spoke, but he didn't realise just how much his nightmare had taken on a new dimension.

Chapter Three

Gordon's head, resting on Tania's left breast, rose and fell gently with her breathing. They were lying on the settee while she watched a cookery programme. She spent a large part of most days watching television, following the leading chefs and their demonstrations almost obsessively. It seemed to him there was always someone promoting a new way of eating healthily or dieting, showing how to create easily a scrumptious meal in less than ten minutes, how to feed a hungry family of five with two eggs and a cabbage.

He had little interest and was happy to have his back towards the set in the corner of the sitting room. Lying like this, nestling into the curves of Tania's body, was what he enjoyed most. He hugged her tightly and she stroked his hair. Relaxing his arms again he let his mind wander and it drifted back, as it still did at moments like this, to that morning shortly before his eighth birthday.

His parents had closed the kitchen door, a clear sign they were going to discuss a subject that small boys were not meant to overhear. He thought it might be to do with presents, so had crept along the corridor. Even at that age he had felt that these private conversations, when he had occasionally listened, were not really discussions, but rather opportunities for his father to further dictate to his mother what she was allowed to do. Gordon picked up the end of a sentence, the Scottish accent coming clearly though the door.

'... stop all this mollycoddling.'

'No. It's not right, Angus. He's only seven.'

Her voice was raised, which scared Gordon far more than if it had been his father's. Such a response was tantamount to a rebellion. It must be extremely serious for her to answer like that.

'I'm not having him growing up to be queer and that's what's going to happen if you carry on the way you are, Margaret. You're too affectionate. He needs to be toughened up. You're doing him no good. I hope you're listening to me. You know what I say is always for the best.'

Gordon didn't catch any reply and after a while he heard weeping. His mother was the gentlest soul in the world, but she was stoical almost to the point of martyrdom and it was rare indeed for her to cry. The sound made him lose his nerve and he slipped back quietly to his bedroom. It was such an odd bit of conversation that he couldn't make any sense of it. Who was getting too much affection? Why would this make them queer?

That evening, for the first time, Gordon had to sort himself out when it came to having his bath and there was no bedtime story. There wasn't even a goodnight cuddle. He had changed into his pyjamas and climbed into bed as normal, then simply been left alone to go to sleep.

However, it was the next day that he was confronted with the greatest shock. He had managed to poke himself in the eye with a toy. It wasn't anything really, but he burst into tears and ran to the kitchen where he knew his mother was making lunch and flung his arms around her waist.

After a short while, when he had quietened down, he realised that she hadn't hugged him. There were no words of comfort. Gordon had pulled back and looked up at her, mystified. She was standing ramrod straight with her arms by her sides, staring above his head at the wall behind him, her dear, kind face a mask of conflicting emotions that made no sense.

From that day, she had never again had any physical contact with him. It was as if she had decided it was all or nothing and even a hand on a stick-like arm was too much. Although he didn't realise, his world had changed forever, and the direction of his life set upon on a course that would invite disaster, pain and despair.

Apart from kissing a visiting aunt on the cheek, or shaking someone's hand at Christmas, Gordon had not touched another human being for years. At school he avoided contact sports, which he hated and was useless at, while the idea of a girlfriend was so unlikely that he never considered it. The occasional punch from one of the local thugs was almost written up in his diary as a high point. They had at least acknowledged that he existed.

When he was seventeen he began to understand how his father's phobia of homosexuals was linked to that childish incident, so long ago. One day around this time he broached the subject with his mother when they happened to be alone. It was a rare event as his father always tried to prevent this from happening. The conversation was not an easy one as such subjects were simply never referred to.

However, after they had spoken Gordon began to appreciate that, although this strange change to family life had been very hard for him, enforcing such unnatural behaviour had been incredibly difficult for his mother. A door had been so firmly bolted shut between them, it could never be reopened.

Gordon met Tania when he was twenty and his world altered completely. She had been hugely affectionate and he brushed aside the hurtful things she said or did. She was his first girlfriend while he was the 'only person who had ever understood her'. There had followed a whirlwind romance, engagement and marriage in little over a year.

But the immense sense of loss he had felt at the age of seven was always hovering around somewhere in his subconscious, so he hugged Tania tightly again, while a voice behind him talked of oven temperatures and cooking times. She ruffled his hair absent-mindedly and he smiled, though she couldn't see it.

Eventually, the theme music for the programme filled the room and she turned off the television using the nearby remote.

'Was it interesting?' he asked, without looking up.

'Yes,' she replied, stretching her arms towards the ceiling.

Gordon had never known her to create a meal that she had seen demonstrated by one of these famous chefs, yet he never pointed this out. There was a small library of cookery books in the dining room and she normally picked a recipe from one of three particular, rather grubby, titles, although much of what they ate came as ready-meals from the local Marks & Spencer.

'What do you want to do tomorrow?' he asked.

'I don't know.'

His wife would never propose doing anything, apart from having people around for a party.

'We could drive over to Amberdale Water and perhaps walk around a bit of it.'

The latter option was extremely unlikely as Tania hated walking. Gordon knew that what they would do is drive there to admire the scenery and birds, then he would suggest a short walk and she would say she didn't have the right shoes. So they would come home again. It was like a scene from a play repeated at regular performances, but he didn't have the strength to rewrite the script by suggesting she put some suitable footwear in the car before leaving.

'We'll see tomorrow,' she said.

This was another scene. Tania never said 'yes' to anything straight away. He would plant an idea then they would come back to it later on. That was how things worked between them. Often the opportunity was lost. If they were in the car and passing near to a friend's house, he would normally suggest they should call on the off-chance they might be in. She would automatically reply 'no'; a reflex action with no thought behind it, then when they were several miles further on, and it was too late, she would say 'well, we could call in I suppose'.

'Amberdale is such a beautiful loch,' he said, keen to get out somewhere that Sunday. He hated being inside too much.

When Tania pushed him off the settee it was so totally unexpected, and with such a sudden force, that his head only missed the empty wine glass by chance. Then she was on her feet, pointing at him with a quivering finger as he lay on the carpet, her nostrils flaring in rage.

'Don't ... you ... call ... it ... a ... loch. It's a lake!'

Stupid. Stupid. Stupid. Why did I call it a loch?

'Sorry,' he said, lifting his head and raising one hand in the air in a gesture of submission. 'It's just a word I've picked up over the years from my dad.'

'But you're not Scottish. You've never lived there. You don't call it a loch, YOU CALL IT A LAKE!' she screamed before storming out, slamming the door behind her.

He flopped back on to the carpet, laying one arm across his eyes and feeling utterly drained.

Stupid. Stupid.

Before initiating any conversation with her Gordon would always try to analyse what he was planning to say, whether in fact he should say anything, when he should speak and how he should do it. In this way, he generally managed to avoid igniting her temper, though he didn't always succeed. It was the everyday conversations that tripped him up. He wasn't fast enough in thinking through his answers to ensure he didn't imply the wrong thing. On many occasions his mistake was never made clear to him.

He curled up on the carpet. It was inconceivable to him how, in the brief moment it took to utter one syllable, a person could change from having an everyday chat about where to visit for a couple of hours to completely losing control.

I'll make a list of words that I mustn't use, write them in the back of my diary. I'll forget otherwise. I'm too stupid.

If any of his friends could see him now they would have been puzzled and shocked, horrified at the sight of a twenty-eight-year-old man lying in a foetal position on his sitting room floor, trying to identify what words he mustn't use in front of his wife. But Gordon no longer considered it unusual. He had ended up like this so often during the latter half of their marriage that it seemed normal.

Tania was in the kitchen. He could hear her. She would be drinking and smoking; activities carried out with great enthusiasm. He found the whole concept of smoking repulsive. When they had been courting she had stopped in response to his requests, but she had restarted only days after their honeymoon. It was for her 'nerves'. Another woman at the office was giving her a hard time. Wherever she was employed, there was someone giving Tania a hard time.

She hadn't actually worked at all for the last three years. But she was very good, because he was so against the habit she never did it upstairs. Not once. He couldn't fault her for that. Really, he was very lucky.

Gordon was too much like his mother; mortified at the prospect of conflict or confrontation. Tania was always telling him he should stand up to people; a rather ironic comment when you considered who was making it.

He decided to lie quietly on the floor. It was mid-afternoon, so she would soon be going for her afternoon sleep, probably when the cigarette was finished. Tania nearly always slept during the day. Sometimes at weekends he would join her because he was so exhausted.

Today he would leave her alone. He would have to work out what words he shouldn't use in addition to 'loch'. It worried him that he couldn't think of any, as there must be plenty that weren't allowed.

Eventually, he heard her slow, heavy tread going up the stairs. That was good. She was merely tired. Gordon thought it might be best to do some tidying in the garden, so that he didn't disturb her. Afterwards she would be alright again, no doubt giving him a huge hug before making dinner then they would watch a film together. Everything would be fine. He just had to try harder and be more careful in future. That's all.

Chapter Four

Tom's evening was becoming surreal and yet at the same time everything that happened was ingrained into his unconscious, so that later he would relive the events repeatedly in minute detail. He pleaded with the policemen not to put handcuffs on him, but they were adamant.

'Health and safety regulations,' said the younger of the two. 'We can't transport you otherwise.'

However, he waited until they were in the hallway so Amy didn't witness her father's disgrace. The handcuffs were double-locked, so that they fitted tightly and allowed him very little movement. A few of the neighbours' curtains twitched across the road as he was put into the police car and his shame was so great it seemed to crush the very essence of him, everything he believed in and stood up for ... integrity, right and wrong, fair play.

The police station was bustling: drunks; youths trying to prove their toughness by shouting abuse at those who had arrested them; defeated men staring at the floor. Tom was forced to sit on a long wooden bench next to an old man singing 'We'll meet again' until it was his turn to be taken to stand in front of the charge bar, which was a huge desk that dominated the custody suite to which he had been brought.

'Remove his cuffs,' said the sergeant to the young policeman who had accompanied Tom to the station. 'What are the circumstances of this man being here?'

'I attended a call of domestic violence,' replied the policeman. 'Upon arrival this man's wife claimed to have been assaulted by him. He showed aggressive behaviour ...'

The sergeant was sitting at a computer further along the desk and was protected from attack by a thick glass panel. He was even bigger than Tom and studied him with an expression of loathing, as if he would quite like to take him around the back and dish out a taste of what it was like to be on the receiving end of punches from someone more powerful. Strong men who beat women were high on the sergeant's list of low-life species. However, he remained seated and keyed in the answers Tom gave in reply to questions about his name, where he lived, date of birth, occupation etc.

'You don't have to say anything unless you wish to do so, but anything you do say will be recorded and may be given in evidence,' said the sergeant, reading aloud the text that was on his monitor.

It almost seemed to Tom that he had accidentally walked on to the set of a television drama and had been mistaken for an actor. Somewhere there must be a cameraman and a sound technician.

'What's going to happen?' he asked.

'You're being detained while we investigate this matter further, in order to decide whether you should be arrested and a report sent to the Procurator Fiscal. If you are arrested, you will then either be bailed or held in custody until you appear in court. We can hold you in detention for up to twelve hours with the option to hold you for a further similar period if felt necessary. In a nutshell, you're going to be put in a cell for a while then you'll be interviewed sometime later this evening.'

The sergeant stood, picked up a set of forms and walked over to stand opposite Tom across the charge bar. He then began working through what turned out to be a long list of questions.

'Do you have any injuries?'

Tom considered this. He had some fading bruises, but decided not to acknowledge anything.

'No.'

'Have you used alcohol in the last twenty-four hours?'

'No.'

'Do you have any thoughts at present of self-harm or suicide?'

'No.'

'Do you have any dietary requirements ...?'

The questions went on and on so that in the end Tom wanted to bang his fists on the desk and scream 'NOOO!' However, he kept his composure while the remainder of the forms were completed.

'You have the right to have a solicitor informed of your detention. Do you wish a solicitor to be advised of your detention?'

Tom's head was spinning, but he was innocent and would fight his own corner, as he always had done.

'No,' he said eventually.

'You also have the right to a private consultation with a solicitor before being questioned by the police, and at any other time during questioning. Do you wish a private consultation with a solicitor before you are questioned?'

'No.'

'You have chosen not to have a solicitor informed of your detention, or to have a private consultation with a solicitor. Signing here in no way prevents you from changing your decision at a later time.'

The sergeant turned the sheet around and slid it across the desk so that Tom could sign where indicated.

'Do you wish to inform anyone of your whereabouts?'

Gemma knew where he was and Tom couldn't think of anyone else he wanted to know. As far as he was concerned the fewer people aware of his humiliation the better.

'No,' he replied, 'no one.'

'Empty your pockets,' said the sergeant.

Tom didn't have much, but laid out what he had on the desk.

'Remove your belt, shoe laces, watch and wedding ring.'

He did as instructed and the young policeman put on rubber gloves before searching him. His possessions were placed in a plastic wallet, which was sealed and put in a nearby locker. Tom's heart was pounding at the realisation that he was going to be taken to a cramped, locked room. In his confusion, he hadn't appreciated what was about to happen. Since childhood he had feared enclosed places and feelings of panic danced around the edges of his mind as he was led along the corridor.

The closeness of the entrances to the cells indicated their smallness. Every door had a toilet roll stuck on the handle, which looked slightly bizarre. The sergeant stopped and indicated a particular cell. Tom stood in the doorway, one hand on the frame while he surveyed the interior. The room contained a stainless steel toilet with no seat, one blanket and a thin mattress covered in blue plastic.

'I'm claustrophobic,' he said.

It was more of an apology for appearing to disobey the officer, rather than that he expected the man to do anything about it.

'Do you know I've done this job for ten years and almost every single person detained during that time has suffered from claustrophobia. You wouldn't believe there was so much of it about. In you go.'

Tom entered and was greeted by a faint smell of vomit and unwashed bodies. When the heavy metal door slammed shut he had to put a fist to his mouth to prevent himself from crying out. The ceiling contained two air vents, but apart from these and the entrance, it was a sealed container.

Little more than a coffin.

He paced back and forth. One section of the concrete floor was about three inches higher than the rest, just big enough for the mattress to fit on. His only options were to stand, sit on the edge of the toilet or lie down. Despite the efforts to remove sharp objects, previous occupants had scored messages on the walls and floor. He was surrounded by a mixture of obscene sentences, some not completed and many with words spelt incorrectly.

In an attempt to distract himself he tried to analyse the day's events. Gemma had lost her temper earlier that afternoon when he had reminded her there was a rugby match the next morning. The atmosphere had deteriorated rapidly. Although she hadn't attacked him her flashes of temper became worse as the hours passed: Why did she have so much of the housework to do? Why did he have to work so often? Was he having an affair? Why did she have to do the shopping by herself the next day, with Amy hanging on, whinging about having to walk around the supermarket?

How had he ended up here?

Tom was a proud man. From fairly humble beginnings he had worked his way up to the position of production director at a local manufacturing business, in charge of more than forty people. He was on numerous local committees, including the Rotary Club, and regularly helped to generate funds for various charities. What had he done wrong except raise his voice in the kitchen of his own home, whereas he had been chased up the stairs by someone clutching a carving knife, screaming that she was going to kill him?

But Tom could see how it looked to the two policemen who had brought him in. Just what had Gemma told them and perhaps more importantly, why? This strange ... punishing him if he didn't do what she wanted had become increasingly severe, until she was likely to throw a cup for nothing more than that she thought he hadn't cleared away properly.

The first incident to occur was when his wife had slapped his face for arriving late home one evening. She had prepared a nice meal and he wasn't there to eat it when she wanted. Gemma had immediately burst into tears, said that she had had a terrible day and was sorry. Of course, such a dreadful act would never ever happen again.

The impact of that slap was not her hand on his cheek, but rather that part of the foundations of his life shifted, so he felt unbalanced and no longer walked with the same certainty. Since then, every punch and scratch, each object hurled at him or used to hit him with, moved those foundations more out of alignment until at times he felt that he was staggering through life, increasingly losing his self-respect and sense of worth.

It was as though he was being ... rubbed out, as if he was no more than a pencil drawing on a scrap of paper, and bit by bit she was gradually erasing the person he used to be, then redrawing him to create a new character. He generally bowed to her wishes in an attempt to keep everything on an even keel, but this seemed to make the violence worse, the boundaries of what she could get away with being pushed outwards every time he caved in.

He had been raised never to hit a woman. As a lad, fights with other boys were part of growing up, but his father would have leathered him at the idea of lifting a hand to a girl. Such a cowardly, despicable action was beneath any real man. Tom could easily fend off Gemma's blows if he saw them coming and had, on several occasions, pinned her arms so that she couldn't move. She had always calmed down, eventually, and he would let her go.

Even before they were married she had revealed flashes of temper, but these incidents had always been over quickly, with never a hint of violence or what was to come in future years. The two of them used to have such great times together. Gemma was a stunning brunette and sex had been wild, even after Amy came along.

Tom thought of his daughter, who was the centre of his life. She was the one firm thing that he could rely on. As far as he knew Amy was unaware of this aggressive behaviour. Without making it obvious he had started to check Amy at bath time to make sure there were no bruises or marks that didn't match what one would expect from normal childhood accidents. He had never found anything and she hadn't commented about being hurt in any way.

However, now that he considered it again, perhaps Amy was not quite as happy as she used to be. Had she heard Gemma's screams, the sound of plates smashing against walls? Their daughter was bright and although the attacks always seemed to happen when she was in a different part of the house or outside, maybe he shouldn't assume his little girl was unaware of what was taking place around her. Though he always tried to hide it, the atmosphere on occasions was unbearable.

He didn't know what to do for the best. And what was going to happen to him? Would he be charged and have a criminal record? Tom didn't know if he could face the shame. It had only been concern for Amy that had made him call the police in the first place. And what was his wife saying, while he was held at the police station? Was she telling terrifying bedtime stories of Amy's evil father?

Tom could feel the walls of the cell moving inwards. He knew it was an illusion, but that didn't stop it appearing real. He considered calling out, but what good would that do? They weren't going to release him because he said he was frightened. For the first time in his life he was faced with a glimpse of the despair that could overcome someone in such a situation, and understood why the police removed any items that a person might use to harm themselves.

Gemma knew he would be terrified of being in a confined space. Surely it wasn't possible that she had engineered this to happen from the very beginning. Was this some new form of punishment?

She was breaking him into pieces and he was powerless to prevent it from happening.

He reconsidered the idea of asking for a solicitor to be present, but somehow involving such a person would seem like an admission of guilt. After all, he hadn't done anything wrong. With no clock or watch it was difficult to gauge how long he had been held, but after what seemed like an hour he was taken to be interviewed. He sat at a table opposite two young policemen, one of whom had put the handcuffs on him at the house.

The room was small. Cameras, mounted near the ceiling on two walls, were pointed directly at him and in the corner was a DVD system, which he assumed was for recording interviews. However, the officers ignored this and instead each had their notebooks in front of them on the table. One of the men said who he was and where the interview was taking place, then allowed the other officer to say who he was before Tom was asked to identify himself.

'You are going to be asked questions about an incident of domestic violence,' said the first policeman. 'You are not bound to answer, but if you do your answers will be noted and may be used in evidence. Do you understand?'

For the first time since arriving at the station Tom answered 'yes' to something.

'Earlier this evening your wife made an allegation against you of assault. Can you explain to us what happened at your home during the course of this evening, and any other relevant events that took place earlier today?'

Tom believed in telling the truth, but he had decided to be extremely cautious in what he revealed, and certainly wasn't going to be rushed into providing answers. So, now he knew that Gemma had accused him of assault. The fact that he had made the telephone call and had said in the kitchen that his wife was the one always beating him up appeared to have been ignored, at least for the moment.

However, two things held him back from explaining how

Gemma had chased him with a carving knife. Firstly, he realised that this would be a very serious claim, which would almost certainly result in her being detained for questioning at the station, just as he was being. Despite everything that had happened between them, he didn't wish this. Also, she would *never* forgive him for such an action, and there was a danger that this would be the catalyst for a new level of abuse.

The second reason he held back was shame. He felt so totally humiliated and to have these two young men writing down how his petite wife had been assaulting him for more than two years was more than he could own up to. It was hard enough to admit it to himself. Would he later on in the evening be the butt of jokes in the canteen? 'You should see the big guy in cell three, and the size of his wife! What a pathetic wimp.'

But he had to say something. Tom guessed that while he had been in the police station someone had been sent to interview Gemma. His instinct told him she wouldn't press charges; that this was some sort of new game being played out between them, and she wouldn't want him to actually be arrested. In which case, it would be a disaster for their relationship if he made a claim of assault against her, while she retracted what had been said when the police first arrived at the house. Then again, he could be totally wrong and was walking straight into a cleverly planned trap.

'We had an argument,' he said eventually. 'It wasn't about anything in particular, but we were both tired and overreacted. There was no physical violence on either side, just some shouting. Nothing more.'

'But you did make a call to the emergency services and claimed to the police officers who arrived on the premises that your wife had previously beaten you up.'

'I'm sorry for that. My mistake. It was just an argument that I made more of than I should have done.'

Tom suspected they didn't believe he was telling the truth

31

and the lies stuck in his throat, but he had to consider the 'bigger picture'. Whatever it took, he had to do and say what was necessary in order to remain close to Amy.

'Can you tell us about other arguments between you and your wife?'

'There's nothing I can say.'

'We will be speaking to your wife so you might as well give your side of events, otherwise we will only have her version.'

'There's really nothing further I can add, other than to apologise for wasting your time.'

The officer tried a few more questions, but Tom remained silent and about ten minutes later he was back in the cell, wondering if he had just made one of the biggest mistakes in his life. If Gemma didn't withdraw her accusation he would be hung out to dry. However, what had been said couldn't be unsaid so he would have to face the consequences.

He resumed his pacing, trying not to think about the prospect of spending an entire night in the cell. Another hour or so went by when the door opened and he was instructed by one of the policeman who had taken part in the interview to follow him. Moments later he was back in the custody suite, opposite the sergeant once again.

'There is insufficient evidence to charge you,' he said. 'But if I ever see you in here again I'll push the Procurator Fiscal to throw the book at you. Check your possessions then sign here.'

The sergeant slid across the desk the plastic wallet containing Tom's watch, wedding ring and other items. He put them on and signed the form to show he agreed that nothing was missing.

'You can leave. Follow the officer and he'll show you the way out.'

'Your wife's in reception,' said the policeman as he led Tom along the corridor.

'Is she?'

'She said that you both simply overreacted and doesn't want any further proceedings to be taken. But like the sergeant says, don't end up back here again.'

When she saw them coming towards her Gemma stood and walked slowly to the exit. Tom caught up just in time to open the door for her.

'Thank you,' she said walking outside.

He felt that he had been wrong-footed again. Now he had to be grateful to her for not pressing charges, even though he hadn't done anything to deserve them. The truth was, though he hardly wanted to admit it, he was grateful. The demons of his claustrophobia had almost overwhelmed him and he was badly shaken by those few hours in the cell.

'Where's Amy?' he said as they walked away from the building.

'She's fine; fast asleep in the back seat. I think we should put this whole episode behind us. It shows how passionate we are about each other that we can get so emotional,' she said. 'I'll drive. You look terrible. You'll not be fit for the match.'

Tom had forgotten about the game. She was right. It was already well after midnight. He would be no benefit to the team at all.

'Yes. I'll ring Jim first thing in the morning and tell him I can't play.'

She was at the driver's door and spoke to him across the car roof.

'The three of us can go shopping instead, and then go out for an early dinner tomorrow evening. That would be pleasant, wouldn't it?'

'Yes ... whatever you think,' he replied.

Chapter Five

The social worker and policewoman, the latter introducing herself as a domestic violence liaison officer, sat in two armchairs opposite Tom and Gemma, who were on the settee. It was a few days after his evening at the station and, unknown to them, the sergeant had submitted a child concern form to the relevant local authorities.

The telephone call the previous morning, arranging the meeting, was a complete surprise, and resulted in a hastily organised sleepover at a friend's house for Amy. She would be away until the following afternoon.

Gemma wasn't happy. Nothing happened in her life without it having been planned meticulously, each conceivable outcome explored and prepared for, no matter how unlikely. She was a teacher and when marking schoolwork always had several pens lined up in a row in case not just the one she was using ran out, but the one after that. Most of her life was dedicated to ensuring that she had as much control over what happened around her as possible, and Gemma took delight in pushing the boundaries of what was possible.

But she hadn't planned this visit and therefore felt uneasy. However, she kept her real feelings hidden, maintaining a light and friendly tone with the two visitors. Tom found it harder to be amicable. The weekend — being chased with a carving knife, his shame at hiding in the bathroom, the call of desperation to the police followed by being taken to the local station — had unnerved him severely. He felt disorientated and confused, and now here were these two strangers, sitting in the lounge.

He couldn't help feeling that when they looked at him their

expressions and manner altered minutely compared to when they spoke to his wife. The change was so slight, so almost imperceptible that it could have been his tired imagination. But he couldn't shift the sensation. The social worker was talking to him and there it was again; an underlying hint of suspicion.

'You understand that our main concern is Amy. She is our priority.'

'Yes, of course,' said Gemma, though the point had been directed to him. 'She is by far the most important thing in our lives.'

'Often,' continued the woman, 'people think children are unaware of difficulties between parents and that they are not affected by arguments or unpleasant atmospheres in the home, but they are highly sensitive to these situations and can become quite emotionally disturbed without it even being obvious.'

'Amy is a lovely, happy child and we have no more ups and downs than any normal married couple. Do we?' said Gemma.

She had deliberately sat away from Tom on the settee so that it was easier to look him in the eye and watch his face while they were talking. It was easier to dominate him.

'No,' he said, the word sounding slurred, as if he had just woken up. 'We are a good family unit. Amy is the apple of my eye and I wouldn't let any harm come to her.'

His comment was true, though it came across rather defensively, as though it was a challenge to them all. It was, in one sense, a warning to his wife never to turn her violence on their daughter. The social worker continued and he thought the two women must have agreed beforehand which one should drive the meeting.

'Have you noticed any changes in her behaviour? Has she, for instance, become unusually quiet or even aggressive? Has her schoolwork deteriorated?'

Tom and Gemma agreed that there had been no alterations to her moods, but they would keep an eye on her.

'We will check, quietly, with her teachers at school,' replied the social worker.

'There's really no need, but if you think it's a good idea then, yes, anything for her best welfare,' said Gemma.

'Perhaps we could see her room?'

'Of course,' said Gemma, standing up immediately, keen to be helpful.

The social worker stood up, however, the policewoman remained seated.

This was planned to split them up.

His wife hesitated, not sure what he might say while she wasn't there, but she couldn't do anything about it as the other woman was waiting for her to lead the way.

'I understand you made a claim that there is some problem with domestic violence,' said the officer when they were alone.

Tom wasn't sure how to reply. Did he tell her everything or did he deny there was anything wrong? Since being detained by the police the fear that something might happen to take Amy away from him had grown in his mind until the idea invaded and influenced every thought.

'Sometimes ... Gemma is violent towards me.'

It was the eyes that gave away her true feeling. Disbelief.

'Is there ever any violence towards Amy?'

'Never.'

'What sorts of things happen that make your wife respond in this way?'

Tom forced his mind to work more effectively. He thought about the question. It seemed to him that the implication was that if she was violent he must have done something really awful beforehand, perhaps even been aggressive towards her.

'Nothing. It just happens. Like being late for dinner.'

'You mean, if it's a meal for a special occasion and you've forgotten?'

'No ... just dinner.'

'I see. And what might she do?'

'Slapping, punching, throwing objects.'

'Do you do the same to her?'

'No never.'

'You've never hit or pushed her?'

'No.'

'Never held her violently?'

'Well, I've restrained her sometimes.'

'And has this resulted in injuries to her?'

'Bruising sometimes, on her arms.'

There was silence in the room while the policewoman studied him. He wondered what was happening upstairs.

'And have either of you required medical treatment for these injuries?'

'I've been to the local hospital a few times.'

'Did you ever report the reason to the medical staff?'

'No.'

'Did you not think it was important?'

'It was a private matter ... something I was ashamed of.'

Tom didn't dislike the woman sitting opposite him. It was just that he was certain she didn't believe much of what he said.

'Perhaps you and Gemma might benefit from visiting one of the many excellent organisations there are for couples who are experiencing difficulties. I've known many who have found them to be very helpful. I'll leave you this list.'

She removed a leaflet from a folder she had brought and left it on the arm of the chair. He thought it might be a good idea, but he was pretty certain of what reaction this would generate.

'What happens next?' he asked.

'Someone will have a word with the school and we may want to talk to Amy. Then we'll see.'

The atmosphere in the house had been oddly calm since the visitors left. Tom busied himself with jobs in the garden while

Gemma was inside. He wondered what she was thinking and was astonished that she didn't grill him the instant they were alone on what had been said with the policewoman. In a way the silence was far more unnerving than a confrontation.

The first time they were together was early in the evening, after he had washed and she was finishing preparations for dinner. When he entered the kitchen she was leaning with her back against one of the units. There were several pans behind her, ready to go on the cooker. He guessed the meal included carrots because there was a slice lying on the floor.

'So,' she said, 'what exactly did you chat about while I was busy upstairs?'

For the last couple of hours he had been planning what to say.

'She was mainly concerned there was nothing happening that would be harmful to Amy.'

'Yes, that came up before I left the room. What else?'

'She thought it might be a good idea for us to attend one of the organisations that help couples who are having a few difficulties. She left a list of contacts.'

'Now, why would she suggest such a thing?'

He was nervous. Gemma's voice sounded falsely bright and friendly.

'I mentioned that we had had some problems ...'

'Oh, did you say I had been nasty to you?'

'That you sometimes lose your temper with me.'

'Everyone loses their temper. And did you tell her that I hit you?'

'Yes.'

'I see. Well, you may be right,' said Gemma, wiping her hands on her apron as if she had just noticed they were dirty and the conversation was really of little importance. 'Maybe we should go to Relate or one of those other places. You read a lot about how helpful they can be. Perhaps you could look into it.'

Tom was amazed and breathed a huge sigh of relief.

'I'm glad you see it that way. I had thought you might be angry, but I really think it's the best thing, to get some outside professional help.'

'Alright. Would you set the table?'

Gemma made a half turn as if she was going to put the pans on the cooker and he bent down to pick up the slice of carrot before getting the cutlery out of the drawer. She had positioned everything with great care. The end pan was empty as she had worked out earlier that she couldn't wield a full one with sufficient speed to take him by surprise.

Tom caught a movement out of the corner of his eye and turned to look, which meant the pan caught him not on the side of the head as intended, but just above his left eyebrow. He grunted and sank to his knees, putting a hand up to his brow.

'Don't you ever tell anyone about what happens in this house! Do you understand? Are you fucking hearing me down there?'

She held the pan high, ready to bring it down again. Tom looked up and saw the implied threat. He felt waves of nausea wash over him and fought the urge to vomit on the kitchen floor.

'Yes, I understand,' he gasped.

'What do you understand?' she shouted.

'That I mustn't ever talk to anyone about what happens in this house.'

'That's good,' she said, putting the pan down on a nearby unit. She leant over and pulled away his hand. 'That's a nasty cut you've given yourself on the cupboard door. That'll need stitches. Here, take this tea towel. I don't want to see blood anywhere. I'll get the car keys and run you to hospital.'

Then she was gone. Tom moaned, not with the pain, which he could handle, but with despair. How could she defeat him so easily? He was intelligent, well-respected in the community.

Tom backed down to no one if he thought he was right, and not many men would pick a fight with him. He felt that he was becoming so weak.

Amy.

Amy was his saviour, his purpose in life. She was what he needed to focus on, to be strong for. Tom held the tea towel hard against his head and stood up slowly. There was blood on his clothes, but he couldn't see any on the floor. He heard Gemma shouting from the front door that he should hurry up so that they could get back and have dinner.

The drive to the hospital seemed completely surreal. His wife chatted on as if they were going out for an evening to the cinema or to meet friends, and appeared unbothered by his lack of response. She read a magazine while they waited in casualty then a nurse appeared and led them to a cubicle. Gemma explained cheerfully how clumsy her husband was: 'turn your back for an instant and he's banged himself again'.

The nurse smiled. Her patient was obviously one of those men who needed looking after, despite his size. When he was sitting on the bed the woman started to wash away the blood so that she could more easily examine the wound.

'So how did you do this?' she asked.

Tom glanced at his wife sitting in the corner.

'I hit my head on a cupboard door.'

'Were you unconscious at any time?'

'No.'

'Have you felt dizzy or sick since this happened?'

Tom hesitated for a moment. The sickness he had initially felt had gone, though it had been replaced by a thumping headache.

'No,' he said.

'That's good. Well this looks to me like a straightforward stitching job. I'll just get some things then I'll fix this up for you. Is that okay?'

'Thanks.'

He knew he sounded surly and ungrateful. He had incurred worse injuries on the rugby pitch and made lighter of them; had more than once joked with the hospital staff about getting mud on their sheets while he lay in his rugby strip and they patched him up. But this was an injury to his spirit that the nurse couldn't mend. He doubted if anyone could.

Chapter Six

Tania and Gordon planned to host a party on the Saturday before Christmas. Their events were popular and they expected at least two dozen to attend, mainly neighbours or members of the choir in which he sang. People knew that the dining room table would be laid with an enormous array of food: quiches, pizzas, baked potatoes, a couple of the biggest pans containing something hot, a massive cheese platter and, of course, lots of alcohol.

Many of the different groups of friends had got to know each other because of these events, which always included several musicians. Guests loved the live music that would invariably take place during some part of the evening. Gordon would get out his violin, but he never instigated a session. His wife didn't like it, so he would let the other musicians start before joining in, taking care always to be positioned unobtrusively in a corner of the sitting room.

Tania had also played the violin and when they were courting he had loved the idea of duets. But she was nowhere near as proficient and often became angry at his far greater skill. As the months passed he had started to deliberately make mistakes then he would apologise, pretending a particular passage was difficult and asking for her advice, which he didn't need. This tactic generally mollified her and it had become a habit.

She hadn't bothered once they were married and over the years he had almost given up as well. Tania always accused him of 'showing off'. He couldn't see the logic of her comments because whenever friends played their instruments they were performing, entertaining others or simply having a good time, but whenever he took out his violin he was 'showing off'. In the end, it was easier to leave it in its case. The only exceptions were the parties at the house, which was one of the reasons he enjoyed them so much and agreed immediately whenever Tania suggested holding one.

He slid out of bed that Saturday morning and went to the spare bedroom to dress. All his clothes were in this room, so that during the week he could get ready for work without disturbing her. Downstairs he put on the kettle. His day would be spent, as they always were when people were coming around, cleaning and tidying. It would take him until about six o'clock then he would just have time to shower and get ready before the doorbell began ringing with the arrival of the first visitors. It was a pretty set routine.

When he had made his tea he started dusting as this wouldn't make any noise. Most of downstairs had been completed when he heard Tania in the bathroom and when she came down the stairs he was in the hallway polishing the harmonium that he had inherited when his grandmother died. He loved it; part instrument, part furniture, its beautiful dark mahogany provided a perfect contrast to the neat row of ivory keys and stops, each one of the latter displaying in copperplate writing the sound effect that would be created if you pulled it out: *diapason bass, seraphon, viola dolce, tremolo.*

It was in perfect condition. Such instruments, which rarely came up for sale, were generally in poor shape. Even good ones didn't cost much because people simply didn't want them. They were too large for most modern houses and there were horror stories of harmoniums being smashed up. He wished he could rescue them all, hide them away until a time when their true value was recognised.

Tania stopped when she was two steps from the bottom and he was engulfed by the scent of the cheap perfume that she

43

dosed herself with each morning. It made his eyes smart.

'Hello, love,' he said. 'Shall I put the kettle on? I was just about to have another cup.'

'Don't think you're singing carols tonight.'

'What?'

'I don't want you starting carols this evening when everyone is around.'

He couldn't believe what he was hearing. What was more natural than a few hymns sung around a harmonium at Christmas? She knew that he had been practising half a dozen tunes over the previous weeks and had even made photocopies of the relevant pages so that people had the words.

'But why not?'

'I don't want people being offended.'

'Offended?'

He couldn't follow her line of thought. They didn't have any multicultural friends and although few of those coming to the party were religious, Gordon couldn't see how such an activity would upset anyone. For years they had sung hymns at the party they held nearest to Christmas.

'Who's going to be offended? If people don't want to join in they'll simply stay in the kitchen.'

'You're not doing it.'

Tania wasn't angry. In fact, she had an odd little smile on her face. But there was an edge to her voice that warned of danger. This was turning into a disastrous start to the day. He didn't want to back down, but if he pressed on too much she was likely to fly into a rage. She remained on the step, which gave her the advantage of height, and waited for his answer. He picked his words carefully.

'Well, I won't play it, but if anyone else wants to then I'm not going to prevent them. I can hardly do that, can I?'

She seemed satisfied and headed off to the kitchen.

'I'll make tea,' she said brightly.

Gordon emptied the ash pan and laid the fire. It was only lit at weekends because such an arduous task was too much for his wife. He retrieved the hoover from the cupboard then moved the settee in order to vacuum the nail clippings that he knew would be there. One of Tania's habits was to cut her toenails while sitting by the fire then she would gather up the main bits in her hand, but instead of putting them in the bin or even on the fire, she would always throw them behind the settee. He never tackled her about such behaviour. Instead, he just cleaned and tidied.

While she started making brunch he began on their bedroom, taking a bin liner for the rubbish that would be on the floor by her side of the bed. Generally, he avoided this side of the room.

Gordon was fastidious about cleanliness and he felt slightly queasy at the sight that greeted him. Pieces of cake, pizza and even a fluff-covered lasagne were all mixed up with leftover chocolate bars, sweets and a part-finished packet of crisps, the contents of which were lying loose. She had stood on some and bits of cheese and onion flavoured crisp were embedded in the fibres of the carpet. Some of the plates of half-eaten food had been pushed so far underneath the bed that he had to clear a space then lie on the floor to reach them. There were several glasses of part-consumed liquids. One unfinished glass of orange had begun to go mouldy.

Amongst this mess were seven or eight paperback books, several lying open and nearly all of them stained by food or drink. Tania was always reading, but she often didn't finish a title and could rarely remember anything about what she had read. 'It was just a mindless story,' she would reply whenever he asked her what she had completed recently. He normally received a similar response if he enquired, on arriving home in the evening, what she had been watching on television that day.

He threw all the food into the bin liner, stacked the plates and emptied the contents of the glasses down the sink. Gordon sighed. Apart from stopping for brunch and a coffee break later on, he would be working flat out until it was time for him to get ready for the party.

When he came out of the shower Tania was putting the finishing touches to her make-up. As usual it was extraordinarily thick and stopped in a precise line that ran right around the edge of her jaw. She had two sisters and the youngest had once dared to say it looked like a clown's mask. The idea of a mask had stuck with him. That's what it was in a way.

Throughout the entire evening she would be all laughter and fun, constantly throwing her arms around people and topping up their wine glasses. Yet he sometimes wondered if his wife was ever happy, even at those moments when no one else would have doubted it. However, what they saw was the façade, the image she wanted to project. The next day she would remain in bed, probably until late afternoon, too hung over, tired and depressed to get up. It was the price they both paid for holding the parties.

'What are you looking at?' she snapped.

He had been watching her applying bright red lipstick.

'That's a nice dress. Is it new?' he said trying to think quickly of something positive to say.

'Why shouldn't I have a new dress? It was in the sale. Less than half price.'

Tania always said that. It was inevitably untrue. If an item of clothing was in a sale then she wouldn't have wanted it. Whenever he came across a receipt for clothing it was usually for two or three times whatever figure she had told him. Fortunately, he earned good money by working extra hours at the factory, so would always let these incidents go without comment.

The evening was a great success. Everyone made a fuss about the food and when one of the keyboard players suggested singing carols, Gordon invited the man to play the harmonium. People crammed into the hallway and up the stairs and sang their hearts out. Even those few who didn't sing still wanted to be involved, to be a part of what was taking place.

Only Tania and Sally, her friend from along the street, stayed in the kitchen, drinking and smoking. Afterwards, there had been a fantastic music session, which went on until midnight. When the last guest had gone, Gordon could hardly believe the mess.

'Leave all this,' said Tania. 'We'll clear up in the morning.'

It was another of her sayings that had no meaning. What would happen, as it always did, was that he would get up early and tidy around quietly then go to the morning service at the local church. When he came back he would make coffee and take one to her.

'Let's go to bed,' she said.

'I'll have to put some of the food in the fridge.'

'Don't be long.'

She staggered off. Tania would have thrown all the food out rather than bothering to save any. If left to her own she would waste colossal amounts. As speedily as he could he put the remains of the perishable items on plates, covered them with film and put them into the fridge.

He rushed upstairs. It was best not to keep her waiting, though he dashed into the bathroom first to clean his teeth and rid himself of the flavours of the strong cheese he had eaten. She rarely cleaned hers. Gordon couldn't remember when he had last seen her do this. Fortunately, they didn't often kiss.

Of all her habits, the one that he found the most difficult to accept was her unusual attitude to personal hygiene and although she showered every day, Tania had an aversion to washing her private parts. He had been shocked the first time they had slept together, but not having previously had a partner Gordon had nothing to compare this to. He considered that perhaps he was too fussy about such things. Alternatively, he tried not to think about it.

When he entered the bedroom she was standing in her bra and knickers, one hand holding a nearly finished glass of red wine and the other on the mantelpiece for support.

'Where've you been? I've been waiting ages for you.'

'Sorry, I had to put away some of the food.'

'Food,' she repeated scornfully. 'It's not food I want.'

She put down her glass and came towards him, swaying. Without saying anything she put her lips against his and thrust forward her tongue. It felt more like an assault than an action meant to arouse.

Dear God.

Gordon couldn't believe a person's mouth could be so vile. He took a step backwards, but she moved with him, hanging on to his body and pushing her tongue in and out forcibly. It wasn't just a sensation of taste. His lips and the insides of his cheeks were beginning to sting. He guessed it was the stale tobacco.

I'm going to gag.

He twisted his head to one side and gasped. She stopped, looking at him with surprise.

'What's wrong with you? Don't you want me? I thought you'd be desperate for it by now, it's been so long.'

'Hey, a guy's got to breathe.'

'Don't say you're not up to it. I know you don't have much, but don't tell me you're not even going to be able to get it up.'

He had to keep the moment light, stop it from dissolving into something horrible.

'You know I've never had any problems on that score. I just needed to breathe. I'll get undressed.'

'Well be quick or I'll be starting without you.'

He went to the spare bedroom and removed his clothes almost frantically.

Please God don't make me have to kiss her again. I'll do anything but that.

He had heard other men at the factory talking about their wives and girlfriends and it was never like this. They always spoke of desire and pleasure. Not revulsion ... not fear. What was wrong with him?

She was naked, sitting on her side of the bed. From the doorway he studied her back in silence. The heavy drinking and smoking, the unhealthy eating habits and almost obsessive inactivity were affecting her severely, even at the age of thirty-two. He wondered what she would be like in ten years' time. The wine glass on the small cabinet was empty. Next Saturday Gordon would have to clear away that week's pile of half-eaten food, scattered on the floor amongst the paperbacks.

'You've made it then,' she said, not turning around.

'Of course. All yours now.'

He was still desperate to keep the mood light-hearted. She had removed the duvet, which lay in a heap in the corner. He tried to ignore the streaks of dried excrement that criss-crossed her side of the sheet. Slowly, as if it was a great effort, Tania rolled over to face him, her body covering the marks.

'Come here then,' she said.

Chapter Seven

The large frosted window of Alfred's shop separated two worlds; one in which time moved on, seemingly at an increasingly hectic pace, and one where it stood still, refusing, with the utmost politeness, all requests to join in. Strangers stepping into his world were either delighted at the quaintness or slightly put off by the lack of cleanliness. The truth was, he could no longer bend down easily to clean the various nooks and crannies.

An assortment of chairs around two walls provided seating for six people, reminiscent of an era when he could regularly have four or five customers waiting for their turn, chatting amicably amongst themselves and with him because they all knew one another, and there was no rush. Most of those men, like those days, were long gone.

The barber's chair, positioned in front of the one mirror and sink, was an amazing object from the past. Its heavy cast-iron frame was covered in dark green leather that was cracked and worn thin by age and the thousands of bodies that had sat in it over the decades.

There were two internal doors. One led to a toilet and the other into a walk-in cupboard, which was used to house a few possessions and where he would sweep the cuttings from the floor. When the mound became too large to ignore any further, he would gather it into a large bag and put this in the bin. Hair, he thought, was the most useless item on earth once it had been cut; it was no good in the garden, took centuries to rot and stank unbelievably when burnt.

As the front door opened that Christmas Eve, Alfred looked

up from the newspaper he was reading and, when he saw it was a stranger, he reverted immediately into a role that was almost a caricature of the man who had trained him all those years ago.

'Come in, sir, come into the warm,' he said standing up and walking over to welcome the man. 'It's gone bitterly cold, sir, but I suppose we can't expect anything different at this time of year. There's no one else here, sir, so you can go straight into the chair. But let me take your coat first, sir. I'll hang it up here, sir, just on this peg behind you. Now I'll just move the fire around so that you can get a bit more heat.'

The customer seemed bemused at the reception, which gave him no chance to actually speak, but he sat down as instructed and the gown was quickly tucked around him.

'Now is it just a suggestion, sir? Just a suggestion? My old boss used to say that if you could tell someone had been given a cut then you had taken too much off. And he was never pleased at that. Very strict he was. Mind you, sir, it was probably because the customer could wait longer before coming back.'

'Just a tidy, please.'

'Yes, sir, just a tidy; just a suggestion.'

Despite his years, Alfred was quick and had started cutting before he had even been told what was required. The customer was going to get a 'suggestion' whether he wanted it or not.

'And what brings you to this part of Englandshire, sir?'

'We're visiting friends nearby. My wife's gone shopping so I said I would look for a barber's shop. I was intrigued by the outside of yours. You can't tell what you're going to find until you walk through the door.'

'Oh, we're a little oasis of sanity amongst a world gone mad, sir,' he replied, using the plural 'we' when, in fact, there was only him. 'Mind, sir, it's a dangerous thing letting the wife go shopping alone, a dangerous thing. And what line of work are you in, sir?'

Alfred's banter was continuous, accompanied by the *click click* of the scissors. There was a rhythm to it, like a singer with an instrument, as if one without the other was an incomplete performance.

'I'm a fireman.'

'Oh, a fireman, sir. That's a noble profession. Yes, where would we be without our fire service? I remember when it was all done by volunteers around here, sir. Oh, yes. Long ago now. I recall one day old Mrs Thompson had a chimney fire, so she sent her son to gather up the men. Well, it was Sunday lunchtime and they were all in the pub, sir.

'She gave them some stick when they eventually arrived, but up one of them went on to the roof and put the hose into the top of the chimney. Then — hee hee — a few moments later out runs Mrs Wake from next door, screaming blue murder. He had put the hose down the wrong chimney and she was cooking the Sunday roast on the stove.

'Hee hee hee.'

No one knew whether these stories were true. Alfred had been telling them for so long that their origins were lost. But he had the most infectious laugh that the majority of people had ever heard, and it was a rare person indeed who could remain unaffected. Soon the customer was laughing heartily and Alfred had to stop cutting.

'The culprit on the roof was too scared to come down because the two women were threatening murder, whether it was a Sunday or not. Poor Stanley got no lunch that day. The roast was ruined. Hee hee hee.'

Alfred had been concerned that when their daughter Kate and her family were visiting on Christmas day something might happen that would expose the terrible secret he kept. However, Enid had shown no signs of forgetfulness during the morning and everyone had enjoyed the meal. Kate lived nearly three hours away and tried to come over every month or so. Their visits were greatly looked forward to.

These days, Alfred was never completely relaxed; always maintaining a wary eye in case his wife did something dangerous, such as leaving the cooker on by mistake, or becoming angry at not being able to remember a particular event or conversation. Increasingly, she got stuck on a word and could be talking quite normally then stop suddenly in the middle of a sentence because she didn't seem able to remember the name of something. But apart from a few minor incidents, their lives had rumbled along as normal since the other week, when she had punched him in the face. He had told no one.

The two children were playing noisily in the living room with Keith, leaving the elderly couple alone with their daughter at the dining room table, surrounded by the remains of a home-made Christmas pudding.

'That was excellent, Mum, thanks ever so much for having us over,' said Kate. 'Thanks, Dad.'

'Oh, it was nothing. Your mother did all the work. It was a marvellous meal, love.'

Enid smiled fondly and there was a slight pause in the conversation.

'Did you know,' she said to her daughter, 'last month your father went into a gentlemen's toilet and there was actually a machine that dispensed flavoured condoms?'

Kate was quite taken aback at this uncharacteristic topic, especially at the table, and on Christmas day. Alfred was surprised, but played along, although it was years ago when he had told this story.

'It's been a long time since I've asked "something for the weekend, sir" and there weren't any flavours in those days,' he said. 'I'd never seen such a thing. I had just started looking down the list when someone walked in, so I moved away. But I did notice there was a strawberry version.'

'I'm not so keen on strawberries. I've always been partial to rhubarb though. That might be alright.'

'Mum!'

'I could go back and see if there's rhubarb or if not, perhaps gooseberry. You've always liked gooseberries.'

'Dad!'

'But I prefer gooseberries in a crumble,' said Enid. 'I wonder if they had a proper menu ... with main courses.'

'Like steak and kidney,' he offered.

'Fish and chips.'

'With mushy peas.'

'Mum! Dad! I don't know what's got into you. I think you've both been sampling the wine before we arrived.'

'Hee hee hee.'

That was it. Alfred was off and his wife was not far behind.

'I wonder what they do for starters?' she said.

Kate stared at her parents, helpless at either end of the table, and her indignation was swept aside by an eruption of laughter that she could not hold back, despite raising a hand to her mouth in a final, futile gesture to maintain the moral high ground. She was soon as unable to speak as the pair of them. When Keith walked in shortly afterwards, he found his wife and in-laws unable to talk.

'What's going on?' he said, smiling at the unexpected, amusing scene.

Alfred had buried his face in a napkin and his 'hee hees' were muffled through the material.

'I'm sorry, Keith,' said Kate. 'I don't think ... it's a suitable thing ... to bring up at the table.'

Keith watched on for a while, but could see that he was going to get no answers out of any of them.

'I'm going back to play with the children. I'll get more sense from them,' he said.

Enid rested her head against Alfred's chest. It was evening. The family had left earlier, not wanting to stay overnight, and so after tidying up the couple collapsed on the settee in a state of contented exhaustion. However, before leaving, Kate had engineered a conversation with her father when no one else was about and expressed concern about her mother's forgetfulness.

He hadn't realised his daughter had picked up so many clues from telephone conversations during the last month or so, but during November Enid had forgotten one of the children's birthdays and that was unheard of. Alfred hadn't thought to check that his wife had sent a card and assumed it had been posted. She always handled these things.

Kate had not mentioned it at the time, having decided to speak to her father when they met at Christmas. They had always been close. He had tried to reassure her that it was nothing to worry about; that they had had a lot on their minds and as people got older they simply didn't remember as well as they used to. But she wasn't entirely convinced and made him promise to keep a careful watch for any unusual behaviour or symptoms. Kate didn't say of what. She didn't have to.

Alfred stroked Enid's hair and after a few moments he left his hand resting on her head.

What was going on in there? What could he do to help?

It seemed to him that it was recent events she forgot; why she had gone into a particular room, what they needed when they went shopping, or something he had said to her earlier in the day. Over the previous weeks he had talked about events that had happened years ago, to test her memory of them, and she had been as clear as he had.

He left so much of the running of the house to his wife, but decided that it might be a good idea to start making lists, without it being too obvious. And he knew where she kept all the paperwork relating to bills that needed paying, along with the little blue book containing the various dates of birthdays and anniversaries of friends and family. Perhaps he could become more of a safety net, to ensure things happened when they should.

What would he do without her? What would he be?

'Shall I put the kettle on?' asked Enid, without moving from where she was nestled comfortably into him.

They always had a cup of peppermint tea before going to bed. It was one of their little routines that they looked forward to each day. Alfred felt himself getting a moist eye. Gently, he started to stroke her hair again.

'You stay there for a while longer and I'll do it shortly,' he said. 'There's no rush, love.'

They had drunk it half an hour earlier

Chapter Eight

Gordon clutched the letter that had arrived earlier, while he studied his face in the bathroom mirror. A 'friend' had once said to him that when God had been giving out body parts in heaven, he had been at the back of every queue. It was a doubly cruel jibe because the man had known of his religious views, but he acknowledged an essence of truth behind the comment.

Nothing about him seemed to match anything else and this was most noticeable in his face, where his ears and eyes, jaw and cheekbones conflicted vigorously with each other and the rest of his head. He often thought it was indeed as if someone had once said: 'Here's a pair of eyebrows no one wants, just stick them on Gordon's face and somewhere in the corner there's a chin that's been left over'.

You couldn't say he had a disfigurement in any medical sense, but if there was such as condition as 'uglyism' then Gordon had a severe dose. The daily abuse he had received while growing up had been staggering. Strangers would scream insults at him as he walked along the street, and groups of girls would shout obscene comments while he waited at the bus stop.

On one occasion, he had been in a major department store on the High Street and one of the staff had called out derogatory remarks as he passed by, even though he was potentially a customer. The gangs of lads were the most dangerous, because they would sometimes wind themselves up so much by hurling verbal abuse that they would then decide it was a good idea to beat him up.

What hurt the most was the hate that these people seemed to genuinely feel when they knew nothing about him, apart from what they saw. They didn't know if he was a good person or a bad one; they had no knowledge of where he came from or what language he spoke; no idea of his beliefs, hopes and fears; whether he had brothers and sisters; if he liked a particular sport or band. He might have had similar interests to some of those who hurled abuse, but they would never know.

While he was a teenager Gordon had grown his hair long and developed the habit of looking at the floor, often even when speaking to someone, so that his hair hung down and covered some of his features. He still did it.

Perhaps one day the Government would legislate against uglyism ... like racism, sexism, ageism.

A part of him knew that it was personality that really mattered. Any sensible adult would say so. But he couldn't ignore the feeling that a significant part of his character, what he felt about himself and how he related to others, had been moulded over the years by people he had previously never met screaming abuse into his face.

You couldn't detach the physical body from the person inside as if they were two separate entities, no matter how desirable such a thing might seem. A very tall woman could wish with all her heart to be a ballet dancer and might even have the talent, but she would simply be too large; just as a small man might desire with all his being to compete at a sport that he was never going to be powerful enough to do.

Gordon sighed and read the letter again. It was from the local hospital, giving him a date in February to attend for plastic surgery to his nose. A 'rhinoplasty' they called it. His nose was enormous and certainly neither the GP nor surgeon he had seen had hesitated for a moment about the need for the operation. No one had asked, 'Why do you feel you need it done?' So his name had gone on a waiting list and now it was near the top.

Tania wouldn't be pleased. She hadn't wanted him to see the doctor about it in the first place, and had told him that she knew people who had gone through the operation and it was extremely painful. However, he didn't obey her in everything. It was like drink-driving. She had never sat her test. He didn't mind, but he was strict about not drinking if taking out the car. It provided another reason for her to goad him.

'Go on,' she would urge, 'you can have a couple of glasses and still drive. Everyone does it.'

Then when he refused she would start to put him down, even with other people around.

'Don't be such a wimp. You can have at least one glass. You're allowed that much. It's the law. Anyone can have one glass. Why couldn't I have married a real man?'

He would never relent on this point, but she never gave up either, so the conversation became another regular 'scene' to be played whenever they went somewhere where alcohol was available and they had the car with them.

That morning, Tania was at the hairdresser's and had gone before the post arrived. He checked his watch. There was some time before he had to go to his choir practice, but he wanted out of the house so he hid the letter, picked up the black binder containing his music, and left.

Gordon went into the nearby church and sat on a pew. He wasn't sure where his religion came from as neither of his parents were religious in the slightest. The first time he had gone into a church was at the age of fourteen, when he had run through the doorway in order to escape a gang of lads. Fortunately, they hadn't followed him and he had been struck immediately by the sense of peace and safety. His beliefs had come upon him slowly during his teenage years. Surprisingly, Tania didn't mock him for his views. She ridiculed him about most things, but not this. He suspected that secretly she feared to do it.

As he sat in the silence, Gordon thought about his wife. He wished she didn't constantly tell lies. Even after all this time together he couldn't decide whether she believed the stories she made up, or if some part of her deep down knew that they were untrue. Sometimes she said things to him that both of them knew were false as she was speaking the words, but he never challenged her.

At the party she had been telling a couple of the musicians how she had to stop playing the violin because of an injury to her hand, which he had never heard of before. It had been a great disappointment because when she was younger she had reached the level of Grade Eight on the instrument. When Gordon first met her she had told him it was Grade Three. Over the years this had become higher without, as far as he knew, her ever taking any further exams. He often found it difficult to separate truth from fantasy, and he couldn't understand her flashes of wild temper, which had become steadily worse.

Yet not everything in their marriage was bad. If he was really careful about what he said and he kept the place clean and tidy, brought in sufficient money so that she didn't have to work, but could still buy what she wanted ... well, it wasn't so bad. She could be funny and was nearly always affectionate. It had to be better than being alone and he should be grateful that anyone would want him with his looks.

Gordon decided to walk to the nearby hall where the choir practised. As he moved along the pew he saw a woman walking up the aisle. He had noticed the solitary figure when he had entered earlier and deliberately picked a spot away from her. Normally, he wouldn't have acknowledged her presence, but she said 'hello', so he could hardly ignore the greeting. Then he realised it was another member of the choir. There were around forty, split fairly equally between males and females. He tended to stick to the group of men in his section.

'Hello,' he replied.

'I heard someone come in, but didn't know it was you.'

'No.'

'I suppose you're off to the rehearsal?'

'Yes.'

They walked slowly together towards the exit. He guessed the woman was in her early fifties.

'You're a baritone,' she said.

'That's right. And you joined recently.'

'Nearly four months ago.'

'Are you enjoying it?'

'Yes, it's a good choir.'

'Did you sing in one before?'

'I did for many years. It wasn't mixed though.'

'What made you change?'

They had reached the door. She stopped, hesitating for a moment before replying.

'I'm new to the area, so hunted out a group to sing with. It's something I've always loved and at one point I had considered trying to become semi-professional, but it wasn't possible.'

They didn't need to rush so stayed where they were, and even when there were lapses in conversation they both felt comfortable in the silence.

'Will your wife come to next week's concert?'

She didn't miss much.

'No,' said Gordon. 'She came to the first one I was ever involved in, but that was to check out the female members. She must have thought they weren't a threat because she's never been to anything since.'

He wasn't sure what made him make such a comment. Usually, he was extremely cautious about what he revealed of his private life and although he tried to make it sound like a joke, the explanation was true. He was rooted to the spot by the stare the woman gave him. It was as if she had seen beyond his light-hearted jest and found a ghost waiting. She had gone pale.

'Are you alright?' he asked, worried she had taken ill.

'Yes, I'm fine, thank you. Just ... it's nothing, only a passing moment. We'd better get around to the hall, but I've not even told you my name. I'm Jennifer.'

Tania had gone blonde. She was in the sitting room, smoking and drinking strong black coffee. Every few weeks she had her hair dyed and Gordon had given up trying to guess what colour it would be next. It was always something garish and false. She used her hair to make a statement, although these bold colours seemed a contradiction because she maintained that she hated people looking at her. It struck him, as he stood in the doorway, that he couldn't say for certain what her natural colour was.

'Have you had a good day?' he asked.

He had learnt never to refer to the latest style. Whatever he said could so easily be taken the wrong way that he had become adept at not raising the issue, even if she had completely changed colour from the last time he saw her. Maybe she wanted him to say it was nice, to acknowledge the difference, but the risk of sending her into a rage outweighed the feeling that he should at least make some sort of comment.

'Yes. I got some good things in the sale.'

Gordon spotted several bags by the settee from one of the High Street chains. That would be an expensive bill.

'Ah well, as long as you've got something you wanted.'

He couldn't quite bring himself to say 'needed' as she owned so many clothes that she had taken over entirely the wardrobe in their bedroom, and most of the one in the spare room.

'I'll get myself a coffee,' he said.

She followed him into the kitchen. He would have to bring up the subject of the operation. He knew better than to mention anything about meeting Jennifer or he would be accused of having an affair.

Gordon could write out a list of at least twenty women with whom there was meant to have been 'something going on' over the last seven years, including several old enough to be his mother, one of his cousins and his wife's youngest sister.

'I've had a letter from the hospital, giving me a date to have plastic surgery on my nose.'

'When?'

'In three weeks.'

'Are you going through with it?'

'Well, I've come to the top of the list and you know I've wanted it done since I was fourteen.'

'I think you're stupid to do it.'

Tania always thought he was stupid. It was her favourite 'scream' at him. She would draw out the word depending upon her level of anger, so that it often sounded as if she was actually shouting 'Stooopid.' But as he poured milk into his mug she remained quiet, leaning against one of the units, and it wasn't until he had put the jug back in the fridge that she spoke.

'You know when I said that it was a really painful operation? Well, it's not. I made it up.'

This was an extremely rare admission of a blatant lie.

'You made it up. What on earth for? I've spent all this time believing I was going to go through a procedure that would be painful.'

She started crying, a common scenario.

'You'll go off with someone else.'

'Why would not having an enormous nose make me go off with someone else?'

'Lots of women will be after you. You'll not want to be with me anymore.'

He put down his cup and took hold of her in his arms.

'That's just silly. There isn't suddenly going to be a line of nubile young females breaking down the front door in order to get their hands on my weedy body because I've had the size of my nose reduced.'

He nearly said, 'No woman in her right mind would want to be with me.' but stopped as she would take this as an insult.

'You won't love me anymore,' she said, her head buried into his chest.

'Will you love me anymore or any less because my nose is altered?'

'It won't make any difference at all, but that's why I can't understand the reasons that you want to have it done.'

'This is something for me. Come on. Let me fill your mug and you can show me the things you've bought. I'd like to see your new clothes.'

Chapter Nine

Gordon was surprised at the reaction to his news that he was having plastic surgery. Some people were totally against it, saying he should accept what he looked like and was wasting limited NHS resources that should be used for other, more important cases. He suspected they had never been chased down the street by a gang who had decided you deserved a good thumping because of your appearance.

One or two said that they couldn't see why it needed altering. He felt their attempts to be kind were farcically misguided. However, several friends admitted secretly that they would like to have some of their own features altered, but didn't have the nerve to go through with it. They admired him for going ahead with what he believed was right. It was these people who had surprised him, confessing how unhappy they were with a certain part of their body. In every instance he couldn't see that there was a problem, though he made little comment.

He had to approach his boss about taking time off work. The man epitomised so much of what Gordon aspired to be: good-looking, athletic and strong, well-respected by those he dealt with. He was a tough individual, although always fair and courteous with staff.

'I need to take a few days off to have an operation,' said Gordon, when sitting in his boss's office. 'It's to have my nose reduced in size. I'm hoping it might stop people making so many comments about my appearance.'

He had decided to be totally open because the reason would be obvious. Afterwards, as he would be wearing a plaster cast. The man said nothing for a while.

'Do you get any abuse here in the factory?'

'A bit,' he replied cautiously.

'A few months ago, I noticed a couple of lads in the warehouse making gestures behind your back as you passed by. I took them to one side and had a quiet word. Actually, it wasn't so quiet. I won't have staff under my control being disrespectful to one another. I'm sorry if there have been other occasions and I've been lax in dealing with them.'

Gordon was taken aback. He didn't know anything of this particular incident and was touched by the man's concern.

'Thanks,' he muttered.

'Take what time you need, and if you ever get abuse within these factory walls, in any form whatsoever, then I want to know about it.'

The following Saturday Tania went into town with Sally, her 'only real friend'. Gordon had great misgivings about the relationship, which he suspected was based largely on Sally being able to sponge alcohol, cigarettes and other items. He sometimes wondered how much of his hard-earned salary went on clothes for the woman along the street, as his wife always appeared to be showering her with little gifts.

He left home early in order to sit in the church for a while. He had been there for about fifteen minutes, so lost in his own thoughts that he hadn't noticed someone had walked along the pew until the figure sat down next to him.

'Hello,' Jennifer said, speaking softly, although there was no one else around. 'I hope I'm not interrupting you?'

'Hello. No, just thinking.'

'Not worried about tonight's concert?'

'No, I love them.'

'There's never the opportunity to speak to anyone during rehearsals unless they're standing nearby, and even then you can hardly talk confidentially. Gordon, I was concerned about a comment you made to me last week.'

'Something I said?'

'Yes.'

'What was it?'

They had only spoken briefly and he couldn't think what had been conveyed in those few moments that could have made this woman hunt him out before this week's practice.

'You joked that your wife came to look at the women in the choir when you first joined ... because she was checking them out?'

'Well, she can be a bit insecure, that's all. She sometimes gets funny ideas, worries that other women will be after me. It's completely silly when you think about it.'

He was being more than a little conservative with the truth. Tania was constantly checking his post, listening on the extension if she wasn't sure who he was speaking to, forbidding him from attending certain functions. Jennifer sat for a while, studying him without speaking.

'My husband wouldn't let me join a mixed choir in case I got speaking to another man. As a huge privilege, for which I had to repay him, I was allowed to sing in an all-female choir. However, he would come to rehearsals and sit at the back of the hall so that he could take me straight home afterwards. It felt like being stalked.

'People thought it very odd. He was the only person not a member and I had to explain to the conductor that I couldn't attend unless he came. I made out it was because I didn't drive, but that wasn't true, although Derek forbade me to ever touch the car keys so it might as well have been the case.'

Gordon was astonished. Nobody had ever talked to him so openly and for it to be an almost complete stranger, and about such a private subject, made the scene in the church feel slightly unreal.

'I'm sorry,' he said, not sure what else to say.

'This was only the tip of the iceberg of a relationship that was so full of control and abuse. I've had no contact with him for over a year, but even now there are times when I hesitate to do something as simple as go shopping, because previously I would have had to obtain his permission. Sometimes I can spend almost ten minutes talking myself round that it is actually alright to go down the street and buy a newspaper. I appreciate that talking to you in this way must seem very strange and I apologise if I'm making you uncomfortable. I know you will keep this in confidence.'

'Absolutely.'

Jennifer took a deep breath, as if she had prepared a speech and was steadying her nerves to give it.

'Since moving to the area six months ago I've told no one about my past. It was a clean start for me, far away from my earlier life, although I'm still married to Derek because he won't give me a divorce. It's his last bit of control. Eventually he won't be able to stop me.

'I trust you with this knowledge because that comment you made about your wife checking out the women in the choir brought so many memories flooding back. I wondered if you are in a position similar to the one I was in. If I'm speaking out of turn or I have misunderstood the situation then I hope you will forgive me, and not take offence at my forwardness.'

Gordon never talked to anyone about his relationship with Tania, not even friends who knew them both, and he was beset by a multitude of conflicting emotions.

'I've never spoken to anyone like this before and I've had all week to consider how to phrase things,' she continued. 'Don't say anything for the moment if you don't want to. Just know that I am a friend willing to listen in confidence if you need it. I won't judge. If I was to make a guess, then right now you can't speak because you're frightened your wife will find out, even though there's no way she could.'

How did she know that?

His astonishment showed on his face. It was indeed fear that prevented him from talking about his marriage, far more than embarrassment or any feelings that this was a private matter. His concern was surely paranoia. How could Tania possibly learn about anything he said to this woman in the solitude of the empty church? Yet, if he was honest, he was terrified she would find out, that she could somehow read his mind about what had taken place.

'I'm going to the practice. There's a little bit of time left. Why don't you remain here for a while before coming to the hall? Take this,' she said, handing him a small slip of paper. 'My telephone number is easy to remember, so you can memorise it then destroy the evidence. If you ever need someone to talk to, either over the phone or face to face, don't hesitate to ring me, whatever the time of day or night.'

Jennifer stood up, smiled kindly at him and walked out of the church. Gordon had hardly spoken a word, but he was frightened. How could this stranger have so easily sensed an inner turmoil that he barely dared to admit to himself? But was she right? Was Tania like this woman's husband? Surely it was completely different. His wife could be affectionate and loving and he would never be in a situation where he needed permission to buy a newspaper. Such a scenario was ridiculous.

Or was it? Did he do *anything* without checking first? Since getting married he had given up the few hobbies and groups he used to belong to, though this was in part owing to the fact that he felt so exhausted most of the time.

What exactly did he *do?* It seemed, as he thought about it, that a great deal of his time was spent clearing up after Tania, or working out ways not to ignite her temper. In fact, most of his life was focussed on trying to keep her mood even. When she was happy, life was fine. They didn't really go out that much as a couple because she preferred to watch television, but not everything about their relationship was bad.

He had some good friends, although they were fewer in numbers these days, because there were several who he was not allowed to see any more. At times, Tania's jealousy was so bad that Gordon wondered which one of them actually had the least confidence.

He also had to be careful what social events they attended. She hated meeting strangers and would normally prepare for such encounters by getting drunk. Gordon had stopped going to any of the functions at the factory ever since two women had to almost carry his wife from the dinner table to the ladies toilet in the middle of the Chairman's speech.

The man had stopped speaking in order to watch the scene, which ensured that every single member of staff, along with their partners, had also looked on. Gordon had been crimson with embarrassment.

However, he wasn't allowed to attend such functions without Tania. After all, you didn't know *who* he might get talking to. According to her every female under seventy was craving to get their hands on his body.

He looked at his watch. If he didn't go now he would be late for the rehearsal. However, before leaving the church, he unfolded the slip of paper and read the telephone number several times before tearing the strip into pieces that were not much larger than confetti, which he dropped into the bin by the door.

Chapter Ten

Judas. Judas.

It was March and the ground had been frozen for so long that it seemed to Alfred it must surely be impossible for life to ever spring forth from the earth again. But although the weather continued to be an important topic in the little barber's shop, it was old news and the newspapers were full of stories about dramatic global events and the death of various celebrities.

Never in his life had he ever thought he had 'betrayed' someone, but as he sat in the doctor's waiting room the feeling was intense. However, Enid's forgetfulness and odd behaviour could no longer be ignored. She was becoming a danger to herself, so something had to be done. That's what he told himself. And it was true.

Yet there was more to his decision. He was also becoming frightened of her. There had been three more incidents of physical aggression: a couple of times she had done no more than slap his face, but the last time, the previous week, Enid had come at him with fists flying and he had only just managed to fend off her blows.

The incident had begun as a normal conversation, but she had got stuck in the middle of a sentence and he had suggested what he thought she was trying to say. He had guessed wrongly and Enid had shouted, 'No, not that.' Alfred tried another word, also incorrect, then she said 'light bulb', which had nothing whatsoever to do with the subject they had initially been discussing. Both of them had quickly become irritated by the lack of communication, yet he hadn't expected her to attack him.

71

He would speak to the doctor. Perhaps there was some medication that she could prescribe to eliminate these flashes of anger and give him back the woman he loved, the one he missed. The medical profession could do all sorts of amazing things these days.

'Alfred.'

He looked up to see the doctor calling his name. She was a nice woman, about the same age as Kate, always came to the waiting room to collect you. He had watched her do this with other patients and noticed that she let them go in front. He guessed she studied them walking along the corridor, assessing their health before they had even spoken.

'Now, how can I help you today?' she said when they were both sitting in her room.

'Well ...'

It was all he got out before he started crying. This wasn't what he had planned at all. Alfred hadn't expected to cry. He had rehearsed exactly what he was going to say to make the most of his appointment and not waste the GP's valuable time, but all he had managed was 'Well.'

She took hold of the hand that was resting on his right knee.

'Just take your time and let me know what's wrong when you're ready.'

She sat quietly, squeezing and patting his hand kindly. He appreciated the contact, which was comforting, though he suspected that these days there was no doubt a regulation against such actions.

'It's Enid,' he said through his sobs, 'I think she's got ... dementia.'

There. He had spoken his fear aloud and now the secret was out.

'Why do you think she has dementia?'

'She's always forgetting things.'

'Okay. Can you give me some examples of the type of things

that she might forget?'

'It's not just going upstairs and then not knowing why when she gets there or making a meal and missing out part of the ingredients, Enid often doesn't remember that something has already been done or said earlier in the day. She's always repeating herself and she'll use the wrong word for an object or become stuck and not know the name for an everyday item. Then she becomes agitated.'

'Can you tell me about the occasions when she becomes agitated?'

Alfred became quiet. He didn't want to talk about the assaults.

'She becomes frustrated and shouts.'

'Does she shout at you?'

Judas. Judas.

'At times, but she doesn't mean anything by it. She's just not herself.'

'That must be very upsetting when you've looked after each other for so long. Does your wife know that you've come here this morning?'

'No.'

'I think that we really need to see her. Do you feel you could tell her that you've visited me this morning?'

Alfred considered this for a moment, weighing up the various pros and cons of such a revelation. He couldn't stop himself becoming upset again.

'No.'

'That's okay. Don't worry about it. I could ask Enid to come to the surgery to review her medication and while she's here raise the issue of memory problems in way that doesn't arouse any suspicion.'

His face showed the relief he felt.

'Thank you.'

'We have to firstly eliminate other potential causes for her behaviour. It might not be due to dementia.'

'What else could it be?' he asked, not having considered there might be an alternative.

'People can become confused for all sorts of reasons, from an infection to a vitamin or thyroid deficiency.'

'I didn't know that.'

'Well, that's why I'm here, to help. Sometimes changes to a person's normal behaviour can be due to failing eyesight or hearing, which makes them feel isolated and not able to communicate as they used to. You mustn't simply jump to conclusions.'

'Thank you.'

'Leave this with me and I'll work out a ploy to get her to the surgery. Now, tell me, how are you?' she said.

Alfred had closed his shop for a couple of hours to go to the surgery and he went back to complete his day's work before returning home as usual. He had stopped asking Enid what she had been up to because she often couldn't recall and easily became flustered or frightened. Instead, he tended to talk about what he had been doing or he would bring up stories from their past, which she always remembered.

'Hello, love,' he said walking into the house.

Enid came to meet him at the front door. It was almost a ritual, like taking his scarf from him, which was always put on a particular peg on the coat stand.

'How was your day?' she asked, taking his gloves and laying them carefully on top of the scarf.

'It was good. I got talking to a man about that holiday we had once in the Yorkshire Dales at that very nice family-run hotel.'

'Goodness! That was in 1965, the year we bought the Hillman Imp.'

'That's right, love. We had quite a chat about it.'

They reminisced about the holiday over dinner. He had

developed the tactic over the previous weeks, saying that he had been talking to a customer about a certain event that he and Enid had done many years earlier. So far she had always made a connection to the story, so they had a subject to discuss that didn't cause her any distress. He could spin this out all evening if necessary, either pretending that he had talked to another customer about a different incident, or by simply letting the conversation flow naturally between events from long ago.

Alfred couldn't see anything amiss around the house. Sometimes items were in strange places and he would replace them quietly. The meal had also been alright, with no parts of it missing. Enid had made a gooseberry crumble. They were nearly finished and had been talking amicably about old times, as if neither had a care in the world, when she suddenly looked at him blankly for several moments.

'Are you alright, love?' he asked.

'Yes,' she said, shaking her head. 'I was going to say something and it's gone completely out of my head.'

'Oh, I wouldn't worry about it. I almost forgot how to get to the shop this morning.'

'You and your shop. How was your day?'

Alfred kept his expression the same, but while wisps of steam rose gently from the spoonful of gooseberry crumble in his right hand, he was crying inside with anger, despair and frustration.

'It was fine ... I talked to a customer ... about the holiday we had in the Yorkshire Dales.'

'Yes, that was a good holiday. We got the Hillman Imp that year.'

The following week Enid sat opposite the doctor while Alfred was in the waiting room.

'Thank you for coming into the surgery. Every now and again it's a good idea to check the medication patients are on and make sure that what they are taking is still correct. Bodies and situations change over time. So can I do my vampire act and take some blood?'

Enid rolled up her sleeve while the GP sorted out what she needed.

'Have you any concerns at all about your health?' she asked, checking for the best vein.

'No, I'm fine, thank you.'

'Good. Sometimes, when people get over twenty-three ...'

'Only just,' said Enid smiling.

'... they may find that they can become a little forgetful at times. What I like to do when I have the opportunity is to put them in the Mastermind chair and ask a couple of simple questions. Is it alright if we do that once I've taken your blood? It won't take very long.'

'Yes,' replied Enid, slightly bemused at the prospect.

The doctor completed her task, washed her hands and picked up two sheets of questions that were lying on the desk.

'You can take your time in replying. There's no need to worry about not knowing an answer. So, can you tell me what building we're in?'

'It's the surgery.'

'And what town is this?'

They worked their way through the thirty questions that made up the standard mini mental state examination, which provided a guide to the way someone remembered and processed information.

'Thank you,' said the doctor, quickly adding up in her mind the number of incorrect answers or evasive replies given, such as when Enid said she didn't read newspapers in response to a question about the date. 'The test shows that there could be a little bit of problem with your memory.'

'It's not a problem to me,' said Enid defensively.

'Well, that's good. But perhaps it might be worthwhile checking this out further and I would like to suggest that we make an appointment for you at the memory clinic. There's one at the hospital, so you don't have to travel far and Alfred can go with you.'

'If you think I need it.'

'You leave it with me. We'll be in touch. Now, I'd like to check you over physically and before you go I need a pee sample.'

Chapter Eleven

Tom spent a long time trying to decide whether to speak to the solicitor he had met socially through the local Rotary Club, or whether to make an appointment with a firm in another town, where he had no connections and would simply be a stranger seeking advice.

Despite the intense feelings of humiliation that dominated so much of his life these days he chose the man he knew and respected, knowing that whatever was discussed would remain confidential. This was why one morning towards the end of March he sat in the office of Jack, one of the senior partners. They had gone through the normal enquiries about family and health.

'So, how can I help?

Tom guessed the solicitor was approaching fifty and although he wouldn't count him as a friend, he had always enjoyed the older man's company at the various charity events which they had attended. Tom was someone who held his head up and looked people in the eye when he spoke, but he answered by talking to the hands resting in his lap.

'It's extremely difficult for me to explain what has been happening.'

Jack knew better than to interject with comments along the lines of, 'I've heard all sorts of things in here', or a similar bland statement, and remained silent.

'Gemma's been beating me up. We've been married for nine years. She's always had a temper, but over the last two years she's increasingly lost control of it. The first incident was a slap across the face because I was late for dinner. She apologised straight away and I made no more of it, though it shook me a lot. The next time something happened she threw a cup, which hit me on the back of the head, but did no physical damage.

'The violence seemed to ... creep along ... becoming worse almost without me realising. Each time the item thrown was that bit heavier, or it was hurled with greater force, always when I wasn't expecting anything. Shortly before Christmas she chased me up the stairs with a carving knife. I had to lock myself in the bathroom. After a while I was worried that Amy might be in danger, so rang the police.'

Tom stopped and looked up. Jack felt he could speak.

'What happened?'

'I ended up in a cell at the local station. They thought it was me who was violent, but they released me without charge. I want to know what my options are.'

'I need to understand a lot more before I can advise you. Have you ever confided in anyone about this abuse, to a friend or family member?'

'No one.'

'Mmm. So even your own doctor doesn't know and isn't treating you for depression or any other condition, such as stress or anxiety, which could be related to this situation in the home?'

Tom shook his head.

'Have you ever ended up requiring medical attention because of an attack or had to take time off work?'

'I've had to go to the local casualty department on several occasions, but I always made out it was an accident in the house, or an injury from a game.'

'That's a pity, although there'll at least be medical records of the treatment. I would suggest that you confide in a trusted friend and get them to take photographs of your injuries soon after they've occurred. Maintain a log of events in a spare diary and for goodness sake make sure you keep it somewhere secret.

Use it to outline what happened, with as much detail as possible to support the visual evidence. Do you think your neighbours might have overheard any of these attacks taking place?'

'No, we're a bit too far from anyone for that.'

'What about Amy? Is she aware of what's going on?'

'I didn't think so, but I'm beginning to worry that she might know a lot more than I had realised. We had a social worker and police officer to the house a short while after I had been detained at the station. Amy was their main concern as well.'

'Does Gemma work?'

'She's a teacher.'

'Would you say she's a good mother?'

Tom thought about this for a while. In truth, he couldn't say she wasn't.

'Your options aren't great. You could leave the house and pay maintenance and you would probably get regular access unless your wife convinced the court that you were a danger to her or your daughter. That scenario wouldn't be a good one. You could try to win custody of Amy, but that would be a difficult road indeed to tread.

'Firstly, you would have to recount in front of others what has been happening to you in private, which wouldn't be easy. I can make a bit of a guess as to how much courage it's taken you to come and talk to me today, with just the two of us. Then you would have to convince the judge that Gemma was a bad mother and, by your own admission, she isn't.

'It would be almost impossible to get her out of the house, which means that you and your daughter would have to leave and someone would have to look after her when you're at work. Unfortunately, the practicalities work against you. The judge will consider the welfare of the child above everything else and my call would be that he would let them stay in the home and you would get restricted access at agreed times.

'Although these days we're all meant to be equal under the

eyes of the law, I'm afraid old ideas and prejudices retain a strong influence in many situations, and this is likely to be one of them.'

Tom was crestfallen.

'What do you suggest?'

'If you want my honest opinion, and that's what you'll get anyway, I would stay clear of the courts and recommend that you start by getting some emotional support for yourself. At least tell your doctor what's been happening. And, if you can, go along to one of the organisations that provide specialist guidance to couples when their marriage is going through difficulties. There are a lot of very good ones around.'

'That's what the police officer advised.'

'Did you put the idea to Gemma?'

'Yes.'

'What happened?'

'She split my head with a pan and I ended up in casualty.'

'Bloody hell, Tom! What did you say at the hospital?'

'That I'd hit my head on a cupboard door.'

'I don't know how else to advice you at the moment,' said Jack looking at his watch.

'Sorry. I've kept you too long.'

'Bugger the time. Come on. There's a first class restaurant around the corner. I'll stand you lunch.'

Chapter Twelve

Alfred and Enid sat in the reception area for the memory clinic. She had been complaining for days that there was no reason whatsoever for the test, which was a dreadful use of NHS money, but on the morning of the appointment she had come along without any fuss. They had already given their names to the receptionist. Neither knew what to expect and, of the two, he was by far the most nervous.

A short while later, a woman walked up to them and introduced herself as the consultant psychiatrist. Alfred thought she looked far too young to hold the post and must really be some sort of assistant, but they followed her along the corridor and into her room without comment.

'Enid, why don't you sit down there,' said the consultant, indicating a chair facing her own.

'Now, are you happy for Alfred to be here with you?'

It had never occurred to either of them that he shouldn't attend the consultation and Enid looked at the woman as if it was a rather daft question. However, she answered politely. After all, it was hardly her fault she was too young to under-stand that they were never apart. And why shouldn't he be there? There was nothing wrong with her. He sat in the chair that was positioned further away, slightly behind the one his wife was sitting in.

'You've had a little memory test at the surgery and your GP has now eliminated any obvious physical problems,' said the consultant. 'What I'm going to do today is give you a slightly longer test. Then I would like you to lie on a bed while we take some pictures of your head. It's very straightforward and quick.

You won't feel a thing. Would that be alright?'

Enid glanced around at her husband and Alfred nodded encouragingly.

'Well, if it helps, I suppose we can spare the time,' she replied.

The consultant told Enid the names of three objects that she wanted her to remember then picked up some papers.

'Right, we'll make a start. There's no rush and don't worry if you can't think of the answers. Can you tell me who the president of America is?'

'Oh, it's that new coloured fellow. He's got a funny name.'

Enid couldn't recall it.

'And who was the president before him?'

'Bush.'

'And do you remember the name of Britain's female prime minister?'

'Margaret Thatcher.'

The two worked their way through the questionnaire, Alfred remaining quiet, his heart sinking every time his wife couldn't answer. She did well on the subtraction tests – taking 7 away from 100, then reducing the figure by 7 several more times. She had always been good with figures, but she was very confused when asked to write the name of objects against a series of pictures, and thought that the pencil was a toothbrush and the kangaroo was a dog.

'Now, could you draw me a clock face that says ten minutes past five?'

Enid took the paper handed to her and drew a small clock face, but instead of drawing the hands of a clock to show the required time, she wrote out in words 'ten past five' as if it was too difficult to work out where the arrows should go. She did poorly at the visuospatial tests and when the consultant asked her to repeat the three words that she had been told to remember at the beginning of the tests, she couldn't recall a single one of them. When this part of the examination had been completed the consultant examined the forms for a while in silence before putting the sheets back on the desk.

'Have you found yourself becoming forgetful, perhaps not always remembering to do things that you would normally do?'

'Oh, no more than you would expect at my age. We all forget things as we grow older,' said Enid as if the consultant should at least know that much.

'Is it alright if I ask Alfred whether he can think of anything that you forget?'

'If it helps,' said Enid, fidgeting in her seat at the waste of the morning.

The consultant looked at the old barber, who cleared his throat, wondering what on earth he was meant to say. When he spoke, it was to his wife.

'Sometimes, love, you might forget to make a meal and go without eating until I've come home from the shop.'

'Do I? It can't be often I've done that.'

The consultant jumped in.

'Do you find that you've lost interest in cooking and eating?'

'Well, I don't think so.'

'And I've taken on paying the bills and doing some of the shopping,' he said after a slight pause in the conversation.

Enid made an 'Oh' sound as if it was news to her.

'And you're always losing things, love, like your handbag, and then when I find it you often say that money has been taken.'

He wondered how much to reveal, whether this was the proper moment to point out that she didn't wash or change her clothes as often as she should, whether he should mention about the violence. Alfred thought the consultant must have been a mind reader when she asked her next question, but later on he realised that the GP would have sent notes.

'Do you become cross when you can't remember something?'

'There's no need to get angry because you've forgotten to pay a bill.'

'But if you did become cross,' continued the consultant, deftly dodging around her reply, 'would you shout, maybe at Alfred?'

The consultant smiled and spoke softly, but her eyes flicked across the room and she noted the minute nod.

'No, we've never had a cross word ever. Have we?'

She turned to face her husband and, for the first time in the whole of their married life, he didn't know what to say.

'Have you ever, for instance, picked up a cup in anger, and thrown it?'

'We don't go throwing china around in our house,' said Enid, once more facing the consultant. 'What a silly idea.'

She was becoming increasingly agitated and upset at this line of questioning, constantly shifting about in her seat and looking at her watch.

'It's perfectly alright,' said the consultant, leaning forward and taking hold of one of her hands. 'There's nothing for you to be frightened about here. Don't worry about the time.'

Enid said 'Oh', but settled down slightly.

'Do you get sad ... perhaps crying when you don't know why ... feeling almost at times that life isn't worth living?'

Alfred considered this line of questions was completely off the mark and was shocked when Enid broke down in tears. She wasn't a crying sort of person.

'Sometimes ... sometimes I don't want to wake up in the morning.'

'Enid!'

He was horrified at this confession. It was so totally out of character, but what was far worse was that he had not appreciated she had been having such ideas. He got up and stood next to her. She buried her head in his side and he put an arm around her shoulder. The consultant let go of her hand and stood up.

'I'll leave you both for a little while.'

When they were alone he sat in the vacated chair.

'Why didn't you tell me you had being feeling like this?'

'I'm frightened, Alfred. Every morning when I wake I feel that another part of me has vanished. There are more things I don't remember and the emptiness just gets bigger. The world outside is becoming terrifying, but the world inside my mind is worse. I'm lost and alone.'

'You're not alone.'

'Yes, I am. I know you love me and will do everything you can. But I am alone. Every day I recognise and understand less, and one morning I'll not even recognise you. After all our many years together, I simply won't know who you are anymore. Don't ever forget me, Alfred. Please don't ever forget the person I was when I become that other person.'

'Never,' he said, tears falling down his cheeks. 'I promise.'

Later on, the radiographer took Enid to the scanning room, leaving Alfred alone with the consultant. He was badly shaken, though did his best to hide it.

'We will need to keep monitoring your wife, but the results of her tests show that she is having quite severe difficulties with her memory, and in processing information.'

'Does this mean she has dementia?'

'There are various forms of dementia and diagnosing any one of them can be extremely difficult. We can't be certain at this stage. Even the scan may not tell us anything for definite. In the meantime, you have the task of caring and I wanted to know how you are coping.'

'We get by.'

The consultant remained silent.

'At times, she becomes aggressive and that's very hard to handle,' he said.

'It's one of the saddest aspects of this sort of condition, but you must always bear in mind that none of what she says or does is really directed at you. It's just that you happen to be the one around.'

'Yes, in my heart I know that.'

'There are several techniques you might consider using that may help. I'll give you some leaflets before you leave which highlight many of them.'

'What sort of techniques?' he asked.

'Well, never forget that a lot of how we communicate with another person is not by speech, but via body language, such as the expression on our face or by physical touching. If Enid's ability to use and understand words diminishes, so you need to rely more on these other forms. And if she expresses herself in anger, try to work out calmly what it is she might be trying to let you know.'

'I hadn't thought of it in that way ... trying to tell me something. I just assumed she had lost her temper.'

'When you're speaking make sure you do it clearly, while there are no other distractions such as the television. I'm sure you won't, but avoid talking down to her and always keep your voice calm, even if she is shouting. Keep sentences short and simple and don't ask her a complex question, which could easily confuse or make her frustrated trying to understand.

'And don't forget that a hug or taking hold of her hand is a very effective way of letting Enid know that you still love her and that she's safe. Often, people with dementia become aggressive because they're scared.'

'Thank you, doctor, I'll try to remember.'

'I think you've got enough on your plate today. You'll find these points and other good advice in the literature. There are also groups in the local area that can provide support and practical advice. But let's not jump to conclusions. Somebody will be in touch to make another appointment when I've got the results of the scan. It should be over by now so perhaps we better see how she is.'

When they returned home Enid sat at the kitchen table while he made tea. They were both exhausted. He made no comment about the number of packets of cheese or cartons of orange juice in the fridge. Despite his attempts to take over the shopping, she would still go out when he was at work.

While she often forgot to purchase items they needed, she nearly always bought more cheese and orange juice. He had already been quietly giving the surplus food and drink to the family next door, but he feared that if he gave too much away his wife would be compelled to buy even larger quantities to replace it.

They drank their tea in silence. Alfred wondered how much of the visit to the hospital had already turned into mist in Enid's mind, making it impossible to hang on to memories; whether by suppertime she would deny they had even been there. He had to think of practical ways to help and one of the most urgent was to get her to wash. This was not going to be easy. She had slapped his face the previous week when he had told her she needed to have a bath and put on clean clothes.

He acknowledged to himself that he hadn't been as tactful as he should have, but the problem was getting worse. He was certain the consultant must have noticed that his wife was, well, a bit smelly. When they had finished their first cup of tea, he poured her another and went upstairs. She didn't ask where he was going.

He turned on the bath taps, adding large amounts of bubble bath. While the water was running he fetched a towel out of the cupboard. This one was really for guests and was softer than those they used every day. He laid out a set of clean clothes on their bed and took her dressing gown into the bathroom, turning off the taps when the water was at the height and temperature he wanted.

But before going downstairs he went back to the bedroom and put the clothes away. He realised that all he had to do was get the items Enid was wearing into the washing machine. She would then have to get clean clothes out and this was far more subtle than laying out items, which he had never done before.

'I've got a little surprise for you,' he said, standing in the kitchen doorway.

'What is it?' she asked, still sitting at the table.

He walked over and held out his hand.

'Well, you'll have to come with me to find out.'

She looked at him without moving for a moment, but he said 'come on' to encourage her, so she took his hand and he led her up the stairs.

'You've filled the bath. Who's that for?'

Alfred took her in his arms.

'Do you remember how, when we were first married, I used to love to wash your hair while you were in the bath?'

'I remember what always happened afterwards as well. Don't tell me you're feeling frisky?'

'We won't know until we try,' he said smiling.

'Oh, don't be silly.'

Enid hesitated. He knew he had to keep talking, to keep her mind occupied so that everything seemed quite natural.

'In fact,' he said, undoing the top button on her blouse, 'I recall that you always used to let me undress you.'

'What will the neighbours think?'

But she smiled, almost embarrassed, like she was a young girl again. Alfred wanted to cry, but he maintained the act, talking and helping her to undress until finally there was a pile of dirty clothes on the floor and his wife had almost disappeared beneath the water.

'Weeee!' she shouted, flicking suds up into the air.

Alfred laughed, while he moved the little wooden stool into position. He had gathered everything together earlier, her shampoo and conditioner, a jug for rinsing.

He left rolling up his sleeves until he was positioned almost behind her, because he didn't want her to be distracted by the ugly blue and yellow bruises that ran up both arms. She had developed the habit of nipping him, even during the night. There was no warning. He could be walking past her in the kitchen and she would suddenly reach out and nip him, always on the arms. Alfred made nothing of it, but he always tried to hide the marks because she was likely to become upset if she saw them.

Enid sat contentedly while he washed her hair. He didn't wash hair in the barber's shop. If men wanted to be pampered like that then they could go to one of the unisex salons and be charged a small fortune for the privilege. But he had loved to wash his wife's when they were younger. There were still flecks of gold and brown. He remembered a time when there was no grey. They talked about the early years of their marriage. There was a connection and in a strange way they were, for that brief moment, happy.

Enid had always been slender, but Alfred was disturbed at how thin she had become. He thought perhaps he should close the shop permanently so that he could be around all the time and make sure she ate properly. She was beginning to need more care in all sort of small ways. He noticed, as she climbed into the bath, that her toenails were too long and wondered if he could cut them when she slept, the way he used to cut Kate's while still a baby.

He was going to have to ring Kate.

When he had finished, Alfred soaped the sponge that Enid always used to wash herself and scrubbed her back. He kept talking and she made no comment. However, he couldn't wash all of her so in the end he handed it over. This was the moment where his plan could come completely unstuck.

He wasn't sure what he would do if she didn't appear to know how to use the sponge, but without speaking Enid set about her left foot with vigour. She always had a set pattern to washing and he waited for only a short while to ensure that, as usual, she started working her way up her leg. Alfred felt confident that he could leave her to wash properly so he gathered up the clothes.

'I'll put the kettle on for you coming down,' he said as he left the room.

He made no mention of washing and she didn't think to comment about him taking away the items on the floor. So that it didn't look as though he was just doing her clothes he collected other things from the washing basket. As he was sorting out garments he noticed that the knickers he had brought from the bathroom seemed too thick. He picked them up and saw that there were several pairs, one neatly inside the other.

For a few minutes he couldn't understand what she had done. Then he realised that Enid had been putting on clean knickers without removing the ones already on, until she had been walking around wearing four pairs. He separated them. But before throwing the garments into the washing machine, Alfred stopped for a moment to take out his hanky, blow his nose and wipe away the tears that were falling down his cheeks.

Chapter Thirteen

Gordon sat nervously in a corner of the little tea shop. It was on the far side of town from where he knew Tania usually shopped so the chances of her discovering him were sufficiently remote to be acceptable. He wasn't sure just what he expected from this meeting, what he hoped to achieve, but he was desperate to speak to someone who might understand how he felt, though he hardly knew this himself.

Was he unhappy? He didn't know how to judge happiness or what married life should be like; how to gauge what was normal. Could Jennifer tell him such a thing?

The previous day Tania had been screaming at him again. He had been in the sitting room, practising a solo part from *Dies Nox et Omnia*. His wife had been in the kitchen, but burst into the room shouting, 'Stop screeching in that stupid voice!' He tried to explain that he was singing *falsetto*, and she had replied that she didn't care what it was from, the noise was, 'doing her head in.' It was pointless to argue, but this now meant he couldn't rehearse in the house while she was there, which presented him with a huge problem in trying to learn the piece.

He was thinking about the incident and what to do, when Jennifer arrived.

'Hello,' she said, sitting opposite.

'Hello. Thanks for agreeing to meet me.'

'I'm glad you were able to ring me when you needed to. Have you ordered?'

'No.'

'Well, perhaps we should do that and then we can chat. There's nothing I have to be away for so you set the timescale.'

They ordered tea and discussed music until the waitress returned with the tray, so that they wouldn't be interrupted once they were talking about more serious matters. One of his legs jumped up and down, a visible sign of how edgy he felt. Jennifer poured tea and then sat quietly, letting him set the topic of the conversation.

'I don't know what to say or how to say it,' he said.

'Take your time. I know from my own experiences how difficult it is to make decisions when, for years, you've not been allowed to voice an opinion, often not even to finish a sentence. But it's important that whatever course of action you take it's because you have decided.'

Gordon was silent for a while and when he did speak he blurted everything out in a continuous stream as if the words were vital to his very existence, yet had to be spoken quickly or they would be lost forever.

'All through my life I've tried never to hurt anybody. When I was growing up I just wanted to get on without causing pain to anyone, even when people were being offensive to me. I was very alone. I thought being married and having a partner would be so different. However, sometimes Tania is so abusive and controlling that I want to scream with frustration and misery, but then I don't want to hurt her and I'm too weak to face up to her when she's in a rage. I get so angry with myself for not being stronger ... for being too stupid.'

He didn't know whether he had said too much, too little or not even made sense. Jennifer studied him without speaking for several moments.

'I was twenty-two when I met Derek. He was six years older. At the beginning I was flattered that he paid so much attention, always wanting to be with me and even coming shopping when I was looking for a new outfit. He would insist on seeing me wear everything that I was considering in order to give his opinion.

'My girlfriends thought I was lucky to have a man who was so charming and took an interest. I just didn't see the warning signs for what they were, such as the way he would become moody if I bought an item that wasn't his choice, particularly if he thought it was too expensive.

'I've often looked back and wished there had been an older, wiser friend who opened my eyes to the dangers ahead. But there wasn't, or at least if anyone had thought something was wrong they never spoke out. So we got married when I was twenty-four.

'The first time he hit me was shortly after our second wedding anniversary. It was more of a push really, but I was utterly shaken. However, he was so very sorry, begging my forgiveness and saying how much he loved me. He had merely had an extremely stressful day. Such an appalling thing would never ever happen again. I forgave him.

'The next time it was slightly more than a push, but he was so contrite I gave him another chance, thinking that these things happened between couples and you had to take the rough with the smooth.

'And so it went on. The push became a slap, the slap became a punch, the punch turned into a flurry of blows aimed precisely to cause maximum hurt. He was careful never to hit my face. One of his favourite punishments if I had been, in his opinion, particularly bad, was to make me stand upright against a wall while he hit my breasts. The pain was unbelievable.

'As time passed he developed strange obsessions, or perhaps he simply felt in a strong enough position to make them known. Everything had to be kept exactly in a certain place in the house: bottles of shampoo in the cupboard, washing-up liquid under the sink, tins of beans ... they all had to be stored within millimetres of some crazy diagram he had in his head. There would always be trouble if the labels weren't facing forward precisely.

'And he would accuse me constantly of having affairs, over and over again, often with someone that I had had no more contact with than paying them for food over the counter at the nearby shop.

'After eight years he controlled every penny I earned, giving me an allowance out of my own money with which I had to buy food, clothes and items for the house. He would come with me when I went shopping to ensure I bought only the cheapest things.

'Can you imagine a man actually going through the display of sanitary products on the supermarket shelf to select which brand his wife could purchase? Women would look at me sadly as they walked past with their trolleys. It became so bad that he would dictate ...'

Jennifer stopped. She had planned exactly what to say, had agreed with herself what was acceptable to reveal and what was not (there were some things that would never be spoken of) and she had talked calmly, without displaying too much emotion.

She had intended to tell him this next part, but her throat closed up with shame at the memory. Somehow confessing to this was worse than talking about the beatings. It was more degrading than admitting to any of the many other controlling things Derek did to her. She took a deep breath and spoke in a whisper.

'It became so bad he would dictate how many towels I could use in a month.'

She was unable to go on. Torturers had known over the ages that it was often not physical pain that finally broke a person's spirit, but a different punishment altogether. Her husband had been an expert torturer.

Gordon gently laid a hand over one of hers. She gave him a little smile of gratitude. Her feeling that this young man was trapped unhappily in his marriage was so strong that she was compelled to tell her story as a means of opening his eyes. If she could help him, it would mean so much. Perhaps her actions, revealing such desperately intimate details about her past life, wouldn't make sense to anyone, but to Jennifer it would be as though she was in a way standing up to Derek and everything he represented.

She sipped tea while composing herself. Gordon was astonished. No one had ever spoken to him like this before and, feeling completely out of his depth, he didn't know what to say or do.

'After about twelve years, I had no friends or hobbies, no laughter, no hope. I had to come straight back from work each day and wasn't allowed to leave the house again without his permission. If we did go out together he would take delight in putting me down in front of people, sometimes saying quite disgusting lies about our private life together. By this stage, he certainly never bothered apologising for anything he said or did; didn't pretend anymore that he loved me.'

'Why did you stay?'

Jennifer smiled, but it was without humour.

'That's always the big question isn't it? Why simply not leave if it's anywhere near that bad? There are many answers. In the early years I tried so hard to make the marriage succeed, willing to give him another chance whatever he had done.

'And he was inevitably so sorry for his "loss of control", which was due to stress at work or having had too much to drink or ... well, there was always a reason. It's difficult to explain how skilful he was at keeping me in a permanent state of confusion by interspersing violent acts with long periods of being considerate and affectionate, so that I found it easier to block out the bad memories and remember only the good ones.

'It wasn't until much later that I realised he never "lost control" if someone else was around, and that he didn't hit anyone but me. Only upon looking back did I understand how Derek was never more "in control" than at those moments when he was abusing me violently.

'But that was later and for a long time I believed I could help him change. However, as time went by I became so isolated. One of his greatest pleasures was to sit me on a stool and force me to telephone people I had known for years, accusing them of terrible things, stealing, trying to sleep with him or saying that their husband had attempted to rape me.

'Dear friends whom I had known since childhood would be so hurt and shocked on the other end of the line that they would be crying because of what I was saying to them. But they weren't my words and it broke my heart to speak them. They didn't know my tormentor was standing nearby, ready to punch me in the area of my kidney if I didn't sound convincing enough.

'Sometimes, in the beginning, I tried to refuse, but I was too weak and couldn't take the pain. One by one he eliminated my circle of support. However, he was extremely devious with his manipulation, and behind my back he befriended people who I knew, winning over several of them so that they became his allies and not mine.

'In the end I felt so utterly empty, as if I had no substance and was merely Derek's shadow, moving only to his will. Without a shred of self-esteem I lost the ability to make even the most basic of decisions. He invariably blamed me for the violence and I became so indoctrinated that I believed his behaviour was my fault, that I was a bad person, and would apologise for making him so angry that he had to hit me.

'Often he would scream that if I did what he said then he would have no reason to punish me. He was trying to correct the flaws in my character. It was really that simple, only I was too stupid to understand. I wore myself out trying to please him, but, of course, he didn't really want to be pleased. What he wanted was to be abusive. On occasions he would change the rules so that it was impossible for me ever to do what was right.

When he told me that no one liked me, I was worthless, I couldn't possibly survive without him ... I accepted it all as fact without question.

'Then one day I was out by myself and saw in a shop window a poster about a charity for battered women. There was a long list of examples of abuse and reading through them was like picking up the diary of my own life. I was too frightened to use my mobile to ring the number given. He always checked to see if I had called someone. I simply didn't have the courage. There was an old-fashioned public telephone box nearby, but I had no money. Even now I don't know what made me do it. An elderly couple were walking past and I told them I needed to make a call.'

Jennifer couldn't go on. Of all the memories, the hurt and humiliation, despair and loneliness, it was relating an act of kindness that proved too much. A great sob escaped from somewhere deep within her, so loudly that the people on the next table looked over.

'Please don't go on. This is too painful for you.'

'No. I have to finish,' she said, struggling to hold back tears. 'I had been married for twenty-five years. All my chances had gone, having a family, a good career, making something of my singing. It was all over. But I still asked. The woman took out all of the change in her purse and put it in my hand, gently closing my fingers around the coins. Without that generosity I might never have escaped.

'I rang the number. When the call was answered, I simply stood there crying. Eventually, the person at the end of the line got enough out of me to realise where I was and told me to stay there, not to leave under any circumstances. Waiting for her was the longest twenty minutes of my life. Then there she was, standing outside the telephone box; someone who understood.

'With no more to my name than the clothes I was wearing, I was taken immediately to a nearby refuge and never went home again. There was nothing of mine in the house, at least nothing that I had chosen and wanted, so I left it all for Derek. Apparently, he hunted for me for months, wild with rage and frustration, but the charity moved me quickly to a refuge in another town and all communication with him was via a solicitor that they appointed. With no friends, he had no one to threaten into telling where I had gone.

'My parents didn't live in the area and wouldn't have anything to do with him, but I kept my whereabouts vague even from them. It was the safest thing. Now I'm far away, with a new life, house and job. Jennifer is my middle name. I never use the first one anymore. It belongs to the past.'

She blew her nose on a tissue and gradually composed herself. Gordon stayed silent, letting her take her own time to recover. With a small smile she reached over and, using the back of her fingers, tenderly wiped his cheek. It was wet. He hadn't realised that towards the end of her story tears had been rolling slowly down his face, a few of them falling into his teacup, like the first hesitant raindrops of a shower that appear reluctant to leave the sanctuary of the sky.

Indeed, Gordon had been so absorbed that he was completely unaware of anything going on around him in the tea shop; not the young mother feeding a baby nearby, nor the elderly ladies at the next table talking excitedly about their forthcoming holiday.

He was certainly unaware of the woman who had been watching him through the shop window for the previous ten minutes. It was Sally. She had glanced in to see if there were any seats and spotted him immediately. So she had watched, waiting long enough to see Tania's husband take hold of the stranger's hand and for her to stroke his cheek. Sally walked a short distance, took out her mobile and made a call.

'I'm so very sorry,' said Gordon. 'I don't know what to say. Your story is awful. My life is nowhere near as terrible as the

99

description you've just given and Tania does understand me.'

'It doesn't have to be as bad to be wrong,' said Jennifer, ignoring for now the idea that Tania understood him, as she knew this was a point that would require some in-depth discussion. 'There are many forms of abuse that do not include physical violence. No one should feel unsafe in their home, monitoring everything they say and do simply to get through the day. I spoke to many women in the shelters and although their histories varied greatly, they all shared similar fears and reactions.'

Gordon couldn't stop himself glancing at his watch. It was, he realised even as he did it, a fear reaction.

'Don't get into trouble by being late. I'm afraid I've done all the talking, but I hope it may help.'

'I'm sorry. I feel I'm running away and leaving you, but if I'm too late my wife will ask lots of questions about where I've been and it's so difficult not to tell her the truth. I'll think about what you've said and about my life.'

'Don't apologise. Get yourself home. The important thing is for you to be safe. Leave me here. I'll get some more tea so that I can sit quietly for a while. I'll be fine doing that.'

He stood up. They smiled at each other, both still with tears in their eyes then he hurried home.

'Hello,' Gordon shouted as he walked into the house.

No answer. He'd beaten her back. Safe.

He closed the front door, letting out a huge sigh of relief. Hanging up his jacket in the hallway, he walked to the kitchen. She was there, waiting for him.

'Oh, hello, love. I didn't know you were ...'

Tania went for his nose, which she knew was still tender following the plastic surgery. She rarely hit him. It wasn't her preferred method of control, so he was completely unprepared for the punch and cried out, while putting both hands up to his

100

face and bending over to protect it from any further assault. This made it easy for her to grab a handful of his long black hair. She wasn't stronger than him, but she was certainly heavier and madder, so she held him down and began to punch the side of his head with her fist as hard as she could.

'You bastard. You bastard. I'm not having you sleeping around anymore. I'm sick of it. Bastard!'

'Stop it. Stop it.'

Gordon was dumbfounded. Blinded by tears from the pain in his nose and utterly shocked by this unexpected violence, he didn't know how to react.

'No. Stop.'

Tania carried on, screaming abuse and accusations, which he was completely unable to reply to. He was saved in the end because she was so unfit that she ran out of breath quickly and simply let go of him, before walking slowly to the sitting room, gasping and sobbing loudly. When Gordon regained his wits he followed her, though he remained close to the doorway so he could escape if needed. She was sitting in the armchair, crying.

'This is all your fault. You've made me hit you. How can you be having another affair?'

'What's got into you? What are you talking about? What affair?'

'You were seen with your lover at the tea shop.'

Gordon felt his shock and anger melting into fear.

'Who told you that?'

'It's pointless denying it. Sally saw you both, trying to hide in the corner. It's disgusting.'

It could only have been worse if his wife had walked into the tea shop herself. Sally took a perverted delight in feeding Tania's fantasies.

'She saw you holding hands and kissing.'

It was already difficult to pick out the lies from the truth. Gordon knew he hadn't kissed Jennifer, but Sally may have said this or it may be his wife making it up.

'We never kissed.'

'But you were holding hands.'

Tania lying.

'We were simply having a cup of tea together, but she told me a very sad story and I took her hand only for a moment to comfort her as she was crying.'

'I'm not the one around here who's stupid. I thought you might have gone for a younger woman. I gather this one's old enough to be your mother.'

'I haven't gone for any woman. We were having a cup of tea. That's all. A cup of tea in a busy tea shop is not an affair.'

'I knew this would happen once you had your nose done. It's given you more confidence to go out chasing every bit of skirt you fancy.'

'I've never chased anyone.'

'Why didn't you tell me you were seeing her? Why did you keep this such a sordid secret?'

Gordon was on dangerous ground. He could pretend that they had met by chance, but he had no excuse for being in that particular part of town. However, if he admitted they had arranged to meet, then he was on equally thin ice.

'She's just a friend from the choir, but I knew you would make something of it. If we hadn't been seen, then no harm would have been done.'

'Because I wouldn't have known what was going on!'

'There's nothing going on.'

'I've put up with your other affairs because I love you so much and if you cared for me you wouldn't see these other women. You shouldn't need someone else, just like I don't need anyone except you.'

'There haven't been any affairs. In my entire life I've not so much as kissed another woman, never mind slept with one. You must know that's true.'

'Why do I have to suffer so much? No one cares about me.'
'I care.'
'Prove it then by promising never to see this person again.'
But this was the last thing he wanted to do.

Chapter Fourteen

'I see you don't come to the surgery often and yet you're almost a regular visitor to the local casualty department. What brings you here today?'

Tom sat in front of the GP, a woman of about thirty who he had never met. It was largely because of the solicitor's comment that he had made the appointment, although he still wasn't sure how much to reveal.

'I've not been sleeping well,' he said.

'What do you think is causing this?'

Tom hesitated.

'I've been feeling anxious. Now I'm exhausted and finding it increasingly difficult to concentrate at work.'

'How long has this been going on?'

'About seven months.'

'That's quite a specific period. Did something happen to bring on this anxiety?'

This was the moment when he either confessed what was really going on or not. However, if he didn't then why was he there? What did he hope to achieve if he kept the abuse a secret?

'One night, around that time, my wife attacked me in bed.'

'She attacked you?'

'With a cricket bat.'

'What made her do such a thing?'

'I don't know ... something she felt I had done, or hadn't done, earlier that day, or else she simply wanted to escalate the violence to a new level of aggression.'

'How long has this behaviour been going on?'

'For around two and a half years.'

'For more than two years she's been assaulting you?'

'Not severely at first,' said Tom and even to his ears it sounded as though he was trying to defend Gemma with the statement. 'In the beginning, it was only a few slaps or the occasional punch, and she always appeared to be hugely remorseful afterwards. Apart from this, our life together was great. We have a fantastic little girl, Amy, and otherwise everything was good between us.'

The doctor sat back in her chair and studied him. Tom thought she was surprised though not disbelieving, and for that he was extremely grateful.

'So the situation became worse as the months went by?'

'Yes. Gemma kept pushing the boundaries of what she could get away with.'

'Is this why you've been so often to casualty?'

'I've always said it was an accident and no one ever enquired further.'

'Do you have any injuries now?'

'Bruises, that's all.'

'May I look?'

Tom removed his jacket and shirt and she took note of a few fading marks on his back.

'Have you told anyone about this?'

'A while ago Gemma chased me with a carving knife. I locked myself in the bathroom, but I was worried about Amy so called the police.'

'What happened?'

'They took me to the local station believing that I was the abuser, but there was no evidence so I was released without charge. However, a few days afterwards a domestic violence liaison officer and a social worker came to the house, concerned about Amy.'

'Are you worried about your daughter?'

Tom considered this point often, but Gemma had never

demonstrated aggression towards anyone other than him.

'I've never seen any violence towards her and I constantly check for marks on her body that don't look right.'

'Perhaps, without making it obvious, you should talk to Amy away from the house, when there's just the two of you. Find out if she knows what's going on and see if you can ascertain if she's being affected.'

'I'll work something out,' he said, already wondering if he could engineer a reason to take Amy out alone around the time of her forthcoming eighth birthday.

'What about you? This must be affecting your self-esteem.'

He clammed up. The GP waited, letting him find the words in his own time. Tom stared down at his hands, unable to look her in the face any longer.

'I ... I don't feel like a real man. More and more I think I'm worthless, a failure. I've even been dropped from the rugby team because my performance is so poor and without the training I'm losing my strength and fitness. It's as though I have no value.'

She didn't answer for a while.

'Have you ever had thoughts of harming yourself?'

'No,' he said, looking up. 'I'm not that bad.'

'Don't become that bad,' she said. 'At the very first hint of any thought of harming yourself I want you to make an appointment. I'll inform the reception staff that if you call at any time you are to be given a priority slot with me.'

'Thank you,' said Tom, a small smile flickering across his face.

'Where to go from here though ...'

'I wondered if Gemma needed counselling, perhaps some sort of anger management course, although to be honest I don't know if she would attend such a thing.'

'I'm not about to try to diagnose your wife's problems, and it wouldn't be appropriate to do so. I would need her to come and see me and that discussion would obviously be confidential. However, speaking generally about domestic violence based on the examples I've come across over the years, what you're suggesting would only treat a symptom.'

'I'm not with you.'

'People aren't abusive because they're angry. It's the other way around. You have to tackle the root causes, which are the beliefs a controller has that he or she has a right to dominate another person, often to the point of altering them, of turning them into the fictitious character they desire in their head, even though this might have little resemblance to the real person.

'Everyone loses their temper. That's part of life. But the regular outbursts displayed by an abuser are only a means to an end. They're generally a red herring, turned on at very specific moments with nothing whatsoever to do with "losing control". Sorry, I tend to get on my soapbox about this issue. Once you've seen some of the results of domestic violence it's difficult not to feel strongly about it.'

'Yes, I'm sure,' said Tom, realising that this planned "loss of control" seemed to be exactly what Gemma had created.

'I've come across many cases of physical abuse against women and I can usually help,' said the GP. 'There are several very good charities and there's an effective support structure locally, including an excellent safe house. There are also well-structured programmes designed for male perpetrators. You present me with a challenge, Tom. I could prescribe you tablets for anxiety or depression.'

'No thanks.'

'No, they wouldn't remove the cause of your problems. If you ever need them come back straight away. I don't know of any organisations for men. I'm not sure what to suggest, but I'm uncomfortable at sending you away without doing more. I wonder ...'

The GP had faced him throughout their discussion, avoiding

the trap of talking to the computer on her desk. She swivelled her chair around to face the screen before keying "Battered Men" into a search engine.

'Wow. Come closer and look at this,' she said, twisting the monitor so that he could more easily see it.

She spent several minutes scrolling through page after page, clicking on websites that caught her attention. There was a colossal amount of information.

'Well, you're certainly not alone,' she said. 'And I need to do some reading. I had no idea so much research had been done into this subject.'

After a short while she keyed in "charities for battered men".

'Look, there are organisations designed to help men who are being abused.'

They read for a few moments then she refined the search to just the UK.

'Bingo. I'm probably not alone amongst my colleagues in being unaware that these various charities existed.'

'Thank you,' he said. 'I don't want to take up any more of your time. I can easily check out these sites at work. You've been very kind. I can't thank you enough. Having someone believe me and knowing that I'm not the only man in this situation has helped a lot.'

'Make an appointment to see me in a month or so, even if nothing has changed or there have been no major incidents at home. Promise?'

'I promise,' said Tom and left.

Chapter Fifteen

Alfred and Enid sat in the consultant psychiatrist's office. They were there to hear the results of the brain scan. He had told Kate what had been happening, everything apart from the violence. There was no point in upsetting his daughter and she would have felt helpless so far away. However, he had agreed to ring her at the first opportunity once they left the hospital.

'Now, how have you been keeping?' asked the consultant, studying the older woman carefully.

'Fine. Fine,' said Enid, looking at her husband next to her.

The visit had made her nervous and she was irritable.

'And how have you been coping, Alfred?'

'I've closed my barber's shop so that I can be at home, making sure Enid eats properly.'

The consultant didn't miss the fact that he hadn't actually said *how* he was, only what he was doing.

'The tests we've conducted, Enid, show there is a slight shrinkage of your brain, which may result in difficulty in processing information, or in carrying out everyday tasks. Have you heard the word "dementia" before?'

'That's something old people get,' replied Enid, counting herself out of that proportion of the population.

'Yes, it's something that the elderly can develop, although it can happen regardless of age. Do you know if anyone in your family ever had dementia, such as your parents or grand-parents?'

'An old aunt was put away because she kept wandering. She was always going off and being brought back by neighbours or the police, once even by the postman.'

'Some types of dementia are linked to our genes, what we've inherited from our ancestors, and we believe other forms are more connected with lifestyle,' said the consultant. 'What we think you might have is something called Alzheimer's.'

Enid gave a little 'Oh', and started to cry. Alfred put his arm around her shoulder and the consultant leaned forward to take hold of one of her hands.

'It sounds frightening because it's always the horrible stories we hear or read about. But there are lots of things that can be done to help. You are not alone. Never think that.'

'What will happen?' asked Enid.

'We can't cure it, but there are medications that can be prescribed that will slow down its progress, in order to keep you better for longer.'

'I don't know how I've got this. I've always lived a good life and there was only the one old aunt. That was years ago. How have I got it?'

'I'm afraid we simply don't know why some people develop Alzheimer's, while others live to be very old without any effects.'

'It doesn't seem fair to me,' said Enid.

'No, it's never fair,' agreed the consultant. 'It's just life.'

'What are we to do?' asked Alfred, who was trying to hold back his tears.

'Firstly, I would like to arrange for the local community psychiatric nurse to come to your home because she can assess more easily what support you may need. You'll like her. She's really lovely and will be available to give you advice going forward, to make it easier for Enid to remain at home. That is, if this is what you both want?'

They nodded.

'I'll write to your GP and explain what's happening. You'll need to see her to obtain your medication.'

'When should I ring the surgery?' he said.

'Perhaps leave it until the end of the week.'

'I'll call on Friday.'

'That's a good idea. I believe you've got a daughter?'

'Kate. I'll speak to her later today.'

'I'm sure she would want to know what is happening,' confirmed the consultant. 'Alfred, you may have heard of the term "power of attorney". With this in place you become in a sense Enid's legal guardian, so that you can make decisions to ensure any course of action is always for the best. I would recommend you do this soon, rather than leaving it until later when it may not be possible.'

He nodded.

'Now, let me explain about the medication ...'

The community psychiatric nurse arrived the following week, having telephoned first to arrange a convenient time. The consultant was right, she was lovely. Alfred liked the way she dealt with his wife. The previous day had been awful. Enid had sworn her mother had been chattering to her in the living room, and she had spent hours going around the house trying to find her.

Alfred had lost his temper, shouting that she was long dead. He knew it was pointless, but he was so despairing that when she made a move to nip his arm he grabbed her wrist. For weeks she had aimed for the same spot, on the inside of his elbow, and it was so painful that he couldn't stand it *again*, not at that particular moment. So he had caught hold of her and the two of them had spent several minutes tussling in the corridor. Afterwards he had sat in floods of tears in the kitchen, while he listened to her opening and shutting doors around the house, calling out to her mother.

He had found giving up his shop and spending almost all of his time in the house was much harder than he had imagined. It was increasingly difficult to make any sort of connection and he wanted to scream when Enid kept asking or saying the same thing over and over again. He was sinking under the weight of sadness and loneliness. He was lonely. Most of the time the woman he loved wasn't there, just some not-very-clean stranger going around the house unaware of him.

The nurse said her name was Ann and her job was to help them overcome whatever fears or problems they might have. If she couldn't solve an issue then there were plenty of other professionals to call on.

'How have you been managing?'

Ann was sitting almost sideways on the settee, so that she could face Enid next to her and was close enough to take hold of a hand if needed.

'Alright. I don't know why you're here. We're alright.'

Enid spoke to the floor and avoided eye contact.

'Are you taking all your medication as instructed by the doctor?'

She didn't answer, so Alfred, sitting in the armchair across the room, said 'yes'.

'I don't know why I need it.'

'Well, the doctor probably knows best about these things. Alfred, how do you feel you are managing?'

'Oh, we get along,' he said, rather unconvincingly.

'People sometimes fear that they will be forced to go into a home against their wishes, but we're here to help those affected live as normal a life as possible, for as long as they can. There's a wide range of support that can be called upon, from providing meals to helping with washing.'

'We don't need any of that type of interference,' said Enid defensively.

Alfred's simple ploy of getting his wife into the bath by pretending he wanted to wash her hair had worked on several occasions, but not every time, and she had become aggressive during his last two attempts so that he felt more wary of trying.

He wondered if it might be a good idea to leave this to someone with experience in these situations.

'I'll provide you with lots of information about the various options that are available, such as practical and emotional aid, and any financial benefits that you might be eligible for. Firstly, I could do with two favours. I'm gasping for a drink and I could do with using your loo.'

'Sorry,' he said. 'I should have thought to offer you tea. The bathroom is upstairs, second door on the left. I'll put the kettle on.'

Ann followed the instructions. This was an often-used trick. She poked her head into the bedrooms to gain a quick overall impression and went into the bathroom to check how clean it was. She didn't need the loo, but pressed the handle so that no one suspected her real motives and then hurried downstairs to the kitchen. Alfred was standing by the kettle. There were cups on the table, but no milk so without asking she walked over to the fridge and opened the door.

'I'll get the milk, shall I?'

Her experienced eye assessed the contents in the time it took to locate the milk jug.

'Lots of cheese and orange juice,' she said, holding the door open so that the items inside were visible to both of them.

'She keeps buying them,' said Alfred. 'I can't stop her, even if we're together. I tried it once and she became so agitated in the shop that I never said anything again. I just give it away to neighbours. She doesn't seem to notice.'

'It's not uncommon for someone with dementia to keep buying the same products.'

'I guess it's not important. I've stopped bothering about it.'

Ann closed the fridge door and walked over to put the jug on the table near to where he was standing.

'What things do bother you?' said asked.

'She's taken to ringing our daughter several times a day,

including during the night. It's upsetting for Kate to hear her mother talk nonsense down the telephone only for her to call a few hours later and say the same things.'

'Perhaps you could ask Kate what she thinks might help her with regard to these calls. How are you coping?'

'I miss the woman I spent the last fifty-six years with. The one who made me laugh so much.'

'I know. But if you can both still find something to laugh about then that's a great way to connect to each other.'

'There's very little these days to find funny. Yesterday Enid wandered around the house for hours looking for her mother who she was convinced had been here earlier. She died years ago.'

'These are all very common reactions. What did you do?'

Alfred was quiet for a while, ashamed at the memory of the previous day.

'I became angry and shouted that she was dead.'

'That's a natural response. If you can, try not to be so blunt about something you know is incorrect.'

'I'm sorry.'

'That's alright. I've been doing this job for a long time so it's easier for me to know a few alternatives in these sensitive situations. Perhaps if she talks about a deceased relative again, you could point out how they always loved to visit, and ignore the fact that they're no longer alive. This is the sort of tack that will help you communicate. Did you read through the literature from the consultant?'

'Yes, I try to follow the advice about listening carefully, offering lots of encouragement, making physical contact to try to overcome her being frightened or lonely. At times it helps. On other occasions it seems to make no difference what I do.'

'Speaking of lonely, we better not leave Enid any longer, but I did want to speak to you.'

'I appreciate it,' he said.

114

Alfred lay for a long time that night while his wife slept soundly next to him. Ann had assessed their needs and they all agreed that she would arrange for a carer to come to the house for two or three mornings a week. After she left he had called Kate. He suggested that she might want to disconnect the landline when they went to bed each evening and just leave a mobile on as a way to make contact in an emergency, but she hadn't been keen.

Alfred berated himself for his refusal in the early days of his wife's forgetfulness to admit that there might be something wrong. Pretending nothing was the matter hadn't been a wise decision and in the long run it had most likely made things worse by delaying the diagnosis and treatment.

Bloody old fool.

Enid made a moaning noise next to him, but she settled quickly and he went back to looking at the ceiling. At night he left the hall light on and the bedroom door part open because this reduced the risk of her falling over, and it also helped to overcome her fear of shadows and furniture that somehow took on a sinister meaning in her mind if she woke up in the dark.

Alfred didn't even bother to try and go to sleep. Although he was learning steadily how best to cope he always felt he was reacting to a situation, never preventing a problem by foreseeing it. Ann had told him not to be so hard on himself, but he couldn't help it. Feelings of helplessness were never far away. It all seemed so unfair. Enid was only seventy-five. That wasn't old. Not these days. He accepted that people got all sorts of terrible diseases and that tragedies happened to all kinds of folk, but why to them? And why this? It was such an evil condition.

His mind drifted back to the evening he and Enid had met at the dance, when they were teenagers, though no one had such a title in those days. They had often sat around the kitchen table and compared their early lives with today's youth. When they were young they had had a proper childhood, playing innocent, simple games, running around the streets or in the local woods. A trip to the cinema was an event that you talked about for weeks afterwards.

There was a structure and order to life that made you feel safe. Everyone ate their meals at the table and did things as a family. There was a true comradeship, not the virtual friends that youngsters seemed to have now. And when you reached fourteen you were expected to become responsible, find a job and bring in some money. It was all so different.

Where had those years gone?

Alfred thought about the past because he didn't want to think about the present. What future did they have ... misery, pain, despair? That was what lay in store for them. Everyone would no doubt be very kind and all sorts of professional people would give advice and support, prescribing clever treatments developed by clever technicians in sophisticated laboratories. But in the end, it all came down to just Enid and him ... and a darkness that no landing light could diminish.

Chapter Sixteen

Tania let Gordon back into their bed after he had been sleeping in the spare room for nearly a month. She had "forgiven him" for his secret meeting with Jennifer in the tea shop, but walking around on eggshells hardly described the new pressure he felt under while they were both in the house. It was a relief to go to work, though he worried what he was going to find on his return and her telephone calls to the factory to check what he was up to had become even more frequent.

'I'd like to see *Aida* next month,' she said one evening after dinner, a few days after he had moved back into their bedroom. 'I see it's on next month at the Town Hall.'

He was more than surprised. Tania had never shown any interest in opera, but he was pleased that she was keen to go out and do something other than watching television.

'That would be great,' he said. 'When's it on?'

She told him the date.

'That's the night of my concert, when I'm giving my solo.'

'Oh, well, that's obviously much more important than taking me out. I mean, when did we last go out together?'

'Isn't it on for more than one night?'

'I don't know.'

Gordon checked the local newspaper. *Aida* was in the local area for only that one performance. He couldn't believe the unfortunate timing. He desperately wanted to perform the solo, but she was correct in saying they hardly went out together, though, in truth, she rarely wanted to go anywhere. Tania sat on the settee, pretending to ignore him by flicking through television channels, although in reality waiting for his reply.

There were plenty of more experienced baritones in the choir who would jump at the part and were capable of doing it, even at this short notice. However, he knew that pulling out would not go down well with the conductor. The piece presented a huge opportunity and solo spots were unlikely to be offered in the future if he gained a reputation for being unreliable.

He looked across the room from the armchair in silence, the newspaper on his knees still open at the Events page. Tania was doing a good job of making the simple act of changing channels convey a sense of aggression and threat. She had a natural ability to do this.

Even in a crowded room, she could smile at him in a way that no one else would consider for an instant was anything other than an expression of affection, while he would know she was telling him to end his conversation. This control over whom he spoke to had reached the stage where Gordon automatically avoided good-looking young women, so that his wife couldn't accuse him of something later on.

If such a woman came over and spoke to him, he quickly made an excuse to move away, resulting in more than one person thinking he was excruciatingly shy, slightly odd, rude or a combination of all three.

'Well, assuming the Town Hall is not sold out, I'll book two seats.'

'That would be great,' she said, putting down the handset. 'Come here and have a cuddle.'

The tickets had been extremely expensive, but they were the only ones remaining so he ordered them as promised. The conductor had been very unhappy, particularly as Gordon could provide no serious reason for pulling out. However, there had been no major incidents since reserving the seats and he decided to make a greater effort to seek out events that they could attend together. Perhaps it would help to keep her temper more steady if they could do more things as a couple.

They ate dinner early on the day of the performance and Gordon went upstairs to shower while she tidied in the kitchen. When he came downstairs, dressed to leave, Tania was on the settee watching television.

'The bathroom's free. You'll need to have your shower and get ready. We're going to have to be off in thirty minutes at the most.'

Tania replied without looking up.

'Oh, I'm not going to bother. I'd rather have a night in. There's a good programme I want to watch later on.'

Gordon was dumbfounded.

'But this is the opera you wanted to see. You specifically asked me to buy tickets. I've missed the concert to go to this.'

'Well, you can go to your concert. You still have time to get there.'

'I can't just turn up. Someone else is doing the solo spot and I've got two very expensive tickets for *Aida.*'

'I've got a headache. Please yourself what you do,' she said, flicking through channels, conversation over.

He walked into the hall and stopped to consider what he should do. But what could he do? At such short notice, he couldn't even ring a friend and offer them a free ticket.

Had this been planned from the very beginning, when she'd first suggested it?

He paced around for a while, but there was no option other than to go by himself. Gordon returned home around ten-thirty to find Sally and Tania drunk in the sitting room. The air was thick with cigarette smoke and the two of them were laughing raucously. Sally was standing in the middle of the floor holding a banana.

'Gordon, the very man,' she said loudly. 'I was just saying you should have got that surgeon to give you a nose like a banana. That would have been really neat.'

Sally held the fruit up to her own nose. Tania was sitting in one of the armchairs, a glass of wine in one hand and unable to speak for laughing. Two empty wine bottles lay on the floor, a large red stain on the carpet showing where one had been knocked over.

'Just think, you could have made a fortune with a nose like a banana.'

He said nothing. It took a lot for him to dislike someone, but he despised this cruel, coarse woman, who had latched on to his wife soon after moving into the street three years ago. Sally was in her forties and lived alone. She had quickly made her distaste for him apparent, taking her cue from Tania that it was perfectly acceptable to be rude to him.

'Hey, tell me. Does your prick look like this?' she said, holding the banana between her legs. 'Well, does it? I mean, that would be really useful if your prick was long and curved like this banana. You would be able to fuck around corners.'

Tania rocked back and forth in the armchair. Gordon could feel his face becoming flushed with humiliation. Sally put a hand to her mouth and pretended to whisper.

'Does his prick look like this, or do I have to eat some of it to make it smaller?'

'You'll have to eat a lot,' screamed Tania.

The two women were in hysterics at this comment. Gordon watched in horror at the scene taking place in the sitting room. That this vile woman should be able to ridicule him in his own home like this hurt beyond words.

Sally started to rotate her hips as if dancing to music that only she could hear, while peeling the banana seductively and moving closer towards him. When she was almost touching he stormed out, slamming the door behind him.

He decided to sleep in the spare room and avoid having to be near Tania, who would be in a terrible state by the time she got to bed. Earlier in the day he had ironed some shirts though not had the chance to put them away, so he opened the wardrobe door and took out a metal coat hanger. Gordon paused in what he was doing. He felt such anger, frustration and sheer misery that he wanted to scream, 'My life shouldn't be like this.'

Without giving it any real thought, he whipped the coat hanger through the air, bringing it down with all the force he could on to his left thigh. He left it there, resting against the material of his trousers while pain shot up his leg. Slowly, as if in a trance, he raised his arm again. The *swish swish* of metal moving through the air was joined by his desperate sobs of anguish and pain.

It wasn't enough to block out the laugher that rose up the stairs.

Chapter Seventeen

Despite living near to each other Tom hadn't seen his best friend for more than a month. They both had a young family and demanding jobs; time just seemed to slip by. But they had agreed to meet one evening for a beer once the children had been put to bed. After half an hour he brought up the subject that was the real reason he had suggested getting together.

'I want to speak to you about something in confidence.'

'Of course, anything you like,' said Pat, taking a sip of beer.

'This has to be between us. You're not even to tell Doreen.'

'If that's want you want, my lips are sealed.'

'Gemma and I have been having some problems.'

'The two of you always seem so happy together and little Amy. Everyone says so.'

'Yes, I know. And on the whole, we are.'

'Well then, I'm sure any difficulties can be sorted out. What's so wrong that's it's made you this worked up?'

This was the moment he had been dreading. Pat was an average, decent family man. Tom trusted that nothing would be repeated, but his shame fought a battle inside him with the need to know how an ordinary person would react to such a revelation, someone who was not a doctor or solicitor. He also needed to speak to a friend. So he said it, and even to his own ears the words sounded unbelievable.

'She's been beating me up.'

Pat looked at him across the top of his glass, which hovered in mid-air a few inches from his mouth.

'You're pulling my plonker.'

'I'm not.'

'Jesus Christ. You mean beating you up as in bashing you with things?'

'In the beginning it was the odd slap or punch. But over the last couple of years it's become worse, throwing objects, hitting me with pans, trying to kick me in the nuts ... succeeding sometimes.'

'Sorry, mate, I'm finding this hard to take in. You could tuck her under one arm and still drink your beer with the other.'

'I know. That's not the point.'

'I don't get it. Just look at the size of you. How can she do it?'

'She uses surprise, attacks me when I'm never expecting it. We can go for weeks with nothing happening, our lives seemingly normal in every way. We do things with Amy, have a laugh, enjoy evenings out as a couple then suddenly I'm lying on the floor dazed because she's hit me on the head with a saucepan.'

'But why? What the hell do you do to provoke her that much?'

'I don't do anything.'

'Come on, man. I've already promised I won't repeat this conversation so you might as well be completely open. You must do something really bad to wind up Gemma so much that she wants to give you a battering. Women just don't do that. It's not in their nature.'

It wasn't just his words that Tom was hearing; he could see the utter disbelief in his friend's eyes, hear it in his voice.

'I don't do anything.'

Pat put down his glass loudly on the table, angry because either Tom was lying to him, or was only willing to tell a part of the story and not prepared to be totally honest when he had already sworn him to secrecy. It was an affront to his integrity.

'I don't do anything that I'm aware of. She just seems to lose control.'

'I'm certainly not suggesting that you're physical in any way

123

back to her, but have you been?'

'No.'

'Well, I'm glad to hear it, but I don't really know what to say to you. I've never heard of such a thing happening and if I had you would be the last person on the list to be involved. Have you talked to her about it?'

'I've tried ...' said Tom, knowing he sounded weak, feeling that he was losing the respect of a man he admired.

'It seems like you need to try a bit more. Where's your manliness gone? I heard you'd been dropped from the team. I hope you're not going through some strange middle-age phase. You're a bit young for that.'

As he spoke he could see his friend was crestfallen.

'Look, this is a bit much for me. I'm a simple guy. I'm sure all sorts of odd things go on behind closed doors between couples, but your wife giving you a thumping is beyond me. Have you spoken to anyone else about this?'

'A solicitor and my GP.'

'What did they say?'

'The solicitor basically told me to keep away from the courts and the GP hadn't come across such a situation before, but she went on the Internet and found some UK charities specifically for abused men. There's more than one,' said Tom, trying to stress that the problem must be widespread for there to be so many specialist organisations.

'Well, at least you've spoken to people who will keep this confidential, and so will I,' said Pat. 'But you should be careful who you talk to. You don't want rumours like this going around about your home life. It's the sort of story that gets twisted in the retelling, and before you know it you'll be the abuser, because nobody will accept it could be the other way around.

'And if people do believe you, then what? You'll be ridiculed, perhaps not to your face, but no one is going to give you any sympathy for letting your wife knock you around. Society has always looked on the hen-pecked male as something funny, like the seaside postcard showing the big woman with the frying pan waiting at the front door to give her husband a good walloping for being home late from the pub.

'You're on a hiding to nothing with this one, Tom. Most people seeing a man slap a woman in the street would rush over to check she was alright and that it didn't happen again. If a woman slapped a man the majority would probably walk on, while wondering what he had done to deserve it.

'This is what the marketing bods call a "no-win" scenario. If you want my advice, keep your mouth shut. But you need to give Gemma a firm talking to. Stand up for yourself, man. Let her know she can't get away with it. I love Doreen, but she wouldn't kick me around.'

Tom listened carefully to his friend's comments and thought they were probably similar to what he would have once said ... before the first time his wife had hit him.

Tom spent a considerable amount of time trawling through information about battered men on the Internet and studied the websites of charities dedicated to this issue, reading other men's stories of domestic abuse with amazement. He carried out his research at work, so Gemma wouldn't know what he was doing. She had a habit of checking his emails and recently visited websites, although he had no idea what she expected to discover.

Tom closed his office door. He assumed that conversations with the charity were confidential and appreciated that the person on the other end of the line was there specifically to help men in situations such as his. Nonetheless, he felt vulnerable, almost overwhelmed by humiliation. He started dialling the number twice, stopping each time part way through, before finally keying it in full.

It was a woman. He didn't know why he felt so surprised.

She identified the organisation, said her name was Penny and asked how she could help.

'My wife has been violent to me,' he said eventually.

'I must firstly check that you are safe ringing me from where you are?'

'Yes.'

'Are you sure? It is vital that you are not putting yourself in danger by making this telephone call.'

'No, I'm certain.'

'If this situation changes at all during the course of our conversation, please end the call and ring again. Can you tell me where you are ringing from?'

He told her the area of Scotland that he lived in.

'And may I take your name?'

'It's Tom.'

'Thank you. I understand how very difficult this is to talk about, but can you tell me what has been happening to you?'

He outlined the relevant events that had occurred during the last two and a half years.

'Have you told anyone in authority about this, such as the police or your GP?'

'I've recently seen my GP, and I spoke to a friend who is a solicitor.'

'It might be worth considering getting in touch with a police officer who is a specialist in domestic violence. They are very understanding and if you contact your local station they can put you in touch with the nearest one. If you do make a formal complaint, make sure you get a reference number of some sort, so that you have something to refer to in future.'

Tom felt too ashamed to tell her that he had been detained in a cell because the police thought he was violent, so he simply muttered 'thanks'.

'How do you feel now?' asked Penny.

How did he feel?

He considered the question before answering.

'Humiliated ... angry ... frightened ... confused.'

'These are all normal reactions. It's always devastating when a partner in what is meant to be a loving relationship is violent, and for a man to be the victim of abuse from a woman it is especially confusing. Most men simply have no idea how to respond because this goes against everything that we are brought up to believe and expect.'

'The shame and feelings of betrayal hurt me far worse than any bruises or other injuries,' he said.

'That's perfectly understandable. We often hear that sort of comment.'

'Until I started reading about male abuse on websites, I thought I was the only person to be in such a position, that I somehow deserved this punishment for something I had done. It was a strange relief to learn that other men are in similar situations.'

'Even today domestic violence continues to be largely a hidden problem in society,' said Penny. 'People simply find it extremely difficult to admit it is happening and seek help. Men are even less likely to report it and this compounds the notion that such things can't possibly happen. Often it's the mother or sister of a victim who contacts us with concerns about his safety.'

'What do you do?'

'We can listen and offer some guidance, but we really need the person himself to get in touch. What has made you contact us today?'

There was silence on the telephone as he thought about this.

'I guess I had reached a point where I needed to speak to someone who understood, who at least believed what I said without pre-judging that I must be guilty of something terrible to be treated like this.'

'We don't pre-judge anyone, although I know this can be

another hurdle for men who do find the courage to speak out. What do you feel you want to do, Tom?'

'I want to stay with my wife and child, to have a normal life without the fear or threat of violence. I love them both.'

'Can you tell me about your child?'

'We've got a seven-year-old daughter, Amy, nearly eight.'

'They grow up so quickly. Has there ever been any abuse towards her?'

'None.'

'Are you concerned at all that Amy might be in danger?'

Penny spoke to him for several minutes about Amy: had she shown any signs of distress, changes of behaviour, were there problems at school? Tom was impressed at her concern for his daughter.

'Perhaps it might be useful if I gave you a few tips on safety. They may seem rather obvious, but it's surprising how people don't think of them.'

'Yes, thanks.'

'I don't know if there are any collections of items around the house that could be used as weapons, but it's a good idea to make sure they are locked away or even disposed of. Military memorabilia would be top of the list, but there could be other hobbies that provide objects that are too dangerous to have lying about if they're easily accessible.

'Consider the room you are in if your wife looks like she might become violent. The kitchen is generally the most risky. If knives are kept in a drawer, rather than hanging on the wall, then those few extra seconds it takes to get hold of one could provide the time required to escape out of the door.

'Think about each room and what is in it that could be turned against you. Don't ignore the bedroom. It might not seem to be the most dangerous place, but it's often where most abuse occurs. Try to construct a safe area in the house, and when your wife becomes aggressive move there if you can during the conversation without it being too noticeable.'

'I'll give all this some thought. Thank you.'

'I'm throwing at lot at you, Tom. Are you okay with what I've said so far?'

'I'm making notes,' he said, adding, 'and I'll keep them well hidden.'

'Avoid fighting back. Just get away if there's danger.'

'I will.'

'And you might want to consider having an escape plan,' she said.

'An escape plan?'

'Regardless of gender, it's important that the victim puts in place a means of surviving more easily if they have to flee from their home. Some people realise the danger to their life is so great that they never go back. But if you hadn't made any preparations you wouldn't even have a change of clothes, and there might be no easy means of retrieving vital documents such as your passport or bank account details.'

'I see what you mean,' he said, beginning to realise the significance of what she was saying.

'Think through carefully what you would need access to if you suddenly left the house with only what you were wearing. I would suggest packing a suitcase with these items, including some money, perhaps a spare set of car keys and details such as telephone numbers in case you leave without even your mobile. It might be necessary to prove who you are, so you might want your birth certificate and some old bills, and don't forget to pack spare medication if you're taking anything, particularly if it's on prescription.

'However, don't remove anything that could possibly arouse suspicion, such as a favourite photograph, and don't leave the packed case in the house because if you're leaving in such a hurry that you can't grab your wallet or phone then you're unlikely to rescue a suitcase from the loft. Leave it with a trusted friend or family member.'

'Thank you,' said Tom. 'I hadn't considered all this, but I appreciate your advice.'

'I'm afraid there is no accommodation in a safe house for abused men in Scotland, but there are a handful in England and Wales, though you might have to be means-tested to get a place should there be one available.'

'England!

'The nearest one is in Yorkshire.'

'Yorkshire! But I have my family and job. A potential bed hundreds of miles away is no use to me.'

'I'm sorry. We have a website and can offer help on the telephone plus face-to-face meetings where possible, but I'm afraid we can't provide somewhere for a man to sleep.'

'What do men do if they've suddenly had to leave their home?'

'Sometimes they are able to stay with friends or relatives. Being re-housed by the local authority can be a complex issue and depends on where you are. Technically, if someone is escaping domestic violence they should be given priority for accommodation, although we know of councils that refuse housing services in these situations because, in their opinion, the person has deliberately made themselves homeless.

'It's a bit of a Catch 22 situation, but it generally helps if you have a crime reference number from the police as you can more easily show you are a victim of abuse. I'm afraid we know of men basically living in their cars in order to remain near to their children.

'And if you are actually planning to leave, rather than preparing for the possibility of leaving, please be extremely careful who you tell. It's been known even for family members, thinking they are somehow helping, to secretly tell the abuser that their partner is leaving them, with disastrous results for the victim.'

Tom had never considered himself a 'victim'. Or course, he knew there was such a thing as domestic violence. Everyone had seen the images of women who had been beaten terribly by their husbands or male partners for little more than that they didn't like the evening meal. He thought such men worse than despicable cowards. But hearing of escape plans and lists, of not being able to tell family members, made everything sound like a bad thriller.

Then he thought about how much he had hesitated to speak even to a doctor. He had felt so ashamed. How many women suffered in silence, believing they too were alone in their misery, that they were the only woman being beaten and must somehow simply endure it?

'Hello. Are you alright?' said Penny.

'I'm sorry,' he said. 'I was lost in thought.'

'There's no need to apologise. Take as much time as you need. You may want to call back again when you've thought through what I've said, and perhaps have further questions. It's not a problem. Ring us as many times as you need. Do you have a trusted friend or member of the family that you could leave your suitcase with?'

'I have a sister. She's not too far away and I trust her completely.'

Chapter Eighteen

Alfred wasn't sure if his idea was the worst he had ever thought up or one of the brightest, but he was going to do it anyway. He was taking Enid on holiday to the little hotel in Yorkshire that they had stayed in all those years ago.

Their daughter Kate had grave doubts about the plan, but he declined her offer to accompany them. He hadn't told the community psychiatric nurse in case she forbade it, although he didn't know if she had the power to do this. Anyway, it was only for a few days.

Weeks earlier he had contacted the hotel owner and was surprised to learn that Joan was the daughter of the couple who had run it in the 1960s. Apparently, they were still alive and helped out occasionally. She had been so kind to him when he had explained over the telephone about his wife's dementia and why they were coming to stay, and had even suggested that her parents might join them one evening if he thought that was acceptable.

There was a mixture of reasons for the trip. Alfred wanted to see if 'stepping back in time' would help his wife make a connection with pleasant events from when they were younger, although he also feared that taking her away from familiar surroundings might make her more confused.

There was another reason, one that he didn't admit to anyone. He feared that Enid would soon end up in a nursing home and he had a premonition of the enormous guilt he would feel when this happened. He would keep her at home for as long as he possibly could, but each week was that little bit more difficult and even with support from local agencies he knew that the day would arrive when this was no longer viable. So he wanted one last holiday together, in a place where they had enjoyed themselves so much that they still talked fondly about it decades later. Maybe it was selfish of him; he didn't know.

The couple arrived at the hotel late in the afternoon. Enid took longer each morning to sort herself out so they hadn't left quite as early as he had wanted, but she appeared content during the journey, referring often to the lovely scenery. He chatted away, keeping his voice cheery and reassuring even when she said the same thing several times, and the trip passed without incident.

Joan reminded them of Kate and Enid took a shine to her, hanging on to her arm while they were shown around. The building had been decorated many times since their stay although parts of it were quite familiar and the surrounding countryside looked exactly the same to him.

He didn't want to tire his wife, but she was keen to have a walk before dinner so they went out soon after arriving. He pointed out interesting sights without asking if she recalled them, not wanting to press her. Occasionally she made little 'Oh' sounds as if particularly interested in something, and twice she made a comment that confirmed a memory, a connection. He was as content as could be.

That evening Joan's parents came into the dining room and asked if they could join them at their table. As agreed beforehand via Joan, they pretended not to have met so that Enid wasn't under any pressure to remember. They were very kind and when she forgot a word, repeated herself or stopped in the middle of a sentence they made nothing of it. However, the couple were completely lost for a response when, while everyone was tucking into their dessert, she announced, 'Alfred used to shave balloons'.

'Fancy you remembering that,' he said, picking up the story. 'Aren't you clever? Yes, when I was a lad of seventeen, just

133

starting my five-year apprenticeship as a barber, I used to have to shave balloons.'

'Really!' said Joan's father, intrigued by such a revelation. 'I'd like to hear that tale.'

'Except for sweeping up, I wasn't allowed to go near a customer. Part of my training included blowing up a balloon and covering half of it with shaving foam. I would then have to shave off the foam using a Hamburg Ring razor without bursting it. Every time I failed, my old boss would say, "If that was a paying customer you would just have nicked his throat. Blow up another one!"

'It took months to learn the skill and it wasn't until I could achieve the task repeatedly with confidence that I was permitted to try on a real person. And this was long before I ever got to actually cut someone's hair.'

Next to him, Enid was asleep. Alfred stared at the ceiling in the light of the bedside lamp. As promised, he had called Kate straight after dinner and told her what a great success everything had been. He felt exhausted from the journey and the stress of worrying that something might go horribly wrong. However, scenes kept replaying in his mind, keeping him awake; images of the pleasant walk they had enjoyed, the sound of laughter during the evening meal.

The next day they intended to potter around locally so he could have some rest and then they would drive home the following morning. As he drifted off he thought that the worry and planning about the holiday had all been worth it.

Something woke him. He couldn't place the cause, but was immediately aware of being alone. It was just after two o'clock. Throwing back the bedclothes he got up and checked the en-suite. It was empty so he quickly put on his dressing gown and slippers then went downstairs. He had no need to search inside since the front door was wide open.

Another moment and he would have missed her, but when he reached the pavement he caught a glimpse of a tiny figure just about to walk around the corner at the end of the road. He followed as fast as he could, though a brisk walk was the most that he could manage. Enid was standing underneath a street light, staring up at the lamp.

'What are you doing?' he said, taking off his dressing gown and wrapping it around her. 'It's the middle of the night and you've only got on your nightie.'

'I was just going for a walk.'

'But not in the dark. You don't even have anything on your feet. They'll be frozen.'

'I like walking.'

When he tried to put his arm around her shoulder she backed away from him.

'No. I like walking.'

'But not now, love. We'll go out tomorrow in daylight.'

'You can't stop me. You're trying to keep me prisoner.'

'Don't be silly. Come back with me to the hotel.'

As he took a step towards her she punched him in the face. There was little force behind it and Alfred made to grab her arm so she slapped him as hard as she could with her other hand, which hurt him a great deal more. The elderly couple struggled under the harsh glare of the artificial light, her screams echoing along the deserted and otherwise silent street. Eventually, he managed to put both arms around his wife and held her tightly against his chest.

'It's alright. There's nothing to be afraid of. I've got you safe. Why don't we have a little walk together? That would be nice, wouldn't it? Just like we used to.'

Alfred kept talking and she calmed down until he felt it was safe to let go. They were both shaking. He picked up his dressing gown and put it around her shoulders again then took her arm as if they were out for a stroll in the park, making sure

135

they headed back towards the hotel. When they reached the gate, he said, 'After you, love', as he always would do when returning home from an outing. Enid said, 'Thank you', then went back into the hotel as if they had merely been out shopping.

Chapter Nineteen

The weather had turned foul and the inside of the car was filled with the sound of rain pounding on the roof as if it was angry. Tom and his sister were in a supermarket car park. She lived about an hour away and he had called her from work to ask if they could get together in secret.

The venue was roughly half way between them and it gave her the excuse of buying the family's food shopping afterwards. Although her husband John would have been pleased for Rose to meet her brother at any time, Tom had insisted that no one should be told. He had taken an extended lunch and was sufficiently senior in the business that nobody questioned what he was doing.

'I don't think I've ever met anyone in a car park,' said Rose.

She was four years younger than him and it felt strange to be asking for her advice. He had always been the big protective male in her life, the one she had gone to for help and guidance since being a toddler. He loved her dearly.

'Sorry,' he said. 'I can't even offer you a coffee.'

'Don't worry about that. You wouldn't ask for such an unusual meeting if there wasn't something seriously wrong. You know you can tell me anything and if it needs to remain confidential then it will.'

'Thanks. I appreciate it. But it's still not easy to talk about. You'll think badly of me.'

'I won't know what to think if you don't talk to me.'

Tom rested his hand on top of his sister's, which she had placed on his knee.

'Gemma has been beating me up.'

'No! Tom.'

'It's been going on for over two years. In the beginning it was an occasional slap and she always apologised straight away, saying that she had had a stressful day and it wouldn't happen again.'

'What did you do?'

'I was too shocked to do anything. You know Gemma's always had a fiery temper, but it was never like this. I tried to work out if these incidents were related to her monthly cycle. I know some women have a terrible time. But there never seemed to be any connection. In fact, I couldn't link the attacks to anything. They generally came out of the blue as far as I could see, but I thought perhaps I was missing something and being insensitive in some way that I didn't realise.'

'It must have been awful. I had no idea.'

She reached up and stroked his cheek with her free hand.

'You would think given my size that the entire scenario is unbelievable.'

'Gemma knows you'll never hit her back, so your extra strength is immediately neutralised. How serious has this become?'

'The slaps and punches turned into throwing things or hitting me with something. Generally, it's not too bad. I've had worse injuries playing sport,' said Tom, some part of him still defending the actions of his wife, as if the lack of force made the abuse more acceptable.

'But that's not the point, is it?' she said.

Rose held his gaze until he shook his head.

'What does she say when you speak to her about this?'

Tom remained silent.

'You have spoken to her about it?'

'I know it sounds weak, but I've never forced her to sit down and explain what was going on,' he said. 'In the early days I would ask why a particular incident had happened and she would apologise and blame it on stress or tiredness. Later on, she would say she had merely lost her temper and not give any reason.

'But there've been plenty of occasions when it's as if nothing has actually occurred. I could be walking along the corridor and be hit on the back with a thrown object and when I've found her, she would be in the kitchen pretending to be making tea.'

'What would you do in that situation?'

'In the beginning I would ask her what the hell she was playing at and Gemma would answer "making tea", as if she had been standing there all along.'

'Didn't you demand to know why she had thrown something at you?'

'You tend not to demand things,' he said. 'I did try, but could never get a specific answer. It was like running on a sand dune; there was nothing firm to hang on to and these little episodes felt unreal, almost as if I was mad and making up accusations. As time went on, I would simply pick up the object and put it back where it should be, or if it had broken I would clean up the mess, but I stopped asking why she had thrown it.'

'I can't believe you've been reduced to this. You were always so strong, standing up for what you believed in.'

'I know. I said you would think badly of me.'

'No, not badly.'

She reached over and pulled his head towards her so that she could hug him.

'Not badly,' she said again. 'You've reacted honourably, the way she knew you would. But I can't understand her reasons. It's one thing to have a temper, but this seems ... calculating.'

She held him for a while and then he sat back in his seat.

'What are you going to do?' asked Rose.

'I spoke to a solicitor who said I risked having restricted contact with Amy if I left, and I don't want to go.'

'You still love Gemma, don't you?'

He gave her a little smile, the first since they had met.

'Afraid so.'

'And I know how you feel about Amy. You're never going to be parted from her, are you?'

'I don't intend to be. I spoke recently to a charity designed to help men in my situation. One of the things they advised was to have an escape route, so if there was an incident where I was suddenly in so much danger that I had to flee the house, I still had easy access to a change of clothes, documents, spare keys. I've packed all of these items in a suitcase. It's in the boot and I wondered if you would keep it safe.'

'Of course I will. I'll hide it in the loft. It's rare for John to go up there. No one will know. Are you going to tell Mum and Dad?'

'Heavens no! They wouldn't understand at all and it would only upset them. Also, they would find it impossible to act normally when they're with Gemma.'

'I know how they would feel.'

'But ...'

'Don't worry. I guarantee she'll not suspect that I'm aware of anything. I'll give an award-winning performance for your sake. I'm so worried for you and Amy. Do you think she's safe?'

'Yes, I do. But I'm going to take her out soon, just the two of us, and try to discover if she knows what's going on. She seems okay, always the model pupil and the ideal daughter.'

'Children react in all sorts of different ways to problems in the family. Trying to be perfect might be her way of coping, of attempting to heal the wounds between her parents. It might be all she can think of to do, to try to make everything better.'

Tom was shocked. He hadn't considered Amy could be reacting like that and he berated himself for his lack of intuition when his baby sister could immediately identify a possible problem that he had not seen. Perhaps he wasn't the wise person he had always liked to consider himself to be.

'Amy's bright, but she's still so young,' said Rose. 'You must promise to let me know of anything I can do to help. And if you want me to keep her for a while she can stay with us any time.'

'Thanks, sis'. I knew I could rely on you.'

'Look after yourself, big brother. If you and Amy need to escape, you know who to call on.'

'It won't come to that,' said Tom, forcing a smile, but even to his own ears he didn't sound convincing.

Chapter Twenty

Heavily laden clouds were gathering ominously overhead when Gordon saw the vicar. They had arranged to meet at a specific point on the path that ran alongside the nearby river. He liked Celina, who had taken over the local church three years earlier, and had telephoned her to request a meeting.

She was a small woman, whose pale grey eyes were usually full of great mischief and humour. She dished out common sense and a no-nonsense approach to religion that had been well received. The congregation had grown significantly in size under her leadership.

'Thanks for seeing me.'

'Thank you for asking,' she replied. 'I hope that I can be useful in some way.'

When a member of the congregation wanted a private conversation with her, Celina often suggested going for a walk. There wasn't really anywhere suitable in the church to speak confidentially and few town vicars were keen these days to have such meetings in the vicarage. Exercising her golden retriever had an added bonus, because the dog played its own part in helping some people unburden themselves.

She found that being out in the open, side by side with someone, generally made them more relaxed. People didn't have to make much eye contact and men, in particular, seemed to find it easier to admit to problems. These occasions were always about problems, nobody ever wanted to meet her to say how pleased they were with life.

'I'm not happy in my marriage and I don't know what to do,' he said.

'I won't tell you what to do, but I'll certainly listen to anything you want to tell me, and try to help you reach a decision.'

'I don't even know where to start.'

'I've never met your wife. Why don't you explain what attracted you both to each other in the beginning?'

'I'm not sure what she saw in me, apart from my athletic physique,' he said, forcing a nervous smile. 'I guess I saw in her the antidote to my loneliness, my need for affection and love.'

'We all need that. Did you never ask her why she wanted to marry you?'

'She always said she loved me, but then she would do and say hurtful things that were completely opposite to the type of behaviour you would expect from someone who cared.'

'What sort of things would she do?'

'Scream at me that I was stupid and useless, that I wasn't a proper man. Then an hour later she would often be smothering me in hugs and kisses, telling me how nice I was.'

'How did you feel about this?'

'Confused, never knowing what the ground rules were. In the end, I was constantly monitoring what I said or did in an attempt not to make her angry. In recent years she's flown into rages over things that seem meaningless, as if the real purpose was to put me down rather than that she was genuinely upset. I'm starting to wonder whether this was always the case.'

Gordon surprised himself in that it was only as he spoke these words that he fully appreciated how true this was. As he thought about this it did make a perverted logic; that the aim all along had been to dominate him by undermining his confidence and making him frightened of her.

'People sometimes mistakenly believe that if there is no physical violence in their relationship then they can't possibly be experiencing abuse, but that's not the case at all,' said Celina. 'Despite what many believe, domestic abuse isn't determined

143

by age, class or race, and it can manifest itself in a range of forms; financial, sexual, emotional.

'The latter proves the lie to the old saying of, "sticks and stones may break my bones, but words will never hurt me". It's often the words that cause the most damage. Long after bruises have disappeared, the effects of hurtful things said by someone who is meant to love you can continue for years. Such comments are an invisible attack, going straight to the heart, which takes much longer to heal than any punch to the body.

'I've come across this sort of behaviour from men towards women in every walk of life, from doctors to bricklayers, lawyers to dustmen, even fellow members of the clergy.'

'Really?'

'Yes, I'm afraid so. I became involved in helping the wife of one colleague who kept the poor woman totally under his control for years by insisting that it was God's will they stayed together and she did what he told her, no matter how unpleasant she found his instructions. That was a very difficult situation, which really didn't have a satisfactory outcome.

'At risk of sounding as though I'm the one who knows what God's thinking, if anyone ever says that it's His will that they should be abused, controlled or so scared by their partner that they submit to anything, then they're talking rubbish. That's perpetrator-speak.

'I've also come across it going the other way, with women being destructive towards their male partner. Despite the nursery rhyme, little boys are not made of slugs and snails and puppy dog's tails and I certainly know several little girls who do not consist of sugar and spice and all that's nice.'

They stopped for a moment while Gordon picked up and threw the stick that the dog had dropped at his feet.

'My life is spent trying to please her,' he said. 'She doesn't work. Most days she sits drinking, smoking and watching television, so I do most of the housework at weekends.'

'What would happen if you didn't do it?'

'The house would be a pigsty and I couldn't stand it. Tania knows this so she doesn't have to bully me much into cleaning up.'

'And what would happen if you asked her to do it?'

'I tried a few times when she gave up work altogether, but she always flew into a temper, screaming about how tired she was and if I was a proper man I wouldn't ask such a thing.'

Celina waited until they were once more walking before speaking again.

'Has she used physical violence against you?'

'Sometimes, though not often.'

'Have you spoken to anyone else about this, such as your doctor?'

'I've become friendly with an older lady in the choir, nothing improper or anything like that. She had a violent husband and has been giving me some advice. It's really because of what she said that I've started to question my marriage.'

'It sounds to me as though Tania doesn't respect you. Do you have any for her?'

'None whatsoever,' he said.

'And do you love her?'

'In the beginning I thought I did, but, no, I don't love her.'

'I'm not saying you should leave, but what makes you stay? Is it because of your beliefs? I know that many religious people go through agonies of indecision, finding it extremely difficult to consider breaking their vows and constantly referring to passages in the Bible that imply they should turn the other cheek, forgive and try harder to make the marriage work.'

Gordon was reminded of the day he had met Jennifer in the little tea shop and had asked her why she had remained in such an unhappy marriage.

'There are so many reasons for staying and so many for going,' he said, almost as if he was speaking to himself. 'Habit. I suppose it's a case of the devil you know, and I would be throwing away some good along with the bad. Fear of being alone again, perhaps forever, of finding out that she was right after all and I was worthless. Concern over what she might do if I left, that I would have to bear the guilt of her harming herself, maybe even committing suicide, which she's threatened over the years.

'Reluctance to have horrible lies about me told to friends and neighbours. Tania can be very convincing and there would be some people who ended up believing that once we were alone in the house I turned into a terrifying monster.'

They walked in silence for a short while until Celina felt sure he wasn't going to say any more.

'Those sound like negative reasons for staying. If there is no love or respect, then it's hardly a marriage anymore. Despite the passages in the Bible that some people may quote as reasons for staying together, I don't believe God expects us to sacrifice the gift of life, living in misery because we've signed a piece of paper and taken some vows at the altar. If one partner is so abusive to the other then those vows are already broken, and I would make the same comment to a man or a woman.'

She stopped and put her hand on his arm to make him look at her.

'We all have faults and yours don't make you worthless any more than mine do. God loves you. There's no shame and a great deal of courage involved in admitting a mistake. The decision must be yours and God will be alongside you in whatever path you take. Would it help if I met you and Tania together?'

'I don't think so, but thanks for asking,' he said. 'I'm not sure there's anything anyone can say to make one person love another, no matter how good at counselling they are.'

They stood facing each other. The dog was at Gordon's feet, wagging its tail and hoping he would throw the stick.

'Abuse is never the fault of the person on the receiving end, no matter how much their partner tries to make out that they asked for it, or are to blame in some way,' said Celina. 'All too often victims end up believing they deserve to be punished because of flaws in their personality that the abuser is merely helping to "correct". Sometimes people survive by focussing on the good times, but often these demonstrations of affection and kindness can be the cruellest actions of all because they're only done as part of an overall plan to control.'

Gordon nodded his head slowly as he took in the many implications of the vicar's comments.

'You know that everything you say to me is in complete confidence,' she said. 'Keep in touch about this and if you want me to make the initial contact with someone in another profession, such as your GP, then I would be happy to help.'

'Thank you.'

'It looks like we're in for a soaking,' said Celina staring up at the threatening sky. 'If we cross the bridge here, we can reach the church in less than fifteen minutes. Why don't we go there together and sit for a while? At the very least we might just avoid the rain ... and you never know, God might be around should we decide to speak to Him.'

Chapter Twenty-One

Amy glided effortlessly around the ice rink, waving at her father as she passed two tottering adults. Tom watched from the sidelines with pride. The few times he had tried skating had been such a disaster that he had vowed never to do it again, and he suspected that, secretly, his daughter preferred to have him as an audience so that she could show off her skills. She was elegant, like her mother, and would grow up to be a beauty.

This was their day out. He hoped to discover if she was being affected by the atmosphere in the house even if she hadn't actually witnessed the violence. Whatever happened he had to protect his little girl at all costs.

Recently, he had been thinking a great deal about his home life. In the early days of the violence his wife always made out that she had simply lost control and was truly remorseful. But when he analysed these incidents, he couldn't help feeling that his sister Rose had been correct and these attacks had been planned carefully.

There hadn't been one occasion that he could remember when anyone else had been present. His daughter had either been in her bedroom, in the garden or away from the premises altogether. It seemed unbelievable that his wife never "lost control" if Amy might overhear, which meant ... well, what did it mean?

It made more sense if she simply had a bad temper, rather than that she was someone conducting a programme of violence for a particular purpose. And if so, what was the purpose? What did she gain from it? If Gemma wanted to punish him for something then why not just say what was bothering her, or tell him what he was doing that was annoying her so much?

All couples encountered problems at times. The solution was communication. He was an approachable guy. People from all walks of life asked his opinion or advice on matters. He was just that sort of person. Tom hated confrontation within the family and normally went along readily if his wife suggested a potential venue for a holiday or a particular colour scheme for a room.

He liked to please her because he loved her. Tom had no hesitation in acknowledging this. Despite the assaults, he loved the woman he had married all those years ago, and who was the mother of his child. If you took away the abuse then the three of them made a tremendous little unit.

The only person who seemed to think otherwise was an old school friend of Gemma's called Amanda. He considered this nervous, dumpy woman to be a very strange acquaintance for his wife who usually selected them with an almost analytical fervour. About a year earlier Amanda had suddenly and quite unexpectedly turned hostile towards him. She stopped coming to the house if he was around and if they bumped into her while they were out Tom always felt that she regarded him as if he was carrying a pitchfork and had two horns on his head.

Amy appeared by the side of the ice rink near to where Tom was sitting and switched from travelling at speed to a dead stop within a few feet.

'Daddy, did you see that?' she asked, excited and out of breath.

'You were marvellous. I don't know how you do it. I can't even let go of the side and that's when I'm sitting down here.'

'You're just silly, Daddy,' she giggled, adding, 'it's eeeasy,' unable to understand how something she found so simple could be difficult for her father, who could do absolutely *everything*. 'Why don't you have another go? I could hold you up.'

Tom smiled, reached over and gently took hold of her nose,

which set off another fit of giggling.

'Listen here, small daughter of mine. You have to leave your old dad with some dignity. Go on, you've only got another fifteen minutes. Make the most of it.'

As she skated off he added 'be careful'. She was always careful. That was her nature, but he couldn't stop himself from saying it.

Like an old mother hen.

He doubted she had heard. How had he been involved in creating something so incredibly wonderful? Tom didn't believe in miracles, but when he looked at her he wasn't so sure that they didn't exist.

An hour later they were sitting in the corner of a restaurant, eating pizza. He had picked a table as out of the way as possible so that she would feel they were more alone and could talk freely. This was going to be a delicate conversation.

'So how has school been?' he asked.

'It's good. Mrs Jenkins says I'm her best pupil.'

Mrs Jenkins was the head English teacher and Amy loved reading a wide range of literature.

'How about we go to the bookshop after lunch and see what new titles they've got.'

She nodded in agreement, a rather overlarge slice of pizza having stopped her from answering properly.

'Don't put so much in at once. No one's going to steal your food ... unless it's me.'

He tweaked her knee under the table.

'So what else has been happening at school?'

'We're all preparing for sports day next week, Peter was given detention and Jonathan's mummy and daddy are splitting up.'

'How do you know about Jonathan?'

'The teacher told us and said that we mustn't mention it and not to ask him what's wrong if he was crying.'

Tom considered that this might give him the ideal opening to steer the conversation in the way he wanted.

'Do you know why his mummy and daddy are splitting up?'

'Ameeeee!'

The shrill voice cut through the sound of conversations taking place at other tables. Tom was horrified. It was his daughter's best friend, Jessica. If the two of them got together he had lost his chance to talk.

'Jessy!'

Without waiting to be asked the girl sat at the table, which was set for four, just as her mother, loaded down with shopping bags, caught up.

'Hello, Tom.'

'Hello.'

In a moment that was approaching panic, he couldn't even remember the woman's name. He saw her glance at the remaining empty chair so stood up to face her.

'Amy and I are having a quiet meal together.'

He knew his response was more than a little rude, but this woman's feelings were not his priority. She looked taken aback at his abrupt tone, which was so out of place, and took hold of her daughter's arm.

'Come on, you've only just seen each other yesterday.'

'But ...'

'No buts,' she said, cutting short the expected protest. 'Say goodbye.'

The girls said their farewells.

'That's a lovely table by the window. Go over there,' she said to Jessica.

Tom was still standing.

'Thank you.'

He spoke with such emotion in his voice that the woman turned back to face him and after a moment she smiled. There was warmth in the smile, understanding.

151

'There are occasions when we all need the chance to be alone with our children. Bye, Amy.'

He was shaking when he sat down and was surprised that such an innocent encounter could upset him so much. Amy was already munching another slice of pizza and didn't notice his distress, so he left her to eat in silence while he composed himself.

'So why are Jonathan's parents are breaking up?'

She swallowed the last of the slice and ignored the remaining quarter.

'Jonathan told us they were always arguing.'

'Oh, that's a great shame.'

'People shouldn't shout, should they, Daddy?'

'No, it's usually better to talk to someone if you want to let them know something, such as how you feel.'

There was a pause in the conversation and he decided to let his daughter make the next comment.

'Mummy often shouts at you ... doesn't she?'

This was more than he expected her to know. He believed there had to be absolute trust between them and that meant no lies, but this was a dangerous ground to tread.

'Well, at times Mummy gets upset with me. But she's not angry at you, poppet. She always loves you, even when she might be shouting at Daddy.'

'But she hurts you and that's not nice.'

Tom's hands were sweating. He felt backed into a corner and didn't know how to answer. Two enormous tears rolled down Amy's cheeks.

'Are you and Mummy going to split up? Am I going to be like Jonathan and have no Daddy?'

'No. No, of course not. Come here.'

She ran around the table and he lifted her up to sit on his knee, facing the wall so that other people didn't see she was crying, which he knew would upset her.

'What makes you think Mummy and Daddy are going to split up? Eh? Who's put that silly idea into your head?'

'But why does Mummy hurt you?

'I don't know, poppet. I don't know.'

'Why don't you ask her then you'll know what to do?'

Jesus Christ!

'I could ask ... if you're frightened,' she said.

Amy had buried her head into his chest and her words were interspersed with huge sobs. Tom stroked her hair to give himself some time.

'Well, there's no need for that. I tell you what. I'll ask Mummy myself and then I'll find out what's wrong. Wasn't Daddy daft for not thinking of doing that before?

'And always remember that it's never your fault or your responsibility for what happens between adults. You mustn't feel that you ever have to behave or act in a certain way because Mummy and Daddy have disagreed with each other. Whatever happens between us we both love you very much and you're not to blame for anything that goes on.'

'And you won't go away and leave me?' said the tiny voice, so vulnerable.

Tom thought of the woman at the charity advising him to have an escape route, of the packed suitcase hidden in his sister's loft, of the abuse and misery he had endured, the trips to the local casualty department. But there was only one answer.

'No, poppet. I won't leave.'

'Promise?'

'I promise.'

However, she continued to cry.

'There, I've said I'm not leaving, so why the tears?'

'You've ... you've not eaten your pizza,' she said, pointing at his plate.

Amy had only left one quarter and he hadn't even finished a quarter.

'Well, that's soon sorted.'

He reached over and stuffed what was left of the slice into his mouth. He didn't actually want any of it. She looked at his bulging cheeks with open mouthed astonishment.

'Daddy! That's naughty.'

Tom couldn't speak so made lots of 'Mmm' sounds, which eventually turned her tears into giggles. He hoped he didn't have to eat any more of it. The cold food made him feel slightly sick. Then again, it could have been what he had just agreed to.

Chapter Twenty-Two

The community psychiatric nurse sat opposite Alfred in his living room. Kate was in the bathroom with her mother who, increasingly, needed help with things, and had recently started to 'go to the toilet' anywhere in the house. The old barber had been shocked and now spent part of each day cleaning up when he hadn't been quick enough to steer her upstairs.

The carer came three times a week, but Ann could tell by the state of the rooms and his exhausted appearance that this would have to be on a more regular basis. His wife was deteriorating at an unusually fast rate.

'How are you managing?' she asked.

'Oh, we get by,' he said.

'There's no shame in admitting you need more help. How has the home carer been?'

'She's a lovely lady, very kind.'

'But perhaps we need to have someone coming here daily?'

Alfred didn't reply. He didn't speak so much these days, needing all his energy just to survive through to bedtime.

'What happened to your eye?'

'Nothing,' he said, but he couldn't look at Ann when he answered and she knew he wasn't telling the truth.

A few days earlier, Enid had punched him with surprising strength. She didn't appear to be affected physically by her condition and, if anything, seemed to have more energy than before and certainly slept less. Alfred, on the other hand, was feeling weaker, less able to fend off her blows if she attacked him. When she had hit him in the eye he had seen the throw coming yet couldn't move his head or raise his arms fast enough. It was as if a part of him was giving up and it was less effort to simply accept the punishment.

'I've heard from the carer that Enid appears more aggressive when you are around her. Is that what you're finding?'

'Sometimes,' he said.

'You have to think of yourself as well as your wife. It doesn't help either of you to become a punchbag.'

'I'm alright.'

'I think Enid needs to start attending a specialist day centre, perhaps a couple of times a week,' said Ann. 'But to start with it might be a good idea for her to have a short stay in a nursing home, where there is professional care around the clock. This will give you some time to rest and recover from what is a very traumatic experience.

'Don't underestimate the stress you're under. Caring for someone with dementia is a tremendous challenge, even for a young person, and it requires more than just physical stamina. The emotional drain is enormous. A few days break might be a good idea.'

'But where would she go?'

'There are several good nursing homes nearby. Why don't I make a few telephone calls and see what's available? If you want you can visit beforehand to put your mind at rest that it's a nice place. How do you feel about that?'

'I guess it's a thought. I'll speak to Kate.'

'How has Enid been sleeping?'

'Not good. She's taken to walking about during the night. She left the house without me realising last week and was brought back by the police.'

'She's wearing the identity bracelet?'

'Yes, fortunately she doesn't try to remove it. Now I lock the doors and hide the keys so she can't get out.'

'But it still disrupts your sleep.'

'I catch up when the carer is here.'

156

They were quiet for a while.

'Do you want some cheese?' he asked, a tiny fragment of his old self trying to elbow its way through the heartache. 'There might be some in the fridge.'

Ann smiled, knowing it wasn't a serious question.

'Walking around during the night is common for those with dementia, but it's normally a phase that passes,' she said. 'We think that sometimes it's caused by simply not having sufficient activities during the day time to keep their mind occupied and tire them out. It's easy to forget that people with dementia can become bored, like the rest of us.'

'She follows me around all the time, even when I go to the bathroom.'

'A few minutes left alone in a room might seem like hours to her,' said Ann. 'She could easily become anxious if not able to see another person, even if they're not speaking to her. It's back to the idea of communication without dialogue, in this case being able to see someone is maybe all that's needed.'

The following week Alfred and his daughter waited together for a meeting with the matron of a local nursing home. They were early so had been put into a quiet room. As there was no one else around Kate thought it was a good opportunity to speak candidly. She was almost as worried about her father as her mother. He was beginning to lose everything that was 'him' and looked defeated, not the man she had known and loved all her life. Her suspicions that her mother was being aggressive at times had been confirmed a few days earlier by the carer.

'I wish you had told me Mum had become violent towards you, Dad.'

'I'm sorry, love,' he said, not enquiring how she had found out. 'There didn't seem any point in worrying you further.'

'But you shouldn't have had to go through all of this by yourself. When did it begin?'

Alfred wished his daughter had not asked the question.

'There were a couple of occasions ... before Christmas.'

'Dad! That was months ago. Why didn't you say?'

'It was only twice, both times over in a few minutes, and she had forgotten almost immediately afterwards. What else could you have done except worry?'

'We could have got help earlier.'

'Yes, I realise that now. I was burying my head in the sand, too frightened to admit what might be wrong. It seemed easier to pretend everything was alright. I know it was a mistake to hide the problem. She could have got treatment earlier. Perhaps I've made her worse.'

Kate took hold of his hand.

'I know that whatever you did was out of concern for Mum. The outcome will be the same, whatever happened in the early stages. But being open would probably have made everything a great deal easier on both of you.'

They sat in silence for a while. She didn't want her father to feel guilty about keeping her mother's dementia a secret. He was beating himself up enough about this as it was.

'We're going to lose Mum, aren't we, Dad?'

'I fear so, love. It seems as though her condition is extremely aggressive, and she's failing much faster than any of us thought when she first had the brain scan.'

'It's more difficult to make any sort of connection. When I was over last week Mum thought at one point I was Granny.'

'Sometimes she thinks I'm her father.'

'It's such a wicked disease.'

Before he could comment further, a woman entered the room and introduced herself as 'Matron' in such a way that it almost seemed as if decades earlier, as a tiny baby, she had been christened 'Matron'. She reminded him of a thinner version of Hattie Jacques, playing the role she was famous for in the *Carry On* films; someone whose orders were to be obeyed without question, but behind whose façade of fierce efficiency lay enormous compassion and wisdom.

'Shall we go to my room where we can talk more easily?'

They followed the woman along the corridor and were soon sitting comfortably in her private office.

'I understand that you're looking for a nursing home for your wife to stay for a few days?'

'Yes,' replied Alfred, adding, 'it was suggested by the nurse,' as if he felt guilty and didn't want her to think it was his idea.

'We often have people staying for a short period of respite in order to let their main carer have a rest. It also gives the person a chance to see how they settle into the environment and for us to assess their needs, should they require a more permanent place in the future.'

'Your nursing home has been highly recommended,' said Kate.

'Well, thank you. That's nice to hear. We try our very best for residents. Some are here for many years. I understand Enid has some memory problems?'

'She has Alzheimer's,' replied Alfred, who still had to force the word out when he said it, as if the letters were so arranged that they were guaranteed to wedge in his throat.

'We have a lot of experience of residents with dementia-like conditions. If your wife comes to stay it might help if she brings some possessions that can be put in her bedroom.'

'What sort of possessions?' he asked.

'It could be anything from a special photograph to books or small ornaments, perhaps even a mirror. It's what matters most to the person themselves. Enid will probably want to bring certain items of clothing and it's important that everything is identified with her name either on a sewn-on tag or written in indelible ink.'

'I can do her washing,' he said.

Kate laid a hand gently on his arm.

'They'll do it here, Dad. You should be having a rest from all that.'

'You would be amazed at how many elderly ladies have the same cardigan or top,' said the matron with a smile. 'And it would help if we knew of any newspapers or magazines that she likes to read, or whether she might want to have her hair done. We also need to know of any special dietary requirements and what medication she is on. Are you planning to go away while Enid is staying with us?'

Alfred looked blank for a moment.

'My daughter has asked me to stay with her, but I thought I would be coming here to see Enid and Kate's house is too far away. When is visiting time?'

'We have a very open policy as regards visiting and there are few set times apart from meals, which have to be fixed for practical reasons. However, that doesn't mean people can't visit even then, and in some cases having a close relative present can be the easiest way to get a resident to eat their food.

'You are obviously welcome to see your wife whenever you wish, but you may find it better to keep these visits very short and to have some days when you don't come at all.'

Alfred and Enid sat alone in the living room that evening. She had been 'reading' a novel for more than half an hour, but was still on the same page and the book was upside-down. There was a time when he insisted on turning such objects the right way up and she would immediately put them the wrong way again, then they would argue and he would storm out of the room in frustration.

Now, he didn't bother. It didn't appear to matter to her. She wasn't really seeing the book anyway. These days she didn't *see* anything. Reality depended upon what was in her head at that particular moment and nobody knew what that might be.

He watched her across the room, sitting in the armchair by

the fire. They had had a real one for all their married life, until a month or so ago. Ann thought it was too dangerous to have a live fire in the house, so a local handyman had boarded up the opening and fitted an electric one instead. Enid didn't seem to notice the difference.

Even though he tried hard not to allow it, he sometimes felt awash with anger and misery. Despair was his constant companion. It was worse if he stopped to rest so he fought his demons by keeping busy, always doing things for Enid or around the house and garden until he almost collapsed with exhaustion. It probably wasn't wise, but he had stopped considering himself to be in any way wise. And what else was he meant to do?

This particular evening it was guilt that consumed him and he embraced the feeling as if it was a punishment that was rightly deserved. He should feel guilty. He was about to put his dear wife into a home and she had no idea that this was being planned behind her back. The stay was only for a few days. In his heart he knew this was only the start. A few days would become a couple of weeks then a month then ...

Then she would be gone for good.

By that stage his wife probably wouldn't even realise that she was going into a home forever, a place where she knew no one and had no connection. How could he do that to her? He had loved this woman and been loved by her for more than fifty years. The logical part of him acknowledged that there was no option. The situation couldn't go on as it had done. Everyone agreed there was no other choice.

However, the part of him that longed to cradle in his arms the woman who used to make him laugh with joy, cried silently in shame for the terrible deed he was about to commit; this sin against an innocent. Enid was no more to blame for her actions than if she had been a small child.

So he should be punished and therefore he did nothing to

fight, with sensible arguments or practical points, the sensation of suffocating guilt that enveloped him ... while across the room Enid sat by the electric fire, nodding at her upside-down book.

Chapter Twenty-Three

Amy was at Jessica's and not expected home for several hours. Gemma was downstairs reading a book, while Tom paced in their bedroom trying to pluck up courage to challenge his wife about her behaviour. This was crazy. He *never* backed down if he believed in something.

'What are you reading?' he said, entering the lounge.

'It's about a group of Italian prisoners of war in Orkney during the Second World War. They build a chapel in their camp, which lets them escape their captivity spiritually, rather than physically.'

'I guess they couldn't dig a tunnel. They're all islands, aren't they?'

'Yes.'

'Can you leave the book for a moment? We need to talk about Amy.'

'Of course. What's the problem?'

'Well, I was asking about school and amongst her normal everyday news she told me about a boy in her class whose parents are splitting up. Then she confessed that she has over-heard some of our disagreements.'

Tom was being extremely careful with his wording in order to make everything sound equal and not allocate any blame, while also keeping his voice friendly and even.

'I hadn't brought up the subject at all,' he continued quickly, 'but she's been worrying, without saying anything, that we might split up.'

'That's silly. Poor darling. Was she very upset?'

'She was for a little while, but she calmed down when I

explained that neither of us is leaving.'

'Well done. You're so good with her.'

'The thing is, I need to understand what it is I do wrong that upsets you so much at times to cause our disagreements. It's not something I'm aware of because I wouldn't do it if I knew. I was hoping you could explain it to me.'

Gemma, made-up as though having just completed a major modelling assignment, looked at him in silence across the room. She was sitting in the armchair by the window and the sunlight streaming into the room illuminated her hair.

'Often it's nothing in particular,' she replied eventually. 'I just lose my temper. Everyone loses their temper.'

'Of course, but they don't hit people, or chase them with a knife.'

'Oh, I wasn't serious with the knife. It was just to scare you.'

'But why did you want to scare me?'

'Why do you think I needed to scare you?'

Tom had no idea.

'I don't know. I'm sure I'm being rather slow on the uptake, so can you explain it?'

She sat without speaking for a moment.

'It was a means of getting you to listen,' she said.

'To listen? But you chased me away. I had to lock myself in the bathroom.'

Tom stopped suddenly because he was beginning to sound angry. Without making it too obvious he took some deep breaths and forced himself to remain calm, so that the next sentence, although bizarre in content, came across as if he was merely making a comment about dinner.

'And if you remember, I ended up in a police cell.'

'You simply took it the wrong way and overreacted. I wasn't going to hurt you with the knife. And you called the police. If you hadn't done that then everything would have been alright. You should have opened the door and spoken to me. That's all I wanted, to talk. What happened after the police arrived was nothing to do with me.'

Tom felt that the conversation was already slipping away from reality. It bore little resemblance to what had actually happened that evening and he certainly wasn't obtaining the answers he needed.

'Well,' he said. 'Let's forget the knife incident for now. Can you explain how hitting me with a pan when I'm not expecting it is going to make me pay more attention? You've almost knocked me out more than once and if you do that then there's no way I can talk to you.'

'Perhaps I've occasionally tapped you a bit harder than I had intended, but you've got a solid head. You always recover quickly and you get worse injuries playing rugby.'

'But ... you shouldn't hit me at all, regardless of the force. What's the point of it?'

'It gets your attention. At least you know I'm around.'

'I still don't understand, Gemma.'

'You are being slow today. You're so busy working that you don't seem to know I'm here anymore. And when you are home you're totally occupied with Amy. It's always Amy this and Amy that. I know what a lovely little girl she is, but as far as you're concerned I don't exist when she walks into the room. When do I get some time, some love and affection?

'I think your priorities in life are our daughter, work, sport and somewhere further down the line after your parents, sister and her family, next door's fucking dog that you like so much, then comes me, if you have any time or energy left. So, yes, sometimes I get angry and perhaps I don't show it in the correct way, but it's my way.

'And that's how it is, Tom. You married me for better or worse and I guess this is a bit of the worse. Life's shit at times, isn't it? Well, I might not be worth much in your eyes, but I've had enough of being at the bottom of the shit pile. And by the way, are you having an affair with someone at the office? You do seem to spend a lot of evenings there and I've not seen much action in the bedroom for a long time. Well ... are you?'

Gemma was breathing heavily by the time she reached the end of her explanation. Tom was speechless. He couldn't work out at all how attacking him with a cricket bat while he slept would improve communication between them, but he tried his hardest to analyse the various points she had made to see where he might have gone wrong, and how he could best put things right. However, his head was reeling with the seriousness and number of accusations.

Had he neglected her so much? Was her violence his fault?

'I hardly know where to start,' he said, 'but I can assure you that I've never had an affair, or any sort of improper relationship with a woman during all the years we've known each other. I'm totally astonished to hear that you could even imagine such a thing.

'As to your other comments, I'm really sorry if you feel I've neglected you so much. I didn't realise you thought this. I wish you had told me before now.'

'Oh, so it's all my fault ...'

'No, of course it's not. I'm just saying that if you had explained how you felt earlier then we could have perhaps avoided this problem.'

'I'm just a problem then. You're meant to understand my feelings without me spelling them out. You're my husband. I shouldn't have to tell you that I don't want to be neglected.'

Tom paused to collect his thoughts and give her a chance to calm down. What he said and did next was absolutely crucial. He walked over to kneel by Gemma's armchair so that he could take hold of one of her hands. Carefully, he took the book from her lap and laid it on the floor.

'I'm just so very grateful to you for putting me right. I've been a dunce, not thinking things through or being sensitive enough to your needs. You're right. I should have realised you weren't getting the love and support you deserve. I'm sorry. Let's have a new beginning. I'll look at my work schedule so that I don't have to spend so long there and we'll make sure between us that we spend quality time together.

'And you must tell me of anything else that bothers you, no matter how small, so that I can understand and correct it, in case I'm being too slow to realise. We have a great life together, don't we? It would be criminal not to make the most of everything we've got, every moment.'

He reached over and stroked her hair.

'You hair looks beautiful in the sunlight. Just like you.'

'I guess you're not a bad husband on the whole,' she said softening, 'you just need pointing in the right direction.'

'You'll simply have to tell me ... without the pans.'

This was a dangerous comment to add and as soon as he had spoken the words Tom feared he had made a terrible mistake, so he moved the subject on quickly.

'And I'm sorry if it has been a bit quiet in the bedroom recently. It's not because I don't love or desire you.'

Tom spoke the truth, and Gemma knew it, but there was another reason that remained unspoken, which was that he was exhausted from the constant tension he felt while in the house with her, the feeling of not knowing what the ground rules were or when there might be another attack.

'I think there's still some life in the old dog yet,' he said smiling. 'You know, Amy won't be back for quite a while.'

They looked at each other. Tom was a handsome man. Gemma hesitated for a moment then leant forward, so that their heads were close. The kiss was tender at first, hardly more than a caress. But then she freed her hand from his, put it behind his head and kissed him hard. His hand was left on her thigh and as their tongues fought a duel of pleasure he pushed back the material of her skirt to reveal the white, delicateness of her skin.

Chapter Twenty-Four

Gordon arranged to meet Jennifer at a service station. He had taken a half-day holiday and covered his tracks at the factory so there was a plausible excuse for him not to speak to Tania immediately if she rang to check up on him. Fortunately, she never thought to monitor the mileage on the car as a means of keeping control of his movements.

The restaurant was busy, but he managed to find a table in a corner and reckoned that the noise of people moving about and talking would give them greater privacy than they had had in the tea shop. Apart from a brief telephone call to agree the meeting he hadn't spoken to Jennifer other than during breaks at the choir practices, but there had normally been other members around so these conversations were generally about the pieces they were singing, families, or what people had been doing apart from music. The rehearsals had stopped after the last concert, the one Gordon had missed, so even this contact had ceased.

He thought over once more what he was going to say and decided not to mention the evening of the concert, when Sally had ridiculed him so mercilessly ... when, in despair, he had thrashed his leg with the coat hanger. He had limped for days, but this had been nothing compared to the shock of his own violent actions. It was so out of character.

Even sitting amongst the bustle of the restaurant he could see plainly in his mind's eye the blur of silver metal whipping through the air, feel again the sharp pain in his thigh, hear the *swish swish*, his cries of anguish and the laughter from the sitting room. The evening had troubled him so greatly that the next day he had tackled his wife about her and Sally's behaviour, but she dismissed his complaint with, 'Can't you take a joke? Your problem is you're far too sensitive'.

In a rare moment of defiance he had continued to sleep in the spare room. She had retaliated, firstly by smoking in their bedroom so that most of the upstairs stank as it did downstairs. Then on a couple of occasions, when he had arrived home late in the evening from work, she had told him to make his own dinner.

Gordon didn't know if she had eaten or had snacked so much that she wasn't bothered. However, when he had said he was too tired to cook and would nip around the corner to buy a takeaway, Tania had forbidden him, saying there was plenty of good food in the fridge and it was a sin to waste it.

She had stood at the front door so that he would have to manhandle her out of the way in order to leave the house. She knew he would back down at the prospect of such a physical confrontation. All she had to do was to stand there long enough and ignore his pleas. When he had retreated to the kitchen she would wait to hear him putting a pan on the cooker before going to the sitting room to watch television.

The humiliation of these memories made him feel as though he was being suffocated. In a gesture of frustration Gordon thrust his hands into his jacket pockets. The fingers of his right hand touched something tiny and he became calmer as he remembered another recent event. When he and Celina had gone to the church after their walk along the river she had asked if he would like to light a candle.

When he had been about to put down the spent match the vicar had suggested that it might be a good idea to keep it as a reminder of the light that had been lit that day. He took the slither of wood from his pocket to study, oblivious to the nearby noisy families on holiday, the couples who were on their way to visit relatives, or the various business people stopping for a rest during their hectic schedules.

There were good people around.

He kept the token in his hand and only returned it to his pocket when he saw Jennifer, who was almost at the table before he noticed her. He fetched a pot of tea and was soon recounting what had happened after they had last met, how they had been spotted in the tea shop by Sally, and Tania's response when he had returned home.

'I'm so sorry,' she said. 'That must have been awful.'

'It was nothing compared to what you've gone through over the years.'

'Whatever the level of aggression, the hurt inside can be immense. Thank you for letting me know what happened. You must at all times take the greatest care.'

'I can't tell you how much I appreciated your honesty and trust in explaining about your life with Derek. I understand you did it to make me analyse my own marriage, to question my relationship with Tania.'

'It was the best way I could think of to help you.'

'I would like to tell you some of my story.'

'And I would like to hear it and if I can help in any way then I will.'

Gordon didn't start by talking about his married life, but by recalling the memory he had of when he was seven and how his father had stopped his mother from showing any affection because he thought it would make him grow up to be a homo-sexual. Jennifer had to wipe away tears when he got to the end of the tale.

'You know,' she said, 'I spent several months in safe houses after I escaped and I heard many women's stories. Apparently, it's not unusual for very controlling men to prevent partners showing physical love towards their children. The idea is so totally abhorrent to any mother that it's one of the greatest punishments they can dish out. If a man can make a woman obey him with such extremely unnatural behaviour then he has gained absolute power over her. It's almost as though it's a test.'

He was astonished to hear that such things occurred. Gordon had always believed he was rather odd in the way his life had changed overnight into one of 'non-touching' and he had never doubted that his father's reasons were tied up with his obsessive phobia of homosexuals. But to learn that this situation was not uncommon in certain relationships gave a new slant to his childhood experience.

'I don't think I could have taken more punishment from Derek,' continued Jennifer after they had both been silent for a while, 'but when I heard about the lives of some of the others in the shelters I cried and cried for what they had been through. Some of the depravity they were forced to endure made me feel sick.'

They both sat quietly, drinking tea and reflecting. He picked up his story again, explaining about the insults and ridicule he had grown up with because of his appearance.

'That's so sad,' she said when he had finished.

'The saddest part of it all is that I have let the course of my life be determined by strangers in the street, screaming abuse into my face as though they were doing nothing more than making a comment about the weather,' he said. 'Then when I was twenty, along came Tania.'

'You were vulnerable,' she said. 'People who have grown up in homes where there is excessive control of one person over another, or even of the whole family, often accept those characteristics in their partners as being normal. They don't grow up to become an abusive adult, but the husband or wife of someone who is and unless people are exposed to something different then they have nothing to compare this type of environment to.

'You were even more vulnerable because you were so desperate simply to be held by another human being. We all

171

need that. You can't blame yourself for grabbing what must have seemed at the time to be great good fortune.'

'Yes,' he replied. 'But even though I had never had a partner before and knew very little of relationships, I saw warning signs of Tania's instability quite early on. I shouldn't have ignored them. I simply didn't want to acknowledge what they might represent.'

'Many battered women could probably make a similar admission.'

'I've tried to be analytical in my feelings and the answers I come up with aren't positive,' he said, pausing to collect his thoughts before continuing. 'Her extreme laziness and the way she tells lies as part of everyday conversation have killed any respect, and I can't tell her anything in confidence because she'll repeat it when she's drunk.'

'That's a huge obstacle to exist between two people,' she said. 'If there's not enough trust to say something privately then communication is reduced to a superficial level.'

'I used to think Tania's jealousy — checking my post and the numbers on the telephone bill, reading my emails — that they were just distorted ways of showing love. But when you look at these actions from an alternative perspective, as someone who is trying to dominate another person, they take on a much more sinister meaning.

'It's this constant need to control me. She's chipped away at my confidence, which was already low enough as it was, continually telling me I'm stupid, screaming at me to either do or not do something, using the affection I craved as a bargaining tool to mould me into *her person*, not the one I really am. In the end I became frightened of her without realising.'

He was quiet, looking down at his empty cup.

'All abusers rely on fear,' said Jennifer. 'It's a key weapon in their corrupt arsenal. They depend on the fear of ridicule and rejection, of loneliness and shame, of pain. They steal our money and friends, trample our spirit joyfully into dust, destroy our dreams, until we believe ourselves to be so worthless, creatures so unlovable, that we are totally dependent on them for everything, and even accept we deserve the punishments they hand out.'

She took hold of his hand.

'But you are lovable. You're a good, kind person. Over the years, you've accepted all the insults and criticism as fact, but they're not. You're not to blame for the abuse you receive. Nobody is. It took me more than a year to accept that I wasn't responsible for the situation I was in, and this was with the enormous support of the people at the shelters. You know, those strangers who screamed insults in the street are like Derek and Tania, trying to control another person.'

He had never considered such a link.

'But why would strangers want to control me? What benefit is it to them what I do, as it's so unlikely we would ever meet again?'

'That doesn't matter to people who are overwhelmed with the need to dominate. They'll cast their web in all directions in order to catch as many victims as possible, to infect them with their influence. They're consumed by the need. When we went out in the car, one of Derek's favourite tricks was to flash at a female driver then wave his fist angrily as if she had done something terribly wrong. He always picked the moment carefully, normally when someone had just made a manoeuvre.

'He would drive on smiling, knowing that at least some of the people he did this to would agonise for ages, trying to understand what they had done so incorrectly that another motorist had been irritated to such a degree. With hardly any effort Derek had got inside their head and manipulated their thoughts and feelings. I wanted to hug those women, to reassure them that they hadn't made a mistake and it was just a sick game of my husband's.'

'I remember ...' he said.

'What?'

'It's a silly example, but it's just come to mind.'

'I won't know if you don't tell me.'

'Once, when I was seventeen, a group of five or six lads gathered around me at the bus stop and started to make insulting comments. It was a common scenario. I tried to ignore them and after a few minutes they became bored. But just before they moved on, one of them said, "He enjoyed that". I thought it was an extraordinary statement. Why should this complete stranger believe that I enjoyed such treatment?'

'He sounds like an abuser in the making,' said Jennifer. 'It's a classic tactic to make out that the victim *likes* being tormented. I pity any woman who ever became involved with that lad when he was older.'

'I never really understood why people were so compelled to ridicule me the way they did.'

'I don't know. Perhaps, like all bullies, it's only by putting others down that they can hope to feel good about themselves. There are lots of characters around like it and you'll come across this type of behaviour in all walks of life, just like domestic violence.'

She removed her hand from his and poured more tea. It was going cold, however, they were so wrapped up in each other's stories that neither of them wanted to leave the table to get more.

'There's one thing about Tania that you've not commented on,' she said.

He looked at her without speaking.

'You don't say whether or not you still love her. Despite everything that is done to us, we so often believe we love someone, that they are truly remorseful and will change if we allow them another chance ... if we only give even more of our love.'

174

He knew the answer without having to consider it.

'No. I don't love her. Perhaps in the beginning, but there's nothing left now except concern that she might hurt herself if I leave, and my own fear of being alone.'

'Do you believe she would harm herself?'

'She's said that she would, but it's impossible to know.'

'Maybe it's just another way of controlling you, playing to your caring nature.'

Gordon shrugged his shoulders.

'One woman in the shelter told me she left her husband when she realised she didn't want to grow old with him, that the hurt could be endured day-by-day, but when she considered the idea of being with him in twenty or thirty years' time, of being *old* together, the image was so awful she left the house that very afternoon and never went back. And I don't think you need to fear being alone. Many women would snap you up.'

He managed to smile at this observation.

'How do you feel now?' she asked.

'Terrified,' he said, but the smile had not completely gone away. 'I know what I have to do. I just have to find the courage to do it.'

Chapter Twenty-Five

Enid took a long time to get ready on the morning that she was going into the nursing home. Alfred wondered if this was a demonstration of reluctance or merely that every day she needed longer to prepare herself before breakfast. Their social worker — they had their own social worker now — had explained patiently that she was to have a few days' holiday in a very nice home. Enid had never said much about it and he wasn't sure if she really understood.

She no longer wandered around much during the night and had gone from ringing Kate constantly to hardly ever calling her. The old barber didn't know what to make of these changes in behaviour, whether they signified a new phase in the condition. He didn't sleep much better, even without having to track her down during the early hours.

The only item she wanted to take was a small green elephant, which was about two inches high and made of pottery. Kate had bought it as a present when she was four using her own money, which had made it a treasured gift. The ornament had been given pride of place on the mantelpiece ever since, even though it clashed with almost everything else on display.

Alfred had been forced to select the clothes and items his wife might need for her five-day stay. It had all fitted into two small suitcases, which were ready at the front door as they waited in the hallway for the taxi. It was no longer safe for him to take her in the car in case she became agitated.

He felt apprehensive, the sort of feeling he had when one of them had to go into hospital for an operation and the other would be leaving them behind once they had unpacked. Enid hadn't spoken since they had got up and didn't speak while they drove to the nursing home. The taxi driver was very kind. He had taken enough people to the building over the years to know that if there were any suitcases then one person was remaining.

The two of them stood in the reception area, feeling lost. She took hold of his right arm, the first sign that morning of acknowledging him in any way. He patted her hand. It was only moments later when they saw a figure striding towards them, a human version of the *Flying Dutchman* at full throttle.

'Hello, Enid. I'm Matron. You've timed your visit well. I was just about to make a pot of tea. Shall we have a cup together?'

She held out her arm. Alfred's wife hesitated for a moment then gently slid hers out of his. He appreciated this was probably a ploy of the matron's and whenever a new resident arrived it would be time for a cuppa. It was meant to reassure and he thought all the more of her for the gesture.

But as the two women walked slowly away he felt a tiny part of his heart breaking. For sixty years it had been *his* arm that Enid had held on to, it was by *his* side that they had faced life's challenges together. They had always been a team. It was as though she had let go of him in more than just a physical sense. He was cast adrift and the ocean was vast, cold and threatening.

They walked slowly along the empty corridor, the matron chatting away, talking about the garden and how a group of children from a local school were giving a small concert after lunch. Alfred was about to reach down for the cases and follow when a man he had not noticed, a porter or nurse of some sort, appeared by his side.

'Here you are, mate, I'll take those,' said the man cheerily. 'You don't want to let them get too far ahead otherwise Matron will eat all the best cakes.'

Much later that afternoon Alfred sat alone in the little kitchen at home. Kate had wanted to help get her mother into the nursing home, but he'd insisted they would be alright so instead she was coming the next day to clean and tidy. The house wasn't quite as it should be, despite the assistance from various people.

Alfred had never felt so lost. He kept reminding himself that Enid would be back by the end of the week and he should make the most of the short break to rest, and enjoy time with his daughter. But as he sat at the table, none of these thoughts helped. He just wanted back the woman he loved, the way she used to be.

Kate arrived shortly after nine o'clock and the two of them set about the rooms like demented demons, as if through physical activity they could find some inner peace. It worked, to a degree. His daughter made a salad for lunch and then told him to sit in the armchair while she sorted out washing.

There were some items that just never got done, like his old yellow scarf. Alfred was worried it might run and spoil other clothes and it was hardly worth doing by itself. He kept forgetting to check with someone who would know about such things and so for weeks it had lain at the bottom of the coat stand, dirty and unused.

How many months had it been since Enid had greeted him at the front door on his return from the barber's shop, taking his scarf and gloves and putting them carefully on the peg that she always put them on? How many thousands of times had she done that over the years? Occasionally, she would announce with fierce determination, 'Goodness, you can't possibly keep wearing those old gloves. I'm going to buy you some new ones tomorrow.' It was pointless to argue. How he loved her.

He hadn't sold the shop, only closed it down 'until further notice'. Well, he suspected that regular customers had heard about his situation by now. He wondered where they had all gone, if they were enjoying having their hair washed by a pretty young girl at one of the nearby unisex salons. Apparently, they gave customers a head massage as well. What would his old boss make of that?

If you included his time in training, he had recently passed his sixtieth anniversary as a barber. Alfred had tried to make a little celebration of the occasion. Enid had been pleased and it had been a nice evening, albeit that they had simply stayed at home.

Where had those years gone?

Despite spending so many decades cutting men's hair, it seemed that all this had taken place so long ago and represented only a minute fraction of his life. Memories were fading in his mind: the happy family times; the birth of the grandchildren; christenings; special parties; the joy of just being together. The images that invaded his thoughts these days were those of recent events: Enid being lost in the street; crying non-stop because she had forgotten something or couldn't make him understand; images of her fist coming towards his face.

Kate stayed that night and the following morning the two of them went to the nursing home. Just like the previous occasion, Matron appeared within a few moments of them arriving in reception. They went to her office.

'How's my mother?'

'She's been fine. She loved the children's concert yesterday and spent a lot of time walking around the garden. She knows a lot about plants.'

'She hasn't been upset?' asked Alfred.

'No, not once.'

'I see,' he said, not quite certain what to make of this information.

'You know, we often find that when people become aggressive, because of a dementia-type illness, that it is those they love most, and are the closest to, who get the brunt of their anger,' said the matron. 'That's how life is normally amongst families and it doesn't alter because someone has Alzheimer's.

'It's very difficult, but please don't have any negative feelings about this side of your wife's behaviour. You may find that she is not aggressive here, but may become so again once she returns home. We try very hard to spot and eliminate the triggers that lead to frustration, which in turn can result in agitation. Obviously, our staff have a lot of experience in this and if we learn anything during the next few days that may be useful we'll certainly let you know.'

The three of them talked for a while before hunting out Enid who was sitting in the lounge, listening to another resident talking excitedly about her various grandchildren. The woman politely excused herself as they walked over.

'Hello, Mum.'

'Oh.'

'Hello, love,' said Alfred, kneeling awkwardly by her legs so that he could take hold of one of her hands. 'How are you feeling today?'

'Have you been in the shop?' she said, patting him on the head as if he was one of the 'pat dogs' that were brought around regularly by local volunteers.

'Later,' he replied, having learnt not to say the business was shut as this tended to upset her. 'I wanted to see you first. Are you eating well?'

'Yes, it's nice. But it's not home.'

'We'll have you back on Saturday. That's only a few days away. Kate's been helping me spruce up the place.'

'That lady has grandchildren. We've got grandchildren.'

'We have, and they both send their love, Mum.'

'I've forgotten their names.'

'You've having me on,' said Alfred, trying to make light of the comment. 'You know it's Peter and Laura.'

'They've written you a card, Mum.'

Enid took it, smiling, but not seeming able to read the words. Kate told her the message, which she knew by heart. They chatted amicably until the matron appeared at the time they had secretly agreed earlier. She had explained that it was often a good idea for a resident to be distracted when visitors were leaving so that they didn't think they were going as well. This often prevented potential distress. So Alfred and Kate left, but they felt like thieves in the night for not saying goodbye.

Chapter Twenty-Six

The day came in July when Gordon had to face up to once more being alone. Those years of never having any physical contact with another person were still as fresh in his mind as when he lived through them and the memory haunted him. But what was the alternative?

Jennifer had asked whether he wanted to be with his wife in twenty years' time; did he see himself going happily into middle age and beyond with her? He had never considered their relationship in such a black-and-white way, but he had no hesitation in answering 'no'. And now this thought had been planted, he couldn't get it out of his head. So why was he staying?

Jennifer had opened his eyes to the fact that his life wasn't what it should be. Perhaps part of him deep down had known, but he had ignored the feelings, had not been strong enough to do anything about the situation. It was far easier to let the months roll by, to try to remember only the good times and not have to face the prospect of splitting up.

Gordon was terrified. He didn't think of himself as a bad man, but a weak one, too afraid of confrontation. That had always been his Achilles heel and people had exploited it to his enormous cost. So what did he do now? Did he put the whole idea on hold for a few months, give her yet another chance; hope that she might change if he tried harder?

He paced backwards and forwards in the kitchen. She would be coming home soon from the hairdresser. Should he say something or wait for the 'right moment'? Would there ever be a right moment for such a painful conversation? Whenever it took place, he would have to be prepared for ... what? Anger? Violence? Threats of suicide?

She had used the latter a few times in the early years of their marriage, not because he had made any hint of leaving but, he realised now, just to put the fear in his head that if he ever did then she would kill herself. As he had never considered such an action, he had put this 'risk' to the back of his mind and it had played no part in their lives.

But recently he had analysed a lot of what had been said during their marriage and had come to understand that this almost unconscious threat had influenced him after all. It was a part of her programme of control. But remaining with someone because you feared they would harm themselves if you left was a desperate reason to stay. In a way he was sacrificing his life for hers.

Jennifer had said that it took a lot of courage to continue living with an abusive person and he should think of himself as brave for surviving these years. But as he paced between the fridge and the sink Gordon didn't feel brave in the slightest. The front door opened.

Dear God, help me now.

Perhaps he should leave everything for a few weeks, until there was a better opportunity to say something?

Tania's hair was red. It looked bizarre and after all the conversations he had had with himself, all the doubts of what he should, or should not, do, it was seeing the colour of her hair that Saturday morning that made him decide. She stood in the doorway of the kitchen, having laid down several bags of clothes-shopping.

'Hello,' he said. 'Do you want a coffee?'

'I thought you would have had one already.'

'No, I was waiting for you,' he said, switching on the percolator, which he had already set up for her return.

'You look worried.'

'Yes, I am to be honest. There's something very important I have to say and there's no easy way to tell you. To be truthful, I've not been happy for quite a while ...'

Say it. Say it.

'... and I think we should have some time apart.'

Gordon had wanted to say they should get a divorce, but thought this might be a cruel thing to blurt out with no previous warning. However, a part of him felt he had bottled out. Tania's face went through a range of expressions, as if she couldn't believe what she had just heard and didn't know how to respond.

Was it going to be anger, violence or threats of suicide?

'Don't be stupid!'

Anger then.

He took a large breath to steady his nerves.

'I'm not being stupid and it's not right that you constantly say I am. I never put you down, while you do this to me all the time.'

'Oh ... don't be stupid, Gordon.'

Tania was so shocked by what he had said that she fell back again on to a familiar phrase, ignoring the fact that he had just pointed out this was not acceptable behaviour.

'You can't leave me. I won't let you.'

'Well, you can hardly lock me in the shed.'

'You're not doing this to me after everything I've given up for you.'

'What things have you given up?'

Tania was completely unused to being answered back, or by him questioning one of her outrageous statements. There was a pause in the conversation while she tried to think of an answer.

'I've given up my career to look after the house so that you can concentrate on your work and not worry about anything else.'

Gordon was taken aback at this as she had only ever held

184

low-skilled office jobs, never showing any keenness to earn her own living, until she had stopped working altogether. She didn't do anything in the garden and, apart from cooking, did almost nothing around the house. However, he was utterly speechless when she continued.

'And I've given up having children so that I can look after you.'

Such blatant lies felt like punches and he reeled from them, unsure how to react. Tania had always been adamant that she didn't want children and he had gone along, feeling they were both still young. She could see he was shaken and pressed ahead with a new line of attack.

'Do you think you're really going to leave me? What woman is going to take you on the way you look? I don't mean to be unkind — because I love you a lot — but nobody is going to want to be with you. You're better off staying here with me.'

This was completely the opposite to what she had said for most of their married life, when every few months she would accuse him of having 'something going on' with yet another woman.

'If you leave me then I would get the house along with everything else. I can't work, so you would have to pay me maintenance. And imagine what your friends will say when they find out how badly you've treated me. They'll all take my side. You'll have no one and no place to stay. If they find out at the factory how you've abused me then you'll lose your job. Have you thought of that? Well, have you?'

She paused, but in a flash of inspiration thought of one more weapon to use.

'And what will your poor mother say when I explain how abusive you've been to me? Think how distressed she would be to learn that her precious little boy was so terrible.'

Tania threw so much at him that he couldn't think straight. Each point on its own was absurd, but hurled at him all together made him start to doubt himself. Would he lose his friends? She looked almost pleased as she faced him across the kitchen. Could he lose his job?

Why couldn't she work?

'Why can't you work?'

Now it was her turn to be caught off guard and she stumbled over a reply.

'You know I can't. I'm not well enough. The doctor says so.'

'When did a doctor ever say that you couldn't work?'

'DON'T BE STUPID!'

They stood in silence apart from the noise of the percolator bubbling and hissing. Neither of them knew where to take the conversation. Tania was reverting to her 'Don't be stupid' response, which was what she always said when he asked her a question she couldn't answer. He had spoken of his feelings and she had basically ignored them. She was still standing in the doorway, but after a while walked over to him, trying a different approach. She was good at this.

'Look, perhaps I have overreacted to some things. But I know you better than you know yourself and I've only got your best interests at heart. I'll let you have your friend from the choir. She sounds like a nice lady. You could bring her around for dinner.

'And you should come back to our bedroom. I won't smoke upstairs anymore and I'll change the bed so that everything is fresh for tonight. It's only because I love you so much that I get worried. You know we get on well together on the whole. Every couple has their ups and downs. Why don't we get our coffee and sit in the garden? It's nice outside.'

She put her arms around his waist, hugging him tightly.

'And I'll make you something special for dinner,' she continued. 'Anything you want. You can invite some of your music friends. How does that sound? We can put all this silliness behind us.'

But Gordon remained standing where he was, arms down by his sides, his eyes fixed on the bright red hair only inches from his face.

Chapter Twenty-Seven

A part of Tom's insides froze when he saw the mark on Amy's arm. He was helping her get ready for bed and was holding her pyjama top. The bruise was just above the right elbow and when he checked he could see a similar one on the other arm. Someone much stronger had held his daughter with significant force.

'That's a funny little bruise,' he said pointing to the spot as she slipped a hand into one sleeve. 'How did you get that, poppet?'

She went quiet, looking down at the floor, half in the top. He helped her finish dressing so that he could lift her up on to his knee and she buried her head into his chest.

'It's alright. You're not in any trouble. I just wanted to know how you managed to get it. You couldn't have banged yourself because you've got one on the other arm just like it. Eh?' he said gently, trying to coax an answer. 'How did you get those?'

'Mummy said not to tell.'

Tom wondered if the small ear resting against his shirt could hear the increase in his heart beat.

'Well, you can tell Daddy. That's what daddies are for, listening to their wee girls. So why did Mummy grab your arms?'

'She was very angry.'

'Oh dear. Why was she angry?'

'I don't know.'

'That's odd isn't it? What did she say to you? Mummy must have said something.'

Amy sat up properly so that she could look at his face.

'She said I was a naughty girl and had to obey her. But I always do what she says,' said Amy, two huge tears rolling down her cheeks.

'And Mummy didn't say at all why she thought you were naughty?'

'No.'

Tom knew the feeling, of being punished and not knowing what for.

'Then what did she do?'

'She let me go and told me to do my homework, which I'd already done. Please don't say anything, Daddy.'

Tom didn't know how to respond. It was the first sign of Gemma doing something physical to Amy. He couldn't let this incident pass, but his daughter, now crying openly, was terrified of him speaking to her mother about the matter. Did he even go so far as informing social services? Various scenarios flashed through his mind as Amy sat on his knee, waiting for him to confirm that he wouldn't let Gemma know she had spoken to him.

The GP he had met was sensible. Perhaps he could get her advice. But then she might be under some sort of duty of care and would be forced to report serious concerns about a child's welfare to the authorities. Maybe this applied even to solicitors. He didn't know. He was tempted to take hold of Gemma and give her more than a talking-to, though he knew he couldn't coldly plan such a course of action. It simply wasn't in his nature.

'Daddy?'

'It's alright, poppet. Daddy's just thinking what to do for the best.'

He pulled the small figure into his chest again and wrapped his arms around her in order to gain time while he considered his options. But as he sat cradling her he was completely at a loss.

Tom did nothing for five days, until Amy was having a sleepover at Jessica's and he was alone with his wife in the house. Since his frank conversation with Gemma about her aggression he had tried to get home earlier in the evenings and he made sure he was on this occasion. He washed quickly and went to the kitchen to help with dinner.

'I wanted to ask if you had noticed those bruises on Amy's arms,' he said, almost casually as he laid out the table. 'There's one above each elbow, as if someone has held her tightly.'

'Yes, I did,' she replied, her back to him while she chopped up vegetables.

'Well, what do you think caused them?'

'I suppose it's like you say. Someone has held her arms.'

Gemma was being evasive and spoke as if they were talking about an episode from a television programme.

'So, do you know who might have done such a thing with sufficient force to leave marks?'

'Yes,' she said, getting a packet of frozen peas from the freezer.

'Who?' he asked.

His patience was cracking under the strain of having such a superficially light conversation about so serious a subject.

'It could've been me.'

'Oh. Why did you hold her so hard?'

'I can't remember.'

She cut the bag with a pair of scissors and poured peas into a pan, apparently fascinated by the miniature green waterfall.

'Well, you must have had a reason. Did you become angry with her?'

'I suppose so.'

'What about?'

'Don't remember.'

'Have you held her like that before?'

'Maybe. I don't know.'

190

'That's not good enough.'

She turned quickly and threw the packet at him, but he ducked and frozen peas scattered around the floor like a small hailstorm.

'Well, you'd obviously decided it was my fault before you began this interrogation so why bother asking me who did it?' she screamed. 'You and precious Amy again. I'm just here to do the fucking cooking.'

He strode across the kitchen. She picked up the scissors lying on the side, but he was too quick and grabbed her wrist as she turned to face him. Gemma screamed and tried to scratch his face with her other hand, but he blocked her attempts until he managed to catch hold of the other wrist.

'You don't hold a child so tightly that you leave bruises! Don't you ever do that again.'

'Fuck you!'

Gemma tried to headbutt him, but he held her off so she lashed out with her foot. The blow caught him on a shin though there was little force behind the kick and he pushed her back easily into the corner so that she had no room to manoeuvre.

'Let me go, you fucking bastard. Let me go.'

Even with his extra strength Tom was cautious. She had bitten him before and he made sure that she didn't get the opportunity on this occasion.

'This violence and aggression of yours has got to stop,' he said. 'It ends now, as of this night. I'm taking no more of it and you are never going to hurt Amy again. Are you hearing me?'

Gemma had once said that to him, after she had hit him with the pan when he was kneeling on the kitchen floor picking up a slice of carrot.

'I don't care if you go for counselling, or whether we go somewhere as a couple, but this is not continuing.'

She was forced to drop the scissors, but struggled wildly, furious at having so little control. Eventually, her chest heaving with exertion, she quietened down appearing to accept that she couldn't win in this position. And Gemma had to win. They stared at each other in grim silence.

'You're hurting my arms,' she said.

'Are you sure you've calmed down enough for me to release you?'

'Yes. Just let go of me.'

'And have you understood that these violent attacks of yours have got to stop?'

'I've heard what you said.'

'What about Amy?'

'She'll be fine. You don't need to worry about her.'

'You know I'm serious. I won't let you hurt her.'

'I should know that much. Yes.'

He let go of her and stepped immediately out of reach. Tom didn't trust his wife not to hit him. As regards his little girl, he didn't know what else he could do. At least he had managed not to reveal that their daughter had spoken to him earlier in the week. That night, he had fudged his answer in the end, not really promising one thing or another and Amy had not been completely satisfied with the reply. She had only settled when he agreed to sit by her bed until she had fallen asleep.

Gemma rubbed her wrists where red marks were already clearly visible against her pale skin.

'You hurt me,' she said accusingly, as if all the times she had put him in the local casualty department were really of no consequence.

'I'm sorry. You know I would never deliberately harm you, but you've overstepped a boundary.'

'I understand that now. And there's no need for me to ever hurt her again, so it won't be repeated.'

Tom didn't quite follow the meaning of what she said, but he assumed it was merely an awkward turn of phrase used in the heat of the moment. They stood facing each other for several moments then, almost brightly, she said:

'Well, do you still want dinner? I've nearly got it ready to put on.'

It struck him as an odd question under the circumstances. How could she think of food after what they had both just been through? His heart was racing yet she seemed to be recovering surprisingly rapidly. He was reminded of the last journey they had had to the hospital, when she had chattered away almost merrily while he held a blood-soaked tea towel to the cut above his eye. The scene in the kitchen had a similar feel about it, as though there was a detachment from reality.

'It's a pity to waste the gammon steaks,' she said. 'They look rather good.'

'I guess,' he replied. 'By the time it's cooked I may feel like something.'

He didn't want to eat, but wondered if this was some sort of peace offering.

'It won't be ready for half an hour. Why don't you go out for a walk and get some fresh air. I'll have everything ready for when you get back.'

Tom stared at her. Was it only minutes ago that she had been like a wildcat, trying to scratch and kick him? But she was right about him needing some fresh air. He turned slowly and headed for the door.

'Red or white?' she called after him.

'What?' he said.

'Wine. Red or white?'

He paused, standing in the doorway near to where the bag of peas had come to rest.

'Red,' he answered without thinking.

'Right then. Make sure you mind the time.'

She turned to the cooker and Tom went into the corridor where he picked up his jacket. It was almost as though she was shouting after Amy, going out to play. '*Make sure you mind the time. Dinner will be in half an hour and then you've got your homework to do.'*

He walked out of the house feeling bewildered. Had he actually won that argument? Had Gemma really agreed to what he'd said? He felt wrong-footed again, like the time she collected him from the police station and he had been grateful to her, even though she had been the cause of him being there in the first place.

As he walked along the street, Tom couldn't shake off the sensation that what had just occurred in the kitchen was exactly what Gemma intended.

Chapter Twenty-Eight

It was the worst journey Gordon had ever made. By nature he was a cautious driver, but he broke the speed limit several times as he raced home following Tania's telephone call. She had taken an overdose. He had been attending an exhibition, a rare event, and was due to return that day anyway, but she had called him in the morning before he had even left the hotel.

The journey there had taken him over five hours a few days earlier so she knew he couldn't get back quickly. Tania said she had made herself sick so there was no need for an ambulance and Sally was with her. The latter thought didn't give him any peace of mind.

It was impossible to know whether his wife had really taken any tablets, had perhaps taken only a couple so that there was no danger yet some truth in the claim, or that she had indeed swallowed a large quantity. The risk was too great not to take seriously so he hurried in the rain at speeds that made him uncomfortable.

There was no sign of Sally when he walked into the house. Tania was in the kitchen, smoking.

'What have you done?' he said

She rushed into his arms.

'It's alright. I'm going to be alright now you're back. I was just so miserable. Without you I'm a wreck. See what such a short time apart has done to me? You can't leave me. I won't survive. I really will kill myself if you go.'

'I've been frantic. I nearly crashed the car twice.'

'That shows how much you care. You wouldn't have rushed back if you didn't love me. It proves we should stay together.'

Gordon pulled himself away.

'Where's Sally?'

'She's just gone, only minutes ago. I told her to go.'

'What did you take?'

'Tablets lying around the house.'

'I think you should see a doctor.'

'No, there's no need. I brought them all back up almost immediately so no damage has been done. But next time ...'

'You can't hold this threat over me. I can't stay with you for the rest of my life because of fear. That would be a terrible existence.'

'I'll change. You'll like me more. You'll see. I'll cut down on my smoking and drinking and lose some weight. I'll get a job. Then you won't have to work so hard at the factory. I'll be a better person. It'll be a fresh start for us.'

Gordon started to pace the kitchen in despair while she lit another cigarette.

'Look,' he said, picking his words carefully. 'People are what they are and shouldn't have to change to please someone else. We're just not suited to each other. The things you desire are not what I want out of life. I'm truly sorry that I'm hurting you. I never wanted to harm anyone, but now I know you can't always achieve that. If I stay then I'll be miserable.'

'It's this new woman of yours!' screamed Tania. 'She's put all these mad ideas into your head. You would never have thought of this all by yourself.'

Gordon looked at his wife without answering. Although Jennifer was hardly 'his woman' there was some truth in the accusation.

'I've realised a lot about us over the last few months and I'm not going to carry on as we are. I'll find somewhere to stay as soon as I can.'

'I'll kill myself if you go.'

He sighed. They were both close to tears.

'You simply have to take responsibility for your own life,' he said. 'You cannot put this on to me.'

'At least stay in the house. You can sleep in the spare room if you want, but you can't leave me at a moment like this, when I'm in such need.'

He knew he was being manipulated, but could feel himself weakening. Perhaps he should remain until he was ready to leave for good. It would be easier to sort everything out if he didn't have the added task of trying to find accommodation.

'Alright, I'll stay if you promise not to take any more overdoses.'

She threw her arms around him.

'Of course. Now that you're here there'll be no need to harm myself. Everything will be fine.'

But he knew in his heart this last comment was untrue, and he doubted that she believed it either.

Chapter Twenty-Nine

The two sheriff's officers were thickset men, used to dealing with trouble. They watched Tom with experienced eyes as he stared at the papers they had thrust into his hands, having just confirmed who he was. 'Served on behalf of the court' might be the legal term for what had occurred, but this description didn't convey any sense of the brutality of the action. It gave no acknowledgement of the horror that was about to unfold. The three of them were standing by the desk in his office.

'What's this?' said Tom, whose brain refused to accept the text that he was reading.

To interdict the defender from molesting the pursuer by abusing her verbally, by threatening her, by placing her in a state of fear and alarm or distress and by using violence towards her, and to grant such an order ad interim ...

'This,' said one of the men, 'is called an Interim Interdict and it means that the local Sheriff is telling you what you can and can't do in regards to your wife. Read it carefully and make sure you follow the instructions or you're likely to end up in even more hot water than you are now.'

'The Sheriff? But why would he do such a thing? I don't understand this at all.'

'Everyone says that,' said the man. 'He's done it because your wife's solicitor has asked him to and he has agreed.'

'Gemma?

Tom looked from one man to the other, his initial confusion turning rapidly into despair, but their faces were expressionless. They were doing their job and had seen this reaction far too often to be affected by it or inclined to offer sympathy.

Jack agreed to see him during his lunch break so they sat in the solicitor's office while he read through the papers Tom had been served earlier that morning. After several minutes the older man put them down on his desk, removed his glasses and rubbed his eyes.

'Bloody hell, Tom. I know this is not your fault, but I warned you about getting involved with the courts.'

'What am I supposed to do?'

'Listen very carefully to what I'm about to say. Whatever you do you must obey these restrictions to the letter. At the moment this is a civil action, but if you fall foul of the conditions it could become a criminal matter. Gemma's solicitor has included in this Initial Writ an exclusion order suspending your rights to occupy the matrimonial home and forbidding you to enter the property without your wife's permission.

'Now, these restrictions can only come into force after you've had a chance to put your case to the sheriff, so they're not actually active at the moment. However, my advice would be to treat them as though they were in place and to have no contact with Gemma until after the hearing. This means no phone calls, emails, texting ... nothing.'

'But if I don't go to the house I might not see Amy,' pleaded Tom. 'I read her a story every night. She won't go to sleep without one.'

'I know it's hard, but according to the Writ your hearing at the sheriff's court is only a couple of days away. When children are involved the authorities are never keen for the situation to continue for any longer than absolutely necessary. In addition, being served with papers like this makes out that you're guilty of a crime you've not had a chance to defend yourself against, which rather goes against the natural laws of Scottish justice.'

Tom was close to tears.

'Amy won't sleep without her bedtime story.'

'Keep away from them for now. I'm sure it can be sorted out.'

'What am I to do, Jack?'

'This is not my field. You need the help of a colleague of mine. She's good. Her name is Frances. I know she's out at the moment, but I'll see if I can arrange a meeting for you early tomorrow morning. Can you get some time off work?'

'Yes. What happens in court?'

'Basically, Gemma tells her side of events and you tell yours. There are a multitude of potential outcomes, but it won't depend on that one meeting by any means. The sheriff will know that you've only been aware of these accusations since being served with the Interdict, so he'll make allowances for the fact that there has been no time to prepare documentation or gather any witnesses.

'The important thing for the moment is to remain calm and stay focused on the task in hand. This is a long way from being the end of the world.'

But Tom put his head in his hands and started to cry.

Rose had seen her brother shed tears before, but nothing like this. He was inconsolable, so she cradled him as he used to hold her when she was young. He had arrived at her house that afternoon. John and the children were yet to return home so she had some time alone with him to try and find out what had reduced one of the strongest and most dependable men she knew to this sad figure, sobbing uncontrollably on her shoulder.

'Tom. Whatever has happened? I've never seen you in such a state.'

He pulled back to face her, his handsome face puffy and tear-stained.

'Gemma's gone to the court and I can't go near the house. I'm not allowed to see either of them or have any contact. I can't even ring to wish Amy goodnight.'

'Oh, dear God. How has she got away with this? And why? What is she trying to achieve?'

'I don't know. I'm not sure what I'm meant to do any more. I can't see my little girl. She'll think I've broken my promise not to leave, that I've deserted her.'

'Amy would never think that. When you next see her you can explain.'

'But what am I explaining? That her father is considered too dangerous to live in the house? That she should be in fear of him because he is such a terrible person? How can I possibly explain to my little girl that I'm not allowed to read her a bedtime story? She won't understand.'

He couldn't speak for several minutes so she held him tightly while they both wept. Rose loved her big brother and seeing him like this broke her heart. And she didn't know what to say. This was all beyond anything she had ever had to deal with.

'Have you seen a solicitor?'

'Briefly, at lunchtime. He's a man I know, but I'm going back in the morning to see a colleague of his who specialises in matrimonial matters.'

'Well then, you'll soon get some professional advice and have a better idea of how to move forward with this. I'll come with you. Perhaps I can speak to Gemma? Surely I'm not forbidden from contacting her?'

'I don't know. What would you say?'

'I'm not sure. We would need to think it through, but I could try to find out what it is she wants, assuming she knows herself. I could go over there this evening. You can stay here with John and look after the kids.'

'Gemma probably wouldn't see you.'

'I could just turn up and perhaps at least try to speak to Amy and explain what has happened.'

'No, thanks all the same. It's probably not a good idea.'

'I just don't know what else to suggest. How has she done this? Surely there would have to be some proof against you.'

'I lost my temper.'

'Oh no, Tom. What happened?'

'I saw bruises on Amy's arms and she said that her mummy had done it, but begged me not to say anything. I kept quiet for several days until Amy was away one night, then I confronted Gemma.'

'Well, did she admit it?'

'It was so odd. She owned up to it quite readily as if she was waiting for me to tackle her about it. Said she had been angry, but couldn't remember why. We started arguing in the kitchen. She picked up a pair of scissors so I grabbed her wrists and backed her into a corner. When she promised never to do anything like that again and to stop the violence against me, I let her go. She calmed down quickly and was soon talking about dinner as if the scene between us had never occurred.'

'When was this?'

'Four days ago. There were marks on her wrists where I held her. I don't know if that's evidence. I can't deny what happened and that she was probably hurt. It wasn't right, but there seemed no other option at the time.'

Early next morning Tom and Rose sat in the solicitor's office. The woman Jack had recommended gave the impression of being slightly irritated at having to fit in this unexpected meeting. However, she had the Interdict on the desk in front of her and had obviously gone through it already.

'Most of the wording in this document is standard,' she said within moments of them all sitting down. 'The parts that are specific to this case are these bits at the beginning and I need you to be completely honest with me about this as we go through these individual points.

'Have you ever been violent towards your wife, or made threatening gestures or comments? She must have had some evidence to back up her claim. The sheriff is highly unlikely to have granted the Interdict without some proof of injuries and probably also a witness.'

Tom explained about the incident in the kitchen. He couldn't think of any possible witness. No one had ever been aware of the many incidents when she had attacked him, so he didn't know how there could be anyone who would testify that he had been violent towards her.

Rose laid a hand on top of one of her brother's.

'Tom, tell Frances your story, about the beatings you've had and all the various trips to the casualty department.'

He remained silent.

'I can't help you without knowing all the facts,' said the solicitor. 'If your wife has been violent towards you and there is evidence then this goes a huge way to forming a case against her, which obviously helps in your defence.'

Tom still hesitated. The last thing he wanted was a legal war with Gemma. He was certain this would drive a wedge between them that could never be removed. It felt almost like the interview at the police station, when he had decided not to reveal she had chased him with a carving knife because such a serious accusation would have resulted in her automatically being detained and questioned.

He had guessed right on that occasion because she had withdrawn her accusation and in the end the police had nothing to go on either way. But this was different. The stakes were so much higher and if he presented no case he could be crucified in the sheriff's court and end up with ... well, what ... a divorce, limited rights to see Amy.

His nightmare was a scenario where Gemma 'announced' that he had been violent to or even molested his daughter. He hadn't voiced this fear to anyone, not even his sister. But such a heinous claim hadn't been made, so he forced the thought away. It would be completely counterproductive to let this concern dominate his mind when he had to concentrate on what he knew Gemma had said. He just didn't know which way to play this stage of the 'game'.

'As you're my solicitor, do you have to do what I instruct?' he asked.

'Well, yes. I will be guided by what you want within the boundaries of the law.'

Tom eventually made his decision. He took a deep breath and began to talk about the beatings, of how a one-off slap had developed into attacks that were increasingly violent and frequent. He told her about the trips to casualty, how being physically intimidated by a woman who had a fraction of his strength made him feel less of a man, that he was turning into a figure of ridicule. Tom explained how he tried ever harder to make Gemma happy, not just by giving her immediately whatever she asked for, but trying desperately to anticipate her demands.

He confessed how much he wanted to recapture the happier times they had had earlier in their marriage, how he still loved his wife and worshipped his daughter. Tom recounted the conversation with Gemma when she told him that she felt 'at the bottom of the shit pile' with regard to his priorities, although in truth he didn't believe this analysis was accurate or fair.

But the greater he tried, the more it seemed that his efforts weren't sufficient, or the ground rules changed so that he often didn't know what he was supposed to do to please her. He talked at length about Amy. Rose cried quietly through most of her brother's explanation. The solicitor made copious notes. She didn't interrupt because he was clear and precise in everything he said and it wasn't until Tom had obviously come to a stop that she spoke.

'Even though you told the medical staff that your injuries were either caused by an accident at home or during a game of rugby, there will at least be records of the treatment,' said Frances. 'Your GP should have access to these notes on her computer system. Have you spoken to your doctor about this situation at home?'

'Jack advised me back in March to get some emotional support for myself so I went to my doctor a few weeks later.'

'The fact that you've spoken to a solicitor and your doctor about incidents of domestic violence quite some time before your wife has applied for an Interdict gives us a much stronger hand. Have you spoken to anyone else?'

'A friend of mine,' said Tom, adding 'Pat' for his sister's benefit. 'He would confirm the conversation we had if I asked him to.'

'And you contacted the charity for abused men because they advised you to have an escape plan and that was before you met me in the car park,' said Rose.

'Yes, that's true,' said Tom, who had forgotten to mention these points.

'You've actually spoken to quite a few people about this,' said Frances. 'I think we have a very strong case to put before the Sheriff. He won't expect you to have sworn statements for the first hearing, but if you're confident you can get them, along with your medical records, then when we go back in front of him for the second time we could really turn the tables.'

'There'll be a second hearing?' asked Rose.

'Yes, if not more further down the line. Because the Interdict is served without warning the Sheriff will expect you to present your evidence on the next occasion.'

'Can you explain the court proceedings?' said Tom.

'As this is a domestic violence case, the sheriff will most likely hear it in his private chambers, which means that no members of the public or other outsiders will be present. It may only be Gemma's solicitor and me who go along, or you could both attend as well. There is an option for you and your wife to speak to the Sheriff without your solicitors being there, although I wouldn't advise that option and her solicitor is

205

probably saying the same. It's not unheard of for the two parties to agree what they want beforehand and then present this as a solution at the hearing.'

'Would the Sheriff agree to such a thing?' asked Rose.

'Oh yes. If it sounds sensible and balanced, so that it doesn't appear in any way that one party has been forced into an unfair position, then if it's what both people want, why shouldn't he agree? He'll always ensure there are safeguards in place for any children.'

'So it doesn't look as bleak as we thought,' said Rose, laying a hand on his arm.

'Not at all,' said Frances. 'We just need to start gathering evidence.'

'No,' said Tom.

'I don't follow,' said Frances.

'We're not gathering evidence against Gemma.'

Rose understood her brother's meaning more quickly than the solicitor.

'Oh no, please Tom,' she said. 'You can't mean not to defend yourself.'

'Potentially, you have a strong case,' said the solicitor.

'Gemma could destroy you,' said Rose, starting to cry again because she knew in her heart what he was intending to do.

'Your sister is right. If we say nothing then you're throwing yourself on the mercy of your wife.'

'She won't destroy me,' he said, although he wasn't perhaps quite as certain as he tried to sound. 'That's not what Gemma wants.'

'What does she want?' asked Frances, slightly exasperated.

'I'm not sure, but it's not that. This is designed to weaken, but not annihilate me. However, if I publicly reveal the violence that has been taking place then she will never forgive me and I will have no chance ever of getting back the woman and the life I used to have. The family unit that we currently are will be gone

206

forever. I won't allow that. You said that you have to do what I instruct?'

'Yes.'

'Then we don't do anything at present. Let's hear what she has to say and see where that takes us. But I'm forbidding you to attack Gemma in court or tell the Sheriff about her violence.'

Chapter Thirty

Tom barely slept the night before appearing at court and felt sick with apprehension as he made his way there. He found Frances in the corridor, which was bustling with a wide cross-section of humanity. As they waited, she explained some of the formalities, such as how to address the Sheriff should he be spoken to, and tried to put his mind at rest. She failed dismally at the latter.

After about twenty minutes Frances heard her name being called out by the clerk and they followed the man to the Sheriff's private chambers, picking up Gemma and her solicitor further along the corridor. Tom hadn't spotted his wife amongst the throng of people.

The room was expensively furnished and the Sheriff was already waiting for them behind a beautiful oak desk. The clerk instructed them where to sit before taking a seat next to the Sheriff. The four legal professionals were dressed in long black gowns although only the clerk wore a wig.

Gemma made quite a display of taking off her coat before sitting. She was wearing a new outfit, which covered most of her while still making a statement about the body inside it. Her make-up was light and her hair done in a slightly different style from normal. The overall impression was one of 'shy beauty' and Tom thought she must have spent hours planning the impression she wanted to present.

'Mrs McDonald,' said the sheriff. 'I believe that you are representing the pursuer in this case.'

Gemma's solicitor stood up.

'Yes, my Lord.'

'Could you please tell me where we are with it?'

'The Interim Interdict was served on the defender on the sixth of September, my Lord, and since that day he has refrained from contacting his wife. You will note the doctor's letter confirming the existence of bruising to my client's arms, consistent with being held by someone with considerable force. There is also an affidavit ...'

While the solicitor checked her paperwork Tom leant forward in his seat in anticipation at who on earth Gemma had been able to get to state in writing that he had been violent.

Amanda!

Suddenly the pieces tumbled into place. This explained why Amanda had turned hostile towards him overnight when he had no idea what he had done to offend the woman. That had been over a year ago. Had Gemma been feeding her stories of his 'abuse' ever since?

'It is only today, my Lord, that we have been in a position to pass on the affidavit to the defender's legal representative. We would ask the court to maintain the Interdict as it is.'

The solicitor sat down and the sheriff turned to Frances.

'Miss Campbell,' said the sheriff. 'Do you wish to make a statement at this stage?'

'My Lord,' replied Frances once she was standing, 'we are hopeful that the two parties will soon be reconciled. My client agrees to comply with all the terms of the Interdict until the next hearing. However, it is paramount that contact is maintained with his daughter and we ask that a date is arranged for the two to get together as a matter of urgency.'

'Mrs McDonald. How does your client feel about this proposed meeting with her daughter?' asked the sheriff.

Gemma and her solicitor whispered to each other before the latter stood to reply.

'No objections, my Lord. I'm sure the legal representatives can agree the details without having to bother the court.'

'Excellent,' said the Sheriff, who then conferred with the clerk before giving a date in October for the next hearing.

It was agreed that Tom and Amy could have lunch the following day. He couldn't pick her up from home because Gemma would be there, but she had agreed for a friend to drop off their daughter at a restaurant of his choice. This person would then bring her home afterwards. Tom wanted more time, not just a meal surrounded by strangers, but he was desperate to keep things on an even keel and Frances stressed that it was probably best to be as flexible as possible.

Tom arrived at the restaurant early and chose a table in the corner. He was determined not to make Amy a ping-pong ball between him and Gemma. He had decided to be extremely careful what he asked her, so that she wasn't pressured into revealing anything. As he expected Gemma to grill her when she returned he also had to be cautious about what he said concerning his circumstances.

Amy was meant to arrive at twelve and by quarter past Tom was ready to explode with frustration. He had agreed that their daughter could leave at two and their precious time together was ebbing away. Then she was there, standing just inside the doorway, and when he saw who was beside her his mouth opened in shock. It was Amanda!

Of all the many friends and neighbours who would have happily brought Amy to him, Gemma had chosen the one person who despised him. At least he now had an idea why she hated him.

Amy spotted her father and squirmed to get free of Amanda's hand, but the woman held on firmly until a waiter had spoken to her. She nodded at the man, then let go and Tom's daughter weaved her way through the tables like a miniature sprinter. He knelt down and she flung her skinny body into his so that he could wrap his arms around her as though trying to protect her from all the evil in the world.

Neither of them spoke. Amy was crying and Tom only just managed not to join in. He didn't want to break down in front of his daughter and the surrounding people, a few looking on with interest at such an emotional reunion between what was obviously father and child.

Above Amy's head Tom watched in growing horror as the waiter led Amanda across the restaurant. There was one table near to them and it was unoccupied. Gemma's accomplice smiled smugly in triumph as the waiter pulled out a chair. She was near enough to hear their conversation. Tom could barely contain his rage. This woman would destroy the short time he had with his daughter and all his feelings of joy were pushed aside by anger.

He had never been accused of being a threat to Amy and it was completely unreasonable for this to be turned into an unofficially supervised visit, as though he had to be monitored because he was dangerous, like some sort of pervert. However, he could hardly forbid the woman from eating a meal in a restaurant and he certainly didn't want to make a scene. For an instant he considered going to another venue, but had a vision of Amanda chasing after them along the High Street and, in addition, this would be breaking the agreement that had been made. The whole thing made him feel impotent.

This had been planned.

Amy was still in his arms, her sobs dying away, and Tom glanced around frantically for an alternative. There was one empty table in the centre of the restaurant that had people all around it. It wasn't such a good spot, but this would certainly be better than letting Amanda eavesdrop and cast her spell of negativity over everything.

'Come on, poppet. Let's go to that table over there.'

'What's wrong with this one?' said Amy, pulling back to look around for the first time.

'Oh, I don't like it anymore.'

The two of them went to the chosen spot and he moved the chairs so that they could sit side by side like conspirators, facing away from the woman now alone in the corner, glaring at his back with an expression of loathing.

'Well, let me look at you properly,' he said. 'Aren't you lovely? Is that a new dress?'

'Amanda got it for me yesterday.'

'Oh,' said Tom.

He had never known this woman to take their daughter out shopping before, but he was careful not to make a judgement one way or the other.

'When will you come home, Daddy? Dolly and I miss our stories and it's not the same without you there. We're both lonely.'

'Well, I don't think it will be long.'

'But why aren't you there now? I don't understand why you had to go away and leave me.'

'Daddy just had to spend a little time apart from Mummy. But we saw a very wise man, a bit like Merlin, who is helping us sort out our problems and I'm sure it will soon be better and we'll be back together again.'

Tom truly believed this because he would do whatever it took to give Gemma what she wanted in order to let him live at home. Whatever bizarre control she craved, she could have it, whatever punishment she dished out to him, he would take it. This was his decision, and no one else's. If physical violence was the price of staying close to Amy he was willing to pay it.

'I still don't understand,' she said, staring down at her hands. 'I thought you had gone because you didn't love me anymore.'

'Listen, Amy. Never, ever believe that I don't love you. Sometimes things happen that we have no control over.'

She continued to avoid his gaze.

'Look at me, poppet,' he said.

212

Amy raised her head.

'Never doubt that I will always love you. Wherever we both are and whatever age you might be, you will always be my precious little girl that I adore.'

Tom didn't speak in order to give her the opportunity to bring up any subject she wanted, but she was quiet, which was unlike her. Normally, Amy chatted away non-stop. He got the impression she was either holding back or had been instructed to be careful what she said. Eventually, however, curiosity got the better of her.

'Will the wizard come to the house?'

'No, there'll be no need for that,' he said smiling, trying to imagine the sheriff with a white gown and staff as though he was Gandalf. 'Although it won't be that long before it's Halloween, so maybe you could be a wizard.'

'Men are wizards. Women are witches,' she said, trying to sound full of knowledge about the subject.

'Oh,' said Tom, thinking that such a statement was probably not politically correct. 'Well, I'm sure there are good and bad wizards and witches, just as there are people.'

He wanted to ask what had been said about him in the house, whether Amanda was spending a lot of time there. However, he knew it would be unfair to his daughter, although he hoped some things might be revealed naturally during the course of their conversation.

'Well, shall we look at the menu?' he said.

Tom helped her go through the various choices and a few minutes later they ordered. He asked about school and what she and Jessica had been up to, which soon had Amy chatting away until their meals arrived.

'Mummy said you had to go away for a few days on business, but Amanda says it's because you've been very naughty.'

Amy had volunteered the information, although she could hardly get out the words due to the food in her mouth.

'Don't put so much in at once,' said Tom, wondering where to take this line of conversation.

'Why did Amanda say I had been naughty?'

'Don't know.'

'So when did she make this comment?'

'When we were shopping yesterday.'

'Mmm. It's an odd thing to say.'

Amy swallowed the food then leant towards him and he crouched down so that their heads were almost touching.

'I don't like her,' she whispered.

'Why's that, poppet?'

'She shouldn't say nasty things about you, and she made me have this dress, but it's not the one I wanted.'

'Well, maybe you and I will go out shopping soon and I'll buy you the one you like. How does that sound?'

'Okay.'

It was the most Tom got out of her about what had been happening in his absence. They had not long finished their desserts when he was aware of a figure behind him. At first he thought someone was having trouble getting past, but then he heard Amanda's voice, which sounded falsely cheerful.

'It's time for us to be going, Amy.'

Tom looked at his watch. It wasn't even two o'clock. He stood up and turned around, inches away from the woman. The only time in his life that he had used his bulk to intimidate someone was when he had come across a man bullying another worker in the factory. However, he glowered at Amanda, whom he dwarfed, and she took a hasty step backwards, a flicker of apprehension edging aside the smug expression that had reappeared on her face.

'Your watch is fast,' he said.

'Well, I'll just go and wait by the door then,' she said taking another step away from him before hurrying over to the exit.

Tom sat down.

'Can't you take me home, Daddy? I don't want to go back with Amanda.'

Amy began to cry so he lifted her over to sit on his knee and cuddled her.

'It's not because I don't want to, poppet, but the wizard says that for the moment it's best I stay at Auntie Rose's house. But I'll soon be reading you bedtime stories again.'

'Do you promise?'

It was that tiny, vulnerable voice again and he was reminded of when they had last been in a restaurant. On that occasion she had also sat on his knee crying and Tom had had to assure her that Gemma and he would never split up. What had happened to that promise?

He hadn't even kept the one he had given the doctor to go back and see her. Tom was no longer the solid, dependable person so many people considered him to be. Maybe no one thought this, perhaps they never had, and it had always simply been a grand illusion that he had clung on to.

'Yes, I promise,' he said and hugged her little body tightly, desperate not to relinquish it into the hands of his enemy waiting nervously at the door.

Chapter Thirty-One

Enid never referred to her stay in the nursing home and Alfred wondered if she had forgotten about it almost as soon as she came home. That was nearly three months ago and these days it was increasingly difficult to tell what his wife was thinking. He tried all the various communication techniques he had read about in the relevant leaflets or that the nurse had advised him of, but she was generally in a world of her own.

He had attended a couple of meetings of the nearest Alzheimer's group. His wife had refused to go, even when he had pretended that they were just going shopping for food. He hated lying to her. They had always been so honest with each other. It was as if she had sensed the suggestion was untrue and they had ended up arguing in the hallway. Alfred had attended subsequent meetings by himself. The people were very kind and helpful and there were several with dementia, some of whom had spoken quite sensibly to him.

A carer visited the home every morning and Enid now attended the day centre at the nursing home three days a week, which gave him a break. Even so, he felt weary to the bone and tired of everything: cleaning up, the fights, the heartache, the sheer gut-wrenching misery of it all.

He had promised to look after her, said the words all those years ago at the altar in front of friends and family. Over the previous months he had whispered it again while she slept next to him in bed. But it was difficult. Even their daughter was becoming worn out.

Enid had started to accuse him of all sorts of things: stealing money, hiding possessions, moving furniture around in order to confuse her. One time, she shouted that he was having an affair with the carer. He had been horrified, but the woman had carried on as if not hearing the comment and, later, had told him quietly that this was not uncommon and he wasn't to be upset.

'I've lost count of the number of elderly gentlemen I'm meant to have jumped into bed with,' she had said, patting his arm. 'Please don't make anything of it.'

The crux came one Sunday during the middle of September. The carer had left and Alfred made a special effort to cook a special lunch. He had gone shopping the previous day to buy what he needed and had spent much of the morning in the kitchen. He didn't really know why he was doing this. Enid didn't seem to bother what she ate.

Perhaps, in his heart, he knew they would soon be parted forever and this could be one of their last meals together. Maybe it was a doomed attempt to make some sort of connection, the hope that through a favourite meal she might reveal a spark of her old self.

When he had finally managed to get her to sit at the table he put across her lap one of their white linen napkins, which Kate had bought them for their Golden Wedding anniversary and that only came out on special occasions. Three tureens of vegetables were already laid out neatly in a line.

'I've made your favourite dish,' he said, trying to keep the mood light, though she hadn't spoken since getting up.

It still troubled him greatly that the carer could more successfully obtain a response than he could. He understood that the woman was highly experienced at her job, but it was him his wife loved.

'I'm sure it's not as good as you used to do, love, but I've tried to reproduce how you cooked it,' he said, laying a plate of steaming lamb in front of her. 'I've put in garlic, rosemary and herbs, the way you like. It's a nice piece. I asked the butcher

217

yesterday for the best he had.'

He picked up his plate from the top of the cooker and sat opposite. Enid bent her head to sniff the food.

'We've had some great meals together in this little kitchen, haven't we? Lots of good times.'

His wife looked at him in silence.

'Do you want a hand, love? Shall I come around and help you with some of it? It's no bother.'

'It's snot.'

'Don't be silly. It's lovely. Why don't you try some, while it's still hot?'

'Hot snot,' she shouted.

'Come on. Eat your dinner nicely. I've made it especially for you.'

Enid put her napkin on the plate and rich gravy soaked instantly through the material.

'Don't do that,' he said, desperate not to shout. 'Take that off your plate.'

She picked up the dirty sopping linen as if she was going to obey him then threw it across the table where it knocked over his water glass.

'Don't throw it. Eat your food.'

Slowly, Enid lifted the plate, holding it flat with one hand underneath so that the contents didn't fall off.

'Put that down. Put it down!'

'Snot,' she shouted and hurled the plate at him so that most of the lamb fell across the tablecloth, their best one, which matched the linen napkins.

The plate missed him and fell on the floor where it broke into several pieces. He looked with dismay at the mess that was suddenly surrounding him.

'What have you done?'

A great deal of anguish lay behind the question. It wasn't just that she had scorned his cooking and broken a plate, or that she had spurned all the effort he had gone to in order to have a pleasant meal together. Despite everything that had happened over the previous months, his wife had just rejected him in a way she never had before.

'What have you done?' he repeated.

Enid picked up her knife and folk and threw them. It was a wild throw, like a small child chucking an object with no aim or power. The knife missed him altogether and the fork hit his chest before dropping on to his plate, splattering even more gravy on to his shirt. It was one of his smartest, which he usually wore when going to church.

'Stop it!'

Alfred's increasingly desperate requests had no effect whatsoever. She picked up her water glass, stood and raised her arm. He ducked and the glass shattered loudly when it hit the cupboard behind him. Shards of crystal joined the broken china and pieces of still hot meat scattered around the floor. The sound seemed to reverberate in his head as he jumped up and ran around the table.

'STOP IT! STOP IT!'

Grabbing her by the shoulders he started to shake, but she managed to bring one hand up and hit him on the chin.

Then it happened.

In all his long life, Alfred would never have believed such a thing could occur. Even as he pulled back his arm, even as he made his hand into a fist, the old barber couldn't acknowledge on any conscious level what was about to take place.

Although the incident lasted only seconds, he would never forget. Of all the memories he had and would have in the future, the image that haunted him the most until the day he lay on his deathbed was of Enid's beautiful, gentle face crumpling under the impact of his punch; the sight of her glasses flying across the kitchen to land by the fridge, the redness of the blood that spurted from her lip on to the pale blue cardigan, the one he was forever having to help her button up.

She screamed in pain and shock and he cried out in horror at the terrible deed he had committed. All of the bad things that she had done to him were caused by her dementia; every single one of them. But his actions were the result of losing his temper. She had lost the ability to make rational decisions whereas he had a choice. And every possible excuse he could make for the act of violence would be no more than that; an excuse.

She fell backwards under the force, her arms flailing in the air as she tried, but failed, to catch hold of the table edge so that she landed her full length on the floor. He was immediately by her side.

'Oh God. What have I done?'

She whimpered, cowering from him, but he managed to get an arm under her shoulders and carefully lifted her so that he could cradle her head as he knelt beside her.

It was over.

His heart was broken in two as surely as if the butcher had split it with a cleaver on the grey marble slab in his shop; as though what beat within Alfred's chest was of no more value than a piece of meat to be chopped in half because it was the wrong size.

He knew this was the end. He had wanted to keep her at home for as long as possible, in order to look after her. Everyone had said how marvellously he had been coping. But in the dead of night, when he had lain awake next to her sleeping body, he acknowledged that his actions had not been entirely unselfish.

Even though mentally it appeared she had already left, he was frightened of being by himself. Looking after Enid was incredibly difficult, but with help from Kate and the various professionals, he had managed. He alone paid the price. It had been his decision ... abuse or loneliness.

She wrapped her arms around his waist.

'Alfred,' she whispered, so vulnerable.

It was the first time she had said his name in months. He realised as soon as she spoke the word. But violence was a cruel way to make a connection with another person, and with someone you love it was a perverted means of communication. This was too high a cost.

'I'm sorry, my dearest. I'm so sorry.'

It was like cradling Kate when she was a small child. He had reduced Enid to this by his aggression, and as he stroked her hair he decided such a hideous event could never be risked again.

Alfred called Ann the following morning and she visited later that afternoon. He had been distraught when admitting to hitting his wife, but the nurse was very kind and agreed that the situation could no longer continue. She made a few telephone calls and as there was a vacancy at the nursing home Enid had become used to it was arranged she should go in permanently the following week.

Kate had insisted she come over to help. Alfred didn't have the strength to argue and, in truth, he needed the support. This time his wife's visit wasn't for a short respite. Daughter and husband packed the various belongings they thought were most needed. It was an upsetting task, like emptying cupboards that had belonged to a recently deceased relative.

Kate, with help from the carer, managed to get her mother into the bath on the morning of her departure. Alfred had given up attempting this. It almost seemed to him at times that Enid didn't like water. While she was occupied in the bathroom, he called the local removal firm. The company had been very understanding the previous week when he had contacted them, and had agreed to allocate two employees who would be ready to come around immediately once the coast was clear.

The men worked quietly, removing a few items of selected

furniture so that they would be in Enid's new bedroom for her arrival. They took several boxes and two suitcases containing her clothes. Matron said she would arrange for these things to be put away neatly as soon as everything arrived.

Apart from liaising about the furniture Alfred had nothing to do and he felt useless as he sat in the kitchen, while the three women were in the bathroom upstairs. He no longer had a function in life, didn't even cut people's hair. What had his life been for if it was to end in such misery?

Worthless.

If he hadn't lost his temper perhaps they could have carried on for a while longer. He hadn't the courage to confess to his daughter what had happened and the bruising on his wife's face had faded sufficiently for it not to be the cause of questions.

Kate drove them to the nursing home. They travelled in silence, the elderly couple sitting in the back. Enid let him hold her hand, though she didn't seem bothered one way or the other. Within moments of walking into the reception area Matron appeared as if she had been watching out of the window for their arrival.

'Hello,' she said as if greeting an old friend. 'I was just about to put the kettle on. We could all have tea together.'

Alfred had an arm looped through one of Enid's and Matron put hers through the other. He wouldn't ... couldn't let go, so the three of them walked slowly along the corridor, Kate following silently behind, carrying the one small case they had brought with them.

Over the months the matron had built up a comprehensive picture of Enid's likes and dislikes, what her normal routine was at home, whether it would be a problem if a male carer was to help her, what types of activities she might be willing, or was able, to be included in.

Alfred had met several of the staff and thought they were tremendous. Their simple uniform made it easy to identify them from visitors. However, no one had worked out what triggered Enid's aggression towards him. He had gone over the potential reasons time and again until his head felt as though it would explode. Perhaps he didn't pay her sufficient attention? Maybe there wasn't enough stimulation in the house, so that she was simply bored? Should he try harder to be clearer in his attempts to communicate?

Alfred had almost become dulled to the pain from the punches and slaps so that he normally continued with whatever he was doing when she hit him. The worst thing was being nipped on the inside of his arm, which she still continued to do, but even then he had always carried on, though he would ask as calmly as he could, 'What is it? What do you need?'

Matron made them tea in her office and chatted as if they were all old friends. Kate sat holding her mother's hand. He noticed that his wife was increasingly unresponsive and, despite the incident over Sunday lunch, she had become less violent during the last few weeks. Perhaps this was a new phase, another stage of slipping further away.

Afterwards, the four of them took a slow walk around the home, ending up, as if by chance, at the bedroom that was allocated to Enid. They went in. The furniture from the house was in place along with some pictures on the walls and a few photographs, including one taken outside the church on the day they married. A blue vase, a gift for their Golden Wedding anniversary, stood on a small table in one corner and Alfred was moved at the huge bunch of fresh flowers displayed in it.

'This is a pleasant room,' said Matron, who had her arm through one of Enid's. 'Look how the sun streams in through the window. Isn't it lovely?'

Enid looked around, but made no comment so it was difficult to tell if she recognised anything. Kate put down the small case she was carrying and took from it a large ball of tissues. Gently, she prized apart the papers to reveal the tiny green pottery elephant. She had to fight back tears as she put it on the mantelpiece.

'There, Mum, doesn't that look nice? It's catching the sun.'

Enid walked over, the first action she had made that day of her own will, and picked up the ornament. She stared at it in her hand and, for the briefest moment, there was the flicker of a smile.

Chapter Thirty-Two

The week after Enid had gone into the nursing home Kate visited with Keith and the children. Alfred was waiting in reception. He had been most days, but his daughter had agreed to rest and spend some time with her family. She telephoned him every evening to find out how he was, and how her mother had been.

Alfred thought Keith was a decent man, a good son-in-law and a caring husband. The two men shook hands. Peter, five, and Laura, eight, were holding on to Kate, the girl looking slightly alarmed, but the boy staring around with wide eyes. Matron had been consulted as to whether the children should come and it had been agreed that it would help them understand what had happened to Grandma.

Matron appeared. Alfred had begun to wonder if there was more than one of her as she always seemed to be in several places at the same time. 'She's settled quite well into the routine of the home,' she said when the necessary introductions had been made. 'It generally takes residents a little while. She loves the garden, so much so that we often have to bring her inside for meals and make sure she's not out there if the weather has turned for the worse.'

'Have there been any incidents?' said Kate, not wanting to use words like 'aggression' in front of the children.

'Only occasionally, and not to any great degree. We're still trying to discover the triggers. But she's been on a couple of trips without any problems.'

'People go out?' said Keith.

'Oh yes,' replied Matron. 'Residents like to get away for a few hours so we organise visits. It might be just to the local garden centre or to go shopping, or to simply walk around the nearby duck pond, but they look forward to these events and it does them good. We've discovered that Enid loves to get her nails done.'

'Does she?' said Kate, who had never known her mother pamper herself with such an activity.

'Lots of our elderly ladies like having things done to their hands and we have several volunteers, including people from the Red Cross, who come on a regular basis to do that one task. It goes down very well.'

'Where's my wife now?'

'I think she's in the garden.'

Peter made more of a connection upon seeing his grand-mother than anyone else had done for weeks. The boy ran over to where she was sitting by the flowerbed and climbed up on to her knee. It was difficult to know if Enid knew who he was, but what elderly lady didn't like being hugged by a delightful small boy, so he chatted away unconsciously and she seemed pleased. Alfred and Kate sat on either side of her on the bench and Keith stood with Laura.

The barber laid his hand on his wife's shoulder, just to have some sort of physical contact with her, though she didn't seem to recognise any of them and was preoccupied with Peter, patting his head as he told her about school, unbothered by the fact she didn't make any response. When he had run out of conversation Kate suggested to her husband that he took the children for a walk around the grounds.

'Bye, Grandma,' shouted Peter, as he was led away with his sister.

Enid smiled and waved. Alfred thought there was no logic to what or with whom she made connections. Kate reached up and stroked her mother's hair.

'Do you know who I am?' she asked.

'We've come to visit you,' said Alfred when there was no response, 'to see how you're doing. It's a nice place, isn't it? Lovely garden. You like gardens, especially the flowers. And look at that hydrangea. Isn't it beautiful?'

Although he pointed at the plant she didn't realise that she was meant to follow the direction of his finger and looked vaguely at another part of the grounds altogether.

'Peter and Laura were so looking forward to seeing you, Mum. Haven't they grown since last time? They're doing so well at school. Laura is near the top of her class in several subjects, isn't she, Dad?'

'Yes. Very bright children. It must come down through your side of the family, love. It's certainly not come from me, I only know about cutting hair.'

Alfred tried to force a laugh, but it came out more like a strangled cough. He and Kate had sat forward on the bench so that Enid didn't have to swivel her head to and fro, but mostly she didn't look at them at all and simply gazed around as if seeing the plants for the first time.

'You look well,' he said. 'I hope you're getting plenty of rest and lots of fresh air. And I've never known your hands look so lovely. Perhaps I'll get mine done.'

A lot of what Alfred said was a repetition of what he had told Enid over the previous few days and it was as much for Kate's benefit that he tried to keep the atmosphere light-hearted. Inside he was crying and he knew his daughter was just the same, though neither of them would allow such feelings to surface at that particular moment. An image of his fist hitting Enid's face came into his mind, but he forced it away. There was time enough for such self-punishment.

'I understand you've got a trip to the local park,' he said. 'That'll be nice. You'll like seeing the ducks on the pond. I remember a small girl who used to love to feed the birds, including once with the sandwich meant for my lunch.'

'I was only five, Dad. It was a long time ago.'

'That may be, but I had been looking forward to eating that sandwich. It's no exaggeration to say those ducks were smiling when they swam away that day.'

Alfred sat alone at the small kitchen table, one of the old photograph albums open in front of him. Since leaving the nursing home and saying goodbye to Kate and the family that afternoon he had been thinking a great deal about her early childhood. They had been such happy years and he tried to relive some of the memories and moods by going through snapshots of the era: ice cream at the seaside; building a sandcastle; paddling in the water. Everything was so simple.

But that time of sunshine was over, along with the innocent joy and contentment. Why had he let it slip through his fingers so unrecognised for what it was? Did everyone do that, let the good periods in their lives merely pass by as though they would always be there? Alfred wished there was some other way of capturing those moments, those feelings, rather than just blurred images in a photograph album that was rarely looked at. How had it all turned into this nightmare that was now his life?

The clock struck eleven. It was late. They had never been ones for staying up all hours and didn't understand how some people managed to do it with no ill-effects. Alfred didn't rush. What was there to hurry for? All that waited for him upstairs was an empty bed.

There had been so many times over the last few months when he had wished Enid wasn't thrashing around or screaming next to him, or that he didn't have to worry about her wandering in and out of rooms in the middle of the night. But in many ways it was worse without her. He would lie awake wondering how she was, if she was safe and fast asleep while he fretted. It was the not knowing. However, he could hardly ring the nursing home at three in the morning to ask about his wife, even though that's what he often felt like doing.

So Alfred sat in the quiet of the kitchen, reflecting on his life, but when the clock struck twelve he decided it was too cold to remain downstairs. Gently, he took hold of one corner of the album and slowly closed it, covering the image that he had been looking at for the last twenty minutes, of a small girl standing by a pond ... feeding the ducks with a sandwich.

Chapter Thirty-Three

The voice of his cousin Marilyn transported Gordon back to the happiest memories of his childhood. They were a similar age and had been constant companions until her parents had moved away when she was ten. After that they met only a couple of times a year, but spoke regularly on the telephone.

She had come to his wedding and the following year stayed with them for a few days, but Tania had soon decided there was 'something going on' so no further contact had been permitted. Gordon wasn't allowed to attend her marriage to Andrew and he had even been forbidden to reply to their Christmas cards, which still arrived every year from Cornwall where they ran a small hotel.

'Gordon! Are you alright?'

'I'm not sure to be perfectly honest. Have you got a few minutes?'

'As long as you need.'

'I'm leaving Tania.'

'Thank goodness.'

'You're pleased?'

'Delighted.'

'Why?'

'I'm going to be blunt. When I stayed all those years ago I saw a great many things that disturbed me. She was manipulating you the whole time and from a couple of innocent comments you made I could see she was gradually isolating you.'

'Why didn't you say something?'

'Would you have believed me? And if you had, would you have done anything about it?'

He thought about this before answering. He had always considered his cousin to be incredibly intuitive about people, but if she had said something detrimental about his wife so early in their marriage ...

'I guess I wouldn't,' he admitted.

'When I stopped hearing from you altogether I knew she was increasingly taking over. Tania's probably accused me of trying to get you into bed, even after I was married.'

'How did you know that?'

'It wasn't difficult to guess. Also, a close male friend of Andrew's was abused by his former partner and we had lots of conversations with him after he freed himself from the relationship. It gave me an insight into something I didn't know much about. During my short stay with you I saw many of the incidents that he spoke about being replicated before my eyes. It was quite a revelation to watch some of his stories played out for real, almost exactly as he explained them. Have you told her your intentions?'

'Well, sort of, but she's basically ignored what I said as if it wasn't important.'

'It's just another way of trying to maintain control. Do you have a plan?'

'I'm putting one together. That's partly why I've called.'

'I'm listening.'

He outlined his ideas and she made a few suggestions, all of which he thought were good. He had forgotten how much he used to rely on his cousin as a sounding board.

'You've taken me up to the point where you get away from the house, but then what?' she asked.

'That part becomes a bit vague. I want to see my parents and I can stay with them for a short while.'

'Come here,' said Marilyn. 'Stay with us at the hotel.'

'Go to Cornwall? But I'll have no job.'

'If you move away from the area as you're suggesting then

you'll have no job anyway. We'll be hectic over Christmas so you can help us out. Don't worry about not having any work, we'll keep you busy.'

'Don't you need to check with Andrew?'

'No, we've talked this over many times and already agreed that if you ever needed a place to stay then you'd be welcome here.'

They spoke for another ten minutes and agreed she would not try to contact him in any way, but when he had more information he would ring her from a telephone that Tania couldn't check up on. He had called from the factory car park, using a mobile telephone that belonged to one of the other workers with whom he was friendly.

Gordon had secretly taken the day off, leaving home that morning as if going to the factory as normal. During the previous couple of weeks he had managed to make several appointments. He acknowledged that he was too frightened of confronting his wife head on without eliminating as many of the 'weapons' she would inevitably use against him.

By mid-morning he was sitting in front of the solicitor who had handled the purchase of his house, which he had bought before getting married. Gordon had never had any dealings with the firm apart from that one transaction, but they had seemed efficient and helpful.

'I want to divorce my wife and I need to understand what this involves legally,' he said to the solicitor, a man who looked little older than himself.

'To be honest it's not really my field. You would be better off speaking to one of my colleagues who specialises in divorces, but I can tell you the basics.'

'That would be enough for now.'

'In crude terms, you could go for a quickie divorce if you can prove your wife has been unfaithful, or if you can show there has been unreasonable behaviour on her part. In both of these scenarios the case would have to go before a judge, although you wouldn't need to be present and it should go through as long as your wife doesn't contest it.

'Alternatively, if neither of you disputes the divorce then it could be completed once you've lived apart for two years. If your wife disagrees, and doesn't want to separate then you would have to live apart for five years before you could force it through. After that length of time she couldn't stop you.'

Gordon considered what he had just heard. Derek was making Jennifer wait five years before she was free of him. Would Tania do the same to him? By then he would be thirty-four and he was desperate to cut all ties with her as soon as possible. In truth, it was impossible to know what Tania would do or say so he decided to press ahead as if she would agree.

'I think I could make a case for unreasonable behaviour.'

Gordon's next task was to organise transferring the deeds for their house, which was currently in his name. She could have the lot, including the contents. When he had thought about what he might want from the home, he realised that there wasn't much he had chosen. It was a similar scenario to Jennifer and Derek. His wife had picked most things and, when he actually analysed it, they were not items he really liked. He would only take his own personal possessions, almost all of which would fit into the car, which had been valued by a local dealer. After lunch he went to the bank where they held a joint account.

He had already spoken to his boss at the factory and they had agreed he would hand in his notice in order to finish work on the day he left Tania. This eliminated any threats she might make of telling his employers that he had been abusive because by the time she knew his intentions he would only have a few days remaining with the firm.

When she realised that he was serious he expected her to start contacting friends immediately, so he had prepared a list of the people he most cared about and would at least put his side of the story to them. There was little more he could do on that score.

He wasn't worried about Tania knowing where he was going to live. Cornwall was too far away for her to follow him. He felt certain that once he physically left then her power over him would be greatly diminished. However, she would try to make him stay at all costs.

Chapter Thirty-Four

Frances wasn't happy. Gemma's solicitor had been in contact to say they wanted to sist the action. She explained to Tom that meant he would have to agree in front of the Sheriff to abide by the terms of the Interdict then he could return home. However, the Interdict wouldn't be destroyed or annulled in any sense, merely 'put on the shelf', which meant that his wife could easily have it reinstated at any time in the future.

'But I could go home and be with Amy?' he had said.

'Yes, though this potential threat will always be hanging over your head.'

'As I never committed any of the offences listed it isn't an issue for me not to do them, so I don't have a problem agreeing to the terms. I just have to ensure that I keep Gemma happy, so she doesn't feel the need to do such a thing again.'

Frances had argued that they could put a strong case in front of the Sheriff that might get the Interdict removed altogether, but all Tom had said was, 'So I could soon be living at home again?' with a light in his eyes that told her he wasn't really listening and she was wasting her time.

So Frances wasn't happy as the second hearing began. It was almost a replica of the previous meeting with all the players sitting in the same places. Within a short while of them arriving at court, Gemma's solicitor was presenting the proposed 'solution'.

'My Lord, both the pursuer and the defender have agreed that the defender will abide by all the terms listed on the Interdict, and that this action should be sisted. Both parties are in total agreement that it is in the best interests of everyone that he should return home immediately.'

'I want each of you to tell me yourself that you are completely certain this is what you want,' said the Sheriff.

Tom and Gemma each spoke in turn and confirmed that this was what they desired. And it was over just like that. When they stepped outside they thanked their solicitors who then went off together, suddenly friends. It was obvious the two women knew each other.

'Well,' said Gemma, slipping her arm through one of Tom's, 'isn't it marvellous to get all this behind us so that we can get back together again as a normal family?'

Tom didn't know how to respond. His wife had spoken as if she had just had an annual check-up at the dentist and was pleased that nothing needed to be done.

'There's a really nice restaurant around the corner,' she continued, steering him along the pavement towards it. 'Why don't I buy us lunch and then I suppose you'll want to go over to Rose's and get your things?'

Tom hesitated. He felt so *uncertain* and almost stuttered when he spoke, which he had never done in his life.

'No, I don't need to collect a few clothes and a toothbrush. Rose can keep them until the next time we meet. I thought perhaps I could pick up Amy from school, if that's alright with you?'

'That's a lovely idea. Amy will be delighted. And you don't need to ask me if it's alright, silly,' she said, patting his arm as though he was a child that needed reassuring.

But Tom knew this wasn't true. From now on he would have to check everything he did in order to make sure it was approved first.

Amy didn't want a bedtime story. Instead she needed to be told that her father would never go away again. Tom lay on top of the duvet and she cuddled into him as if this demonstration of her love could somehow prevent such a terrible event ever recurring. His daughter had barely left his side since he had collected her from school, but it was only now that they had the privacy to talk in confidence.

'What did the wizard say when you and Mummy saw him today?'

'He said that everything will be fine and that I should come home and take care of my little girl.'

'And will you have to leave again?'

'No, poppet. I won't go away again. You know I didn't want to leave in the first place.'

'I still don't understand why you went.'

'I'm not too certain either.'

'Did Mummy make you go away?'

Tom was on dangerous ground with this question and he hesitated. He felt it was important not to apportion any blame to Gemma.

'It wasn't just Mummy's decision. We both felt it would be better to have a little bit of time apart, and the wizard also thought it was a good idea. We could hardly disagree with him, could we? He's very wise. So Mummy got to have lots of time with you and I got to see Auntie Rose. But that period is over and I'm home to stay, whatever happens.'

Tom regretted instantly saying the last few words as Amy was far too bright to miss the implication.

'But what might happen?'

He stroked her hair while thinking of an answer. He could hardly reveal he had decided that whatever violence her mother inflicted upon him, he would bear it in order to remain at home. No one was going to hear such a confession from his lips. In fact, his intention was that this abusive side of their lives was to be buried once more, never spoken about or acknowledged to the outside world.

He had survived three years of it and could put up with more for his daughter's sake. It had only become public because of that one telephone call to the police and they hadn't even believed him, so what was the point?

'Daddy?'

'Sorry, poppet. I didn't mean anything was actually going to happen as nothing is, apart from you going to sleep. It's late and you've had a long day. We'll think of something nice to do tomorrow with Mummy.'

'Will you stay until I go to sleep?'

'Of course I will.'

'And will you still be here in the morning?'

'I won't be lying here next to you, but I promise I'll be somewhere in the house.'

'I love you, Daddy.'

'And I love you, Amy,' said Tom. 'Now turn over and snuggle down. You can't lie like this.'

He tucked the duvet around her, kissed her head and lay back down, putting a muscular arm around her body. She was soon asleep, but Tom remained for a long while, trying to stop himself from crying before going downstairs to have dinner with his wife.

Chapter Thirty-Five

The tiny green elephant was broken. With great care, Alfred picked up the ornament from the mantelpiece and held it in his hand to study. The end of the trunk was missing and although someone had tried to stick together the other parts they had used too much glue so sections of the body protruded, making the animal appear deformed, a grotesque reminder of the delightful object it used to be. Eventually, he replaced it, wondering if the damage had been the result of an accident or something else.

His wife was nowhere to be seen. He had arrived a few minutes earlier and apart from taking off his coat and scarf in reception had come straight up to her room. He dreaded the visits now. It was early November and Enid had deteriorated along with the weather. During the last few weeks she had been completely unaware of his presence, except for the occasions when she had suddenly turned violent towards him.

If her aggression had been on-going, directed at the other people she encountered in the nursing home, it would have hurt him less, but he appeared to be the catalyst and this was more than he could cope with. Matron was very kind, but she had no answers other than to stress that this sort of behaviour did happen at times and it wasn't his fault. It was so often the partner of the person with dementia, the one who was closest and loved them the most, who received the worst treatment.

Opening the wardrobe door he looked at the clothes hanging neatly inside. He remembered when Enid had acquired some of the items because they had been purchased for specific occasions. At one end, next to the flowery dress Kate had bought her mother for his seventieth birthday party, was the blue skirt and top that she had chosen for their fiftieth anniversary.

There were other things, a shawl he had once given her on holiday, the flowery dress she had worn for Peter's christening. A lifetime of hopes, joy and laughter were displayed on a row of plastic coat hangers as if these past events had somehow crystallised into a physical representation of the memories in his head.

He closed the door and walked slowly over to pick up the photograph that had been taken on their wedding day, which was on the little table by her bed. Where was that vibrant young woman, so full of fun? What had happened to that lad, so proud and happy to be marrying the most beautiful girl he had ever seen?

He appreciated that nobody would recognise him today from the black and white image in his hands. No one could hope to look the same as they did more than fifty years ago. That was simply to be expected.

But Enid had altered in a way that was not just physical. You couldn't look at the picture held within the silver frame and make a link with the shambling figure, staring blanking into space, which was his wife today. He yearned for the woman he had married more than he thought was possible to want anything.

Alfred laid the photograph back on the table, although for a few moments he kept two fingers in contact with the frame. He was using up time. The truth was, he feared these encounters. Every visit was like a knife to his heart and he secretly questioned how much longer he could endure them. Matron had suggested it might be better not to come every day, but he still did. What else could he do?

Kate kept telling him he should reopen the barber's shop and he had thought about it. Everything was there, waiting for him, though he didn't know if any of his customers would ever come back.

There was a sound in the doorway and he turned around.

'Hello, love,' he said. 'How are you feeling today?'

Alfred gasped.

'Your hair! What happened to your hair?'

He knew he was, in reality, talking to himself; that she wouldn't answer him with any coherent comment if at all. She walked into the room, looking so strange with her short hair, so ... old. He took one of her hands and led her across to sit on the bed with him.

'That looks very different, doesn't it? I can see someone has cut that properly. It's very nice,' he said, forcing out the word. 'It's chilly today. I've started wearing my yellow scarf again, the one you bought me. It still does a grand job at keeping out the cold. Kate sends her love, and Keith and the children. I saw a couple of the neighbours yesterday. They send their best regards. Aren't people kind? Yes. People are very kind.'

Alfred kept patting her hand and talking. He tried so hard to speak sensibly rather than make meaningless comments, and to follow the advice Ann had given him so long ago with respect to trying to make some sort of contact. But he often struggled and repeated comments, answered his own questions and talked banally about the weather just so that there wasn't silence in the room.

Some days he felt it was better when they met in the lounge or garden as there was always something going on around them that provided a distraction, which made it easier. At other times he wanted her to himself so that he could focus all his efforts on trying to break through the wall of confusion, to get her to acknowledge his presence and speak.

According to one of the nurses he had spoken to earlier in the week, Enid rarely said anything to anyone. He regarded the staff highly for the work they did and his wife was always clean and tidy when he came. They had obviously been more successful than he had in getting her to wash regularly. Perhaps they washed her themselves. Maybe she didn't care enough anymore and let them get on with it.

'I wonder what we're getting for lunch. I must say the food is very good, always hot and tasty. Better than I could give you, love. I hope you'll let me give you a hand, just if you need it of course.'

Alfred often stayed for lunch and would try to help her eat, although sometimes she did it herself without any bother. When she did have trouble, he never knew if she was going to let him assist until he was holding the first forkful. If she let him feed her, he felt that he had some sort of purpose in life and that he had made a contribution. On the occasions when she brushed his arm away, he would usually end up going home, feeling utterly dejected.

They sat in silence for quite some while, side-by-side on the bed, looking at the chest of drawers opposite. They had bought it on their tenth wedding anniversary.

'I've loved you ever since that evening we met, when I was that gangly lad too shy to say "boo" to a goose. There's never been anyone else. Not once in all that time. You've always had my heart, Enid. My feelings gave me the courage to speak to your father about asking you to marry me. It seems so extraordinarily old-fashioned to think of such a thing now. He was a good man. I remember him saying that he had never seen his daughter so happy and that if I didn't ask you to marry me he would want to know the reason why.

'And when you answered yes, I couldn't believe my luck, couldn't understand what you saw that would make such a beautiful girl agree to spend her life with me. I hope you've never regretted it. I haven't. I love you more now than ever.'

Enid turned her head and stared. He smiled. She was looking him full in the face, an acknowledgement of him as a person.

242

'Okay, love?' he said.

'Who are you?' she said pulling away from him.

'It's your Alfred,' he said, taking hold of her hand again.

'No,' she said loudly. 'I don't know you. What are you doing here in my bedroom? It's mine.'

'Don't get upset. You're quite safe. I've just come to visit you for a little while.'

She brought her left hand around in a long swing to strike his head, but there was no power or speed in the blow and he saw it coming so leant back while putting an arm up to his face. Her thin wrist hit his elbow and he was worried she had injured herself.

Then she screamed.

'It's alright,' he said, desperate to reassure her. 'It's me.'

Standing up suddenly she tried to pull her hand free and step away from the bed. Alfred stood up, not sure whether to let her go completely, or try to restrain her even more. He was frightened she might get hurt, but as if his fears forecast the future the next moment they were both falling to the floor.

He didn't know exactly what happened. They just seemed to trip over each other. To his horror, he landed on top of her. Then she was beating her arms at him, and he was shouting for her to calm down while trying to get up, and they were both crying and everything was despair, noise, confusion and pain.

Alfred felt powerful hands slip underneath his armpits and he was lifted clean to his feet as if he weighed no more than a child.

'I couldn't help it,' he cried.

'It's alright,' said the male nurse, helping to lower him on the bed. 'Just sit there quietly. Everything will be alright.'

But he was distraught.

'No, it's not alright. I've hurt her and it's my fault.'

Seconds later, Matron and a female carer rushed into the room. The two women expertly checked over the figure on the carpet before gently lifting Enid into the armchair.

'Take Alfred to my office, Alan,' said Matron. 'I'll be there shortly.'

'Come on, mate,' said the man putting a hand on his shoulder. 'Let's go downstairs and I'll make you a cup of tea. There's nothing either of us can do here.'

He was crying uncontrollably, but let himself be led away without protest. The male nurse stayed with him until Matron appeared about fifteen minutes later.

'How is she?' he asked through his tears.

She sat down opposite him and for the first time since he had met her, she looked tired.

'We've given her something to calm her down. She'll be fine. Can you tell me what happened?'

He outlined, through his sobs, the events that led up to the accident.

'It's over,' he said.

'What do you mean?'

'I'm not coming back anymore.'

'You mustn't let an incident like this be the cause of a hurried decision.'

'No, it's not just this. My visits upset her. I make the situation worse by coming here.'

'You know that's not always the case, not by a long way. I believe your visits are very important. Yes, there have been occasions when she has become aggressive, but not every time. You're overtired, Alfred. Coming every day is not good for you. Have a break, then call me when you're more your old self. We can talk about how Enid is doing and then make decisions.'

Matron was blurred through his tears. She was a kind woman; not many came better than her. But she was wrong in this. He would never return.

Alfred didn't know how many hours he had sat in the old

barber's chair. He hadn't gone home. That was a place of loneliness and sadness, memories of Enid attacking him, of his fist hitting her sweet, gentle face. The shop held no such nightmares so he had gone there and sat, crying softly, until he forced himself to stop, only to restart moments later.

'Bloody old fool,' he said angrily.

The shop was empty like his life, an enormous void of nothingness. He had to remind himself that he still had Kate and the grandchildren, that he was more fortunate than many. There were lots of people who had lived their entire lives alone, never loving anyone the way he felt towards Enid.

But feelings of guilt and betrayal overwhelmed him and no amount of counting the good things helped to relieve the pain he felt at putting his unsuspecting wife in the nursing home, at leaving her there. Was his decision not to return because he upset *her*, or because the visits upset *him*?

'Coward,' he said to the image opposite, which mouthed the word back like an accusation, as if it belonged to a judge sitting in court.

'What is the verdict on this man? Is he guilty of desertion, of hitting his defenceless wife, of poor judgement and weakness, and not being the husband his wife deserved?'

Alfred was silent for a long while then he whispered with despair into the growing darkness.

'Guilty.'

Something forced its way into the part of his mind that was conscious, prizing apart the doors he had closed upon the world and insisting that he pay it attention. Slowly, he turned his head towards the source. Someone was shouting and banging on the frosted glass of the shop front. The only light came from the streetlights. Stiffly and with difficultly he got himself out of the chair, walked unsteadily to the door and unlocked it.

'Are you alright, sir?'

Alfred stared blankly at the young policeman.

'A neighbour called to say they had seen a figure inside the shop and it's been closed for months.'

'It's mine. My shop.'

'I see, sir. It's terribly cold. It hardly looks any warmer inside than out here.'

It was only as the policeman said this that he began to appreciate how chilled he was. When he had arrived hours earlier he hadn't thought to switch on the little heater and although he was wearing his coat he didn't even have his yellow scarf. He had been in such a state when leaving the nursing home that it had been left behind.

'My wife has got Alzheimer's,' he said, as though this presented a perfectly sensible reason for him to be sitting in a darkened barber's shop on a wintery night.

'It's a horrible, cruel disease, sir. My grandmother's got it and she doesn't know any of the family any more. Very upsetting for everyone. Where do you live, sir?'

His brain felt as frozen as the rest of him and it took a few moments to recall the name of the street.

'Well, that's not too far at all. I'm going that way. Why don't we walk together and I'll see you safely home?'

'Go home?'

'You can't stay here, sir. Not in the dark and cold. It's turning into a wicked night. Better to be in your bed. Get yourself warmed up.'

Giving up, letting himself freeze to death in a worn, old barber's chair was a poor way to die. He hadn't lived his life to end it like this. Enid wouldn't have wanted it. He could imagine her shaking her head at him with an expression of disapproval and disappointment. He couldn't let her down, not again.

'Yes, I suppose you're right,' he replied quietly.

So Alfred stepped into the street, locked the door and left the blackness behind.

Chapter Thirty-Six

It was a Wednesday in early December and Gordon had been in a state of near panic since waking up. That evening he would tell Tania he was leaving her on Friday. Two days' notice might seem cruel, but everything had been planned precisely to give him the courage needed to face her.

Shortly after six o'clock he walked into the hallway to be greeted, as usual, by having a glass of red wine handed to him before he had even closed the front door. The glass was filled to the brim and he had to take great care in putting it down on a nearby table before removing his jacket.

Tania nearly always waited for him like this. Constantly thrusting alcohol upon him had resulted in his consumption rising steadily over the years. The previous month he had been appalled when calculating how much he drank during an average week. He could happily live without alcohol, and the significance of Tania saying often that she *needed* a drink had struck him only recently. It was a vital difference between them.

'How was your day?' she asked, retrieving her glass from the harmonium, despite his frequent requests not to put items like that on the instrument.

'Okay. How was yours?'

'Tiring.'

Gordon felt guilty at his deception, but he had to take control as much as possible so he washed and changed, they ate their ready-meals from Marks & Spencer while watching the news then he tidied up in the kitchen. She was lying on the settee when he entered the sitting room. He switched off the set and sat in the armchair facing her.

God help me now.

'What are you doing? I was going to watch something.'

'We need to talk.'

'Can't it wait?'

'Not any longer,' he said, taking a deep breath. 'I haven't been happy for a long time and I've tried to tell you before, but you don't treat what I say seriously. I've come to appreciate that we aren't suited to each other and that this situation will never change, so I'm leaving you.'

'Not this again! I thought you had got rid of that stupid idea.'

'I'm sorry that this will cause pain, but I'm starting a new life away from here.'

'Well, you can't.'

He remained silent.

'What about your job?' she said eventually.

'I finish at the factory on Friday morning and I'll leave here that lunchtime to drive to my parents' house. This evening and tomorrow I'll pack the few things I'm taking. Apart from the harmonium, which is being collected next week, I won't take anything that doesn't fit into the car.'

A range of emotions seared through Tania and she didn't know whether to show fear or anger.

'I'm not going to let you just walk away.'

'How will you stop me?'

Tania struggled with the unfamiliar scenario. She *always* won arguments. It was simply a case of grinding him down.

'What about the house? I expect to get the house.'

'It's already in your name. I've signed the papers. You've got everything, the building and the contents. It's all yours.'

Her mouth opened, but she was stuck for words as the realisation of how serious this was began to dawn on her.

'We both have the same quantity of ISAs and shares so nothing needs to be done there,' he said. 'I've had the car valued. It's worth £4,000, so I've deducted £2,000 from the amount we have in our joint account and taken out half of the remaining figure.'

'I won't let you.'

'It's done. I transferred the cash earlier today into an account I've opened at a different bank.'

Her growing horror showed clearly on her face.

'You'll have to pay me maintenance.'

'No, I've checked this out. As there are no children and you are perfectly fit and well, then you will have to work like everyone else. I'm sorry. I know all of this is very upsetting, but I have to try and find my own happiness and it won't happen here.'

Tania's world was crumbling and she was frightened.

'You can't leave me.'

He remained silent, making it more difficult for her to argue.

'There has to be a woman behind this. Who is it? You tell me who it is!'

Tania screamed the last sentence, trying to use aggression to dominate. This had always worked in the past. Generally, he would end up cowering from her onslaughts and then, later on, he would be so grateful when she 'forgave' him that she could get him to do *anything*. Over the years it hadn't been enough for him to simply do and say what she wanted. Tania needed to control what he thought ... how he thought. Then he would be hers and no one else's, and she might find happiness.

'There's no woman,' he replied.

'Where are you going to live then?'

'I'm moving to Cornwall to stay in Marilyn and Andrew's hotel.'

He was too calm, refusing to be intimidated or react as she wanted, so Tania switched to a different tack, trying to sound reasonable.

'You can't leave me. Your feelings about us are wrong. I know your mind so much better than you. Look, perhaps I have been a bit hard on you at times, but let's talk this through. How about if I agree to let you take up all of the hobbies you used to like? You enjoyed doing so much at one time. That would make life better, wouldn't it?'

'It's not for you to give me permission to do things. You never had the right to prevent me in the first place.'

'You'll be alone. Who will marry you or give you hugs?'

'Yes, I may be alone and be lonely, but I will have gained hope and perhaps, one day, I might meet someone. If I remain with you then I have no hope.'

For the first time in their relationship, she was staring at defeat. By facing his fear of loneliness, he had eliminated one of the most powerful controls she had over him.

'I won't agree to a divorce and you can't make me.'

'You'll receive the initial papers from my solicitor next week.'

'But you can't. I won't let you.'

'I'm divorcing you because of unreasonable behaviour.'

'But you're the only person who's ever loved me, the only one who understands,' she said, starting to cry. 'What will happen to me?'

'That's down to you. Your life is yours. You must learn to take responsibility for it.'

They fell silent, their eyes drawn towards the fireplace even though the ashes, like their relationship, had long gone cold. He wondered if she would ever try to light it once he had gone.

'My only fault,' she said through her sobs, 'has been to love you too much.'

Gordon didn't reply for a while. It was as if the hearth was a work of art and the blackness of the grate was such a fascination that he couldn't tear away his gaze, then he said quietly, 'No.'

'What do you mean *no*? How do you know my feelings? I've loved you too much and this is the payment I get in return!'

He turned his head to face her.

'No. If you love someone you don't constantly lie and abuse

them; you don't hold them back and continually let them down. These actions are the opposite of love.'

In spite of all the hours he had spent over the previous months analysing his feelings, it was the first time he realised that Tania had never loved him. Their marriage had been based on his need for affection and her desire to control and dominate, his wish to work hard and provide a good living, and her belief that everything should be handed to her without any effort. But it wasn't love.

'I've never done those things,' she said. 'I don't tell lies.'

He stared at her and the old question came to him again: did his wife know the stories she told were untrue, or did she believe them? Suddenly, the woman opposite him felt like a stranger.

'I'm going to start packing,' he said.

Gordon went upstairs, passing the glass of wine she had given him, which was still on the table by the front door, untouched. He had never before out-manoeuvred Tania so successfully, but it didn't make him feel good to hurt another person. In the end, when he had eventually confronted her he had surprised himself at handling the situation with so much authority.

It wasn't long before she was on the telephone, crying, ringing friends and neighbours, even people she normally had very little contact with. He caught the occasional phrase about him as he walked along the corridor between rooms and it was never complimentary. More than once he heard the receiver being slammed down and Tania shout 'Bastard!' up the stairs when it became apparent that he had already spoken to the person she had just rung.

That afternoon he had left the factory early and spent more than two hours contacting those on the list he had created, to give them an overview of what was happening. He had been completely unprepared for the number of friends who admitted that they thought he should have left years earlier.

Gordon hadn't realised that Tania's constant insults, put-downs and abusive behaviour in front of people had been noticed by some for what they were. Others were surprised by the announcement, though everyone wished him luck and asked him to stay in touch. In the end, confessing to friends what had been going on in his marriage had been a relief ... and Gordon had revealed only a tiny part of it.

Chapter Thirty-Seven

'How do you feel?'

Gordon and Jennifer were walking along the riverbank, the same stretch he had taken with Celina. The match the vicar had given him was kept permanently in his wallet. It was lunchtime on the day after he had told Tania he was leaving, so it didn't matter anymore if someone saw them together.

'Strange,' he replied, 'frightened, sad, guilty, excited, relieved, probably more of the first two at the moment.'

'You'll go through a mixture of emotions for a while yet. Expect a few big waves amongst the calmer waters ahead. The worst thing is the indecision, wasting years wondering whether to leave someone or stay. Everything will be clearer now that you've actually chosen to go and you are finally escaping.'

'I'll still be glad when I get to my parents' house tomorrow evening. I'm worried what Tania might do as a last-minute attempt to maintain control.'

'She'll likely throw a lot at you.'

'Do you think ...?'

'No, I don't mean physically. But she'll probably use quite severe emotional blackmail to try to make you change your mind. A couple of the women in the shelter said their husbands deserved Oscars for their performances on the day they were leaving. One woman backed down, even though she knew in her heart it was the wrong thing to do, and a few months later she had to go through the whole scenario again when she eventually did walk out.

'At every point tomorrow you must keep safety at the front of your mind,' said Jennifer. 'I know that your wife is not usually violent, but abusers fear being abandoned more than anything, and leaving is normally the most dangerous time for a partner. Even now I shudder to imagine what Derek might have done if he had known.

'You must promise that at the first sign of trouble you will get away from the house as quickly as possible. Don't let yourself become trapped in a room. You might even consider having a friend waiting outside and agree a timescale and a plan beforehand.'

'Thanks. I'll take care. Once I'm away, I'll stop somewhere to let you know I'm safe.'

'Make sure you do. I think I'm almost as scared as you are about this. I'm partly responsible. I won't be able to eat until I know you're away.'

'I'll try my best not to keep you hungry for any longer than necessary.'

She smiled.

'I'm certainly glad I've got Marilyn and Andrew's to go to when all this is over.'

He had spoken to Jennifer several times using a telephone at work, so she knew he was going to live with his cousin in Cornwall.

'I had always accepted that Tania believed there were things going on with other women, a sort of jealousy she couldn't control, but now I almost wonder if she really thought this or whether it was just an excuse to control and punish me? What do you think?'

Jennifer considered the point then expelled her breath in a gesture of defeat.

'We'll probably never be certain and maybe she doesn't even know herself.'

'I guess not.'

'You need to be aware of one thing that might surprise you,' said Jennifer.

'What's that?'

'Be prepared for the fact that you may miss Tania.'

'Miss her?'

'I know it seems unlikely at the moment when all you can focus on is getting out of the relationship, but abusers get into here,' she said tapping his forehead, 'and they get into here.'

She put her hand on his chest.

'She'll still be there even when you've physically left the area. Several of the women I met said they felt such shame and anger with themselves for almost grieving, even after all the abuse they had received.'

They carried on walking. The day was cold, but there was no threat of a downpour as there had been the time that he took this path with Celina.

'Yesterday, I had a moment of ... liberating madness,' she said.

'What did you do?'

'I know it sounds utterly silly and meaningless, but I went to the kitchen cupboard and moved the bottles and tins around so that they were all mixed up, with some items balancing precariously on others and several of them upside down!

'Derek once slapped me because the label on the mustard jar wasn't facing exactly forwards, so I took mine and emptied the entire contents on to the centre of the table then I stuck the spoon in the middle and left it there, pointing towards the ceiling. It's difficult to describe the tremendous feeling of freedom I had afterwards. For hours I floated around the house on air, constantly going back to the kitchen to look again at my creation.

'When I eventually cleared it away the mustard had left a stain, but in a strange way I was pleased. That mark will always remind me of what I've gained by walking away from my nightmare. Apart from you, no one else will know. It would take great trust for me to tell someone else its meaning.'

'I think I understand some of what you're saying,' he replied when they had walked in silence for a while. 'In a way your spoon was like a tiny flag of triumph, flying from the top of a challenging hill that you've just climbed.'

Jennifer was taken aback at the analogy. When she thought about what he said and the image of the teaspoon raised upon the mess of yellow goo, that's exactly what it did feel like. It was a flag of triumph, representing a great emotional hurdle that had been overcome. She was struck by Gordon's perception and grasp of the significance of her actions, which most other people would probably have considered slightly insane.

'Not long after we married, Tania said I was like a bird in a cage, always singing and trying to escape, but only she had the key, and one day, I would simply stop and never sing again.'

'That's a terribly cruel thing to say.'

'No, that's the strange part. She didn't mean it that way. She was sad, as though acknowledging this was our fate if we stayed together, while at the same time implying neither of us was strong enough to be alone.'

Jennifer had no words of wisdom to give.

'I'll miss our talks,' he said.

'You've got my number and you can ring whenever you want. You'll no longer have to find a telephone away from the house. Freedom is such a tremendous gift. All too often people ignore its value because they've never known any different.'

Gordon recalled another scene that used to be played out regularly at home whenever he made calls or answered the telephone. Tania would always allow him a few minutes in order to work out whom he was speaking to, then, depending upon the person, she would go to the extension either upstairs or by the harmonium.

He always heard the receiver being picked up and would say 'Ah, Tania's joined us on the extension' as if this was expected and a completely natural occurrence, like an actor making an entrance to the same cue every performance.

She would immediately take over the conversation, not allowing him to speak and normally leaving the other person slightly mystified as to what was going on. Finally, he would break in with, 'Well, I'll say cheerio'. The next time Tania would do the same thing again. She always controlled his calls like that.

'But that's enough about me,' he said. 'What about you? What will you do now that you don't have me to rescue?'

'Well, I have a bit of news, but it's nothing compared to yours.'

'What is it?'

'I've been seeing someone.'

Gordon stopped and his face lit up in such a beaming smile that Jennifer laughed.

'That's the greatest news I could have heard. When did this happen? Why didn't you tell me? Well ... who is it?' he blurted out.

'The main priority has been to get you sorted and we've only met for a few coffees and one meal so far.'

'And ...'

'It's Julian.'

'Julian?'

'He's in the tenor section.'

'Julian! Yes, I don't know him well, but he seems a very nice man, always pleasant and helpful to beginners.'

'He's kind and gentle.'

'Didn't he lose his wife last year?'

'Nearly two years ago. He's still fragile, so we're both taking things slowly. I told him a little about Derek and he was horrified. He didn't know such cruelty went on between married couples. But he's been marvellous, listening intently when I want to talk about it, but never pushing me for more information than I want to give. I trust him, and there was a time when I didn't think I would ever say that about another man. Perhaps, one day, I'll let him know the meaning of the yellow stain on the table.'

'I can't tell you how happy this makes me.'

Suddenly, without warning, he hugged Jennifer tightly. It made her laugh, a spontaneous expression of joy that came from the very depths of her soul and which was so loud that a pair of nearby mallards took off from the river in fright. She couldn't remember when such an alien sound had come from her. Like so many aspects of her life, laughter had been a prisoner that knew no daylight.

They continued their walk arm in arm, an intimacy they had previously never allowed themselves. Jennifer thought Gordon had absolutely no idea how appealing many women would find him. There was an enormous strength and goodness about his character, and she had seen glimpses of many other traits, such as his honesty and willingness to work hard, his humour and tenderness.

She understood how he had been so knocked down while growing up that he simply didn't realise, even though he once had a large circle of friends, that lots of people really liked him. Tania had picked off so many of them, as if she was merely shooting ducks on a stall at the fair.

Love can take so many forms. Not for the first time Jennifer felt that she would have been proud to have called this man her son. And if she had been twenty-five years younger ...

'I can't thank you enough for your help and support,' said Gordon. 'I'm not sure what would have happened to me if we hadn't met in the church that day, when you asked if my wife was coming to the concert.'

'I remember the moment well,' she said. 'Sometimes a single sentence can reveal an extraordinary amount about a person's life, even without them being aware of it. Your response transported me back to a terrible period in my life.'

'I thought you had suddenly taken ill.'

'Perhaps I had, an illness of the spirit brought on by a memory. But you should never doubt for an instant how much you've helped me.'

'How much I've helped you?'

They continued walking, but she looked into his eyes before answering. There was such potential behind that innocent, eager face. The right woman would allow him to grow into the person he could be, if just given a chance.

'Don't you understand how much you've enabled me to heal? I was getting over Derek's abuse, slowly, bit by bit, but I would never have had the confidence to accept Julian's offer of coffee if you and I had not fought side by side these past months. We've not just been fighting your battles, we've been fighting mine as well. You have given me your trust, respected completely the confidences I have given you and accepted me with an open heart. Haven't you realised ... you're the closest friend I have in the whole world?'

Gordon didn't answer. Jennifer knew he was thinking about what she had said and that it would probably be a long time, perhaps even years, before he truly understood. It didn't matter. He would get there.

They stopped walking and hugged without any words being spoken. This time there was no laughter, just an intense feeling of closeness. They were a similar height and he nestled his cheek against hers, breathing in the faint smell of the scented soap she had used earlier that morning. It reminded him of lilies.

Apart from Tania, he only vaguely recalled ever being held like this: by his mother, Marilyn, a couple of aunts who were particularly fond of him. But these belonged to his childhood, when his perspective on life was so different that they felt like memories belonging to someone else. They weren't his. He had merely borrowed them to look at with mild curiosity, like an old photograph album dug out of the bottom of the blanket box, showing long since deceased ancestors that no one recognises.

Eventually, they pulled apart and stood looking at each other.

'I'll have to head back to the factory,' he said.

'I think we've said what needs to be spoken of for now. But there is one last subject I wish to bring up.'

'What is it?' he asked when she didn't continue.

'I always maintained I would never tell you what to do because any decisions about your life have to be yours.'

'Yes.'

'But there is one option I really want you to consider.'

'Anything. Tell me what's on your mind.'

Gently she placed her hands either side of his head.

'Please think about getting your hair cut.'

Chapter Thirty-Eight

Gordon took his farewells at the factory on the Friday morning and arrived home at one o'clock. In reality, it wasn't 'home' anymore. Once he had collected his few remaining possessions he intended never to return to the area. Despite all that had happened he felt it was only proper that he said goodbye to his wife last, yet he dreaded what awaited him.

Would it be yet another angry encounter, perhaps even violent, or one full of tears and remorse? He had only just walked through the front door when Tania threw herself at his legs, clasping her arms around them so that he almost fell over.

'Don't go. I'm sorry for everything. I'll change. I really will. You can give me one more chance. And I'll pay for the damage so that it's fixed as good as new. I've already started looking for a job to earn the money. After all our years together you've got to agree that our marriage is worth one more chance.'

He didn't want any of this and had no idea what 'damage' she was talking about. Everything was hers now anyway.

'Please don't,' he said. 'Let me get inside so that I can shut the door. You don't want the neighbours hearing this.'

Then he saw what she meant.

Grandma's harmonium.

The instrument lay in ruins. She must have hit it with something far heavier than a hammer to have caused such destruction. Gordon thought it might have been a decorative stone out of the garden, one that would have needed both hands to lift. Shards of creamy ivory lay scattered on the floor amongst large splinters of dark mahogany. All of the stops had been broken off and most of the keys were gone. She had even

261

removed the front panel to attack the internal workings. No hymns would ever be sung around that instrument again.

Gordon wondered if she had cut up his clothes and smashed his violin. She was still wrapped around his legs and he laid a hand gently on top of her head, where the brown roots showed clearly against the bright red of the dye, a tiny piece of reality struggling to be seen in Tania's world of make-believe. He felt a great sadness. There was a time when he had given this woman his love and believed they had a future.

'Come on, let me get in,' he said quietly.

If he had shouted or raved in anger she would probably have clung even tighter, but the calmness of his voice made her look up. She flopped back on to the carpet and he closed the door. Tania was wearing a new outfit that he hadn't seen before and she had on her 'clown's mask'. It was smudged in several places where she had wiped away tears.

'I think it's best that I just collect my things and leave.'

'No, you can't just go.'

She tried to get up, but the combination of drinking and the over-tight outfit meant that she had to crawl on her hands and knees to the nearby radiator to get some support.

'You can't go yet. I've made lunch. You've got to eat something. Let's sit around the table. One final meal together is not much to ask after all these years.'

Gordon moved around her as she was trying to stand so that he could get to the stairs and in doing so he had to walk through the carnage that lay around the harmonium. His foot kicked a broken stop and he bent down to pick it up. The copperplate writing read 'Octave Coupler'. When you pulled this one out and pressed a key, the note one octave higher would also sound as though there was an invisible finger holding it down.

Tania had got up and was standing with one hand against the wall to steady herself.

'I think it's best that I go,' he said.

He put the stop in his pocket and went upstairs, not certain at all what he would find. However, the two suitcases by the spare bed looked just as he had left them that morning. He had already packed several boxes in the car boot, leaving space for his violin case. Gordon would have liked to have taken everything in one go, but there was too much to carry so he picked up a suitcase and his violin. Tania was standing in the sitting room doorway. She had collected a glass of wine and shouted at him even before he had reached the bottom of the stairs.

'My death will be your fault. You'll have to live with that guilt for the rest of your life. Just think what a cross that will be to bear. How will you be able to go to church with my death on your hands?'

He reached the front door without speaking and put down his case to open it.

'How can you face God knowing you've murdered someone? No one will want to know you.'

He picked up the case.

'Nobody will give you hugs like I do. You'll be that little boy again rejected by his mother, all lost and lonely.'

Gordon paused to look at her. He realised that she must have prepared and memorised a list of reasons why he shouldn't leave and was running through them as each one failed to get the reaction she wanted; pleading, then the threat of suicide and subsequent unbearable guilt, now attacking his longstanding fear of loneliness. Walking out to the car he wondered what she would say when he came back. He soon found out. She was standing at the bottom of the stairs so that he couldn't get past.

'I always knew there was something going on between you and Marilyn,' she screamed, pointing at him with a broken stop, the wood making a dangerously jagged spike. 'Now you're running all the way to Cornwall to be with her. Well, that just proves I was right all along ... you bastard.'

She still held the glass in her other hand and red wine spilled on to the carpet as she spoke.

'There's nothing going on,' he said. 'I haven't seen Marilyn for years.'

Gordon tried to keep his voice even and calm, but she was winding herself up into a frenzy of anger.

'That's what you say, but she'll get tired of you and then you'll be out on your ear. Without me you won't be able to survive. I give you a couple of months at most.'

As she spoke she forced him backwards with the broken stop so that they both ended up near the front door. He thought of Jennifer, walking away from twenty-five years of marriage with nothing more than what she was wearing. The only thing left upstairs was one suitcase of clothes. Everything else he wanted was already in the car. He turned around and went outside. His key was still in the lock and he left it there.

'Where are you going? You haven't got everything,' she said, following him out.

'Give the rest to the charity shop,' he shouted as he walked down the path.

The wooden stop hit him on the shoulder, but it was too small and light to do any harm.

'Bastard!' she screamed. 'You'll be back, begging to be let in. Without me you're nothing! Have you looked in the mirror recently? Your new nose doesn't make any bloody difference. No one's going to want you. Ugly bastard!'

The wine glass missed him altogether and shattered on the pavement. Gordon got into the car and started the engine. From where it was parked he could see along the path to the front door and risked one last look. She was sitting on the ground, crying. It was a sad sight and he was certain it would be the last one he would ever have of her.

He hadn't realised how scared the encounter had made him and his hands shook as he drove away. Sally was running up the pavement towards the house. She put two fingers up to him, but then he was past her and down the street ... and out of Tania's life forever.

Gordon drove for ten minutes then pulled into a lay-by. Jennifer answered immediately.

'I'm free and I'm okay,' he said.

'Thank goodness. Are you sure you're alright?'

'Yes, a bit shaky, but I'm starting to settle down.'

He outlined briefly what had happened. They agreed to keep the call short and that he would ring her tomorrow to explain in more detail what had taken place.

'Go on,' he said, 'get something to eat.'

'I will,' she replied. 'It's time to start living, Gordon.'

'I know. You too, Jennifer.'

'Yes.'

There was a slight pause in the conversation, but it was like everything between them, comfortable and safe.

'Become the person that you have the potential to be,' she said, 'and don't let anyone ever put you down again.'

'I'll try my hardest.'

'And remember what I said.'

'Which particular bit?'

'Don't be a victim of domestic abuse ... be a survivor.'

Gordon stopped at a service station. It was the one where he had met Jennifer and he sat at the same table with a pot of tea, reflecting on the events of the last few hours. His life had changed forever. He was surprisingly calm and wondered quite what emotions he was meant to have in a situation like this.

During the last few months he had had his share of sleepless nights, feeling great guilt, being frightened and remorseful, full of doubts and fears. He had also done his share of crying. Now, he simply felt relief.

He knew that being away from Tania didn't mean she was out of his life and that it would take a long time to free himself of the effects of her domination, of the subtle, and sometimes not-so-subtle, control she had exercised over him. But for the moment he couldn't ignore his surprise at the lightness of spirit he felt, so sat quietly and thought about some of the things Jennifer had said.

She had talked to him in some depth about the comment he made in the tea shop that Tania understood him. Jennifer had been angry, a rare flash of the pain she still felt inside coming uninvited to the surface.

'If abusers say they understand their partners it's because they've moulded them into something of their making, it's because they never forget a single comment given in confidence about our fears and hopes, which they store away for future use against us, and it's because they lie. Abuse and lies go hand in hand because an honest person would find it impossible to dominate and control someone. Abusers don't understand their partner or they would never cause the suffering they do, unless they were so totally devoid of humanity that they could never feel a shred of pity for anyone.'

The words had struck home, partly because she had been so passionate while saying them, whereas normally Jennifer was gentle, like his mother. Gordon poured himself more tea and considered his current position.

There was a little over £5,000 in his new bank account plus a few shares, the car, a couple of cardboard boxes, one suitcase of possessions and his violin.

He remembered how he used to love playing the instrument and suspected that any adult, who had no experience of abuse, would find it unbelievable that a musician would deliberately make mistakes in order to pacify the mood of someone. How crazy was that? Sitting in the restaurant, surrounded by people going about their everyday lives, the concept seemed incredible to him even though he had carried out that very behaviour.

After working hard for eleven years he wasn't walking away with much, but he had gained his freedom and this couldn't be measured in material terms.

Driving to his parents' house felt odd. He hadn't seen them since the summer. Tania had never liked staying there and it was too far to visit in one day. His parents had come to them a couple of times in the early years of their marriage, but they hadn't felt comfortable with the atmosphere or her heavy drinking. Normally, when they all got together, they would each travel half way and meet for lunch, but these occasions didn't allow much time for talking and Gordon was never able to speak to his mother alone.

During the previous weeks he had kept them informed of what was going on, without giving too much detail over the telephone, although they knew he was heading for Cornwall. He didn't know what they thought of his departure or his plans.

And then he was there, standing just inside their front door, and his mother was hugging him tightly ... something she hadn't done since he was seven years old. Leaving Tania that day hadn't made him cry, however, being hugged by his tiny mother with such affection made the tears flow down his face.

His father, standing further along the corridor, thought his son's show of emotion was due to what had been happening. He didn't understand it was because his wife had finally decided, at the age of sixty-one, that she would hug her only son if she wanted, regardless of what his orders were. There was more than one rebellion taking place in the family.

Eventually, Gordon was able to come into the house properly and the two men shook hands. It was awkward, the older man uneasy even at such basic physical contact. Soon afterwards, the three of them sat around the kitchen table drinking tea and he recounted some of the events that had taken place. His mother began to cry.

'We had no idea that you were being so mistreated,' she said.

'It's terrible to think that you have been put through all this by someone meant to love and care for you. I'm sorry we never helped.'

'Don't blame yourself, Mum. No one knew. Even I didn't realise that my marriage and her behaviour were so wrong. It's amazing what people accept as normal when they don't have boundaries to use for comparison.'

He looked at his parents and wondered, not for the first time during the last few months, what boundaries his mother judged his father by. He had considered speaking to her, to open her eyes as Jennifer had done for him. But he was certain that his mother would never leave, and his father, at sixty-six, wouldn't change his behaviour or beliefs, so what good would he do?

If she began to feel that a large part of her life had been wasted trying continually to please this domineering, selfish man, yet at the same time could do nothing to change the situation, then all Gordon would achieve was to make his mother sad and discontented. He felt that she wasn't really 'unhappy' in her marriage because it had always been this way and this was what she knew and expected.

This complex family issue wasn't something Gordon could concentrate on during such a short visit and he certainly wasn't going to say anything in the near future. He needed all his energy to get through the coming months, which would no doubt throw heartache and pain at him in many unexpected ways.

He was staying with his parents for a couple of nights before setting out for Cornwall. It would take him more than a week as, on the way, he planned to visit various friends with whom he hadn't been allowed to have contact for several years. They had all invited him to stay during the journey to his new life and as he had nothing to rush for he had readily accepted the offers, glad they had not held his lack of contact against him.

'Well,' said his mother when they were all into their second cup, 'Marilyn has always been very fond of you, dear, and I'm sure she and Andrew will make you very welcome. I'm sorry it's so far away though.'

'Marilyn's already been checking out nearby choirs and music groups for me to join. I think she has a mission to integrate me with local society as quickly as possible, and she's already hinted about dinners with some of her single girl-friends.'

'She's a good soul,' said his mother.

'If it wasn't for their kind offer, I don't know what I would have done. It's having somewhere to live that's as much of a problem as finding a job.'

'There's always a bed for you here,' she said, glancing nervously at her husband to check that she had not over-stepped the mark with such an offer.

'I'm sorry it's been so difficult to get together over the years,' said Gordon. 'Tania never had anything against you both, but she didn't like staying away from home.'

As he spoke he realised this was not quite true. What his wife had wanted was control in every situation, which included stopping him seeing his parents if she so decided. Being allowed to meet them for lunch had been a great 'favour', like Derek permitting Jennifer to join a choir, a gesture that she'd had to repay him for many times over. It struck him that there was probably a great deal he had yet to appreciate about his marriage and the reasons why certain events happened, why he had been prevented from doing particular things.

Jennifer told him that even after a year she was still finding out new facts about her husband; how she could be carrying out a perfectly ordinary task around the house and in a flash of unexpected clarity would suddenly understand the significance of an action he had taken, or a comment made.

Gordon thought he might have a similar, though shorter, period of 'realisation'. He wondered what he would have been like if he had been married for twenty-five years, and marvelled once more at Jennifer's gritty determination. Once he was settled he would invite her to stay. Marilyn would love her to bits.

His mind had been drifting and he realised his mother was speaking to him across the table.

'What are you doing tomorrow, dear?' she said, repeating the question her son had not heard.

'Sorry, Mum. Tomorrow? There are a couple of jobs I want to do and I'll also have to buy some new clothes. I left the suitcase containing a lot of mine at the house.'

'Why did you leave it?' asked his father, joining in the conversation for the first time.

Gordon hadn't told them that the harmonium had been destroyed so he described some of the scene in the hallway that morning, and how he had felt it was safer to leave when he did. The jagged point of the broken wooden stop had flashed past his face a couple of times and he had been concerned Tania might try to injure him so that he couldn't drive. The risk had been too great.

The next day he would post the *Octave Coupler* stop he had put in his pocket to Jennifer. It might seem a strange gift, but in a way it was like them; separated by many years, yet in perfect harmony with each other. He was sure she would regard it in the same way he felt about the match that had been used to light the candle in the church.

'We didn't want to interfere, but we're so glad you're out of that marriage. I never felt she was right for you.'

Gordon was surprised to hear such a bold statement from his mother, who rarely gave an opinion on anything, at least not while his father was present.

'Well, I'm going to start cooking dinner,' she said. 'Why don't you two unpack the car? I'm making mince and tatties.'

Mother and son smiled at each other. As a child, this had

been his favourite dish.

The two men unloaded the car then sat in the living room, so it was to his father Gordon first told in greater detail the story about his married life. The older man listened without making any comment.

Jennifer had made Gordon think about and analyse events in ways that he had never considered before. Across the room sat the man who, so long ago, prevented his wife from showing physical affection towards her son when he was still a young boy, full of uncomplicated love and in need of the simplicity of unrestricted hugs and kisses. It had been a cruel, wicked act.

However, there was more to this than simply wanting to dominate his mother or prove that he had such total control within their marriage. What his father had to be was the centre of attention at all times. Nothing and no one was allowed to compete. Gordon remembered how everything in their family life used to revolve around him; his needs, his moods. With nothing to compare this to he had assumed that all families were like this.

It hadn't dawned on him how strange it was that, while he was growing up, his father had never once given him a word of encouragement or paid him a compliment, whereas he and his mother would have to heap praise upon him on a daily basis, as if they were spooning baby food into a mouth that was *always* hungry.

In his mind's eye he could still see his mother desperately concocting comments to say, or trying to think of things to do that would keep his temper sweet. His father didn't control by shouting or threatening. If he felt that he hadn't been treated properly he would instead become withdrawn and sullen, withholding affection from his wife as a form of punishment.

Friends and relatives weren't made welcome at the house and over the years such visits had dwindled away, so that even at Christmas there was just the three of them. It had been a classic abuser's tactic of isolating the person they wanted to dominate.

His poor mother was so downtrodden that even if he wasn't watching the television she would never dare ask whether she could switch on the set to see a particular programme. She knew he would reply that he was about to watch something, even if this was blatantly untrue, or he would ask if she didn't have some work to do around the house. He rarely did any.

Gordon chastised himself for not identifying the abuse that had gone on unchecked between his parents; for never doing anything to protect his long-suffering mother. It was only at the age of twenty-nine that he understood why his father had said and done some of the things he had over the years. Now it was obvious to him. But Gordon had been so wrapped up in the whole *process* of abuse that he hadn't seen it for what it was, just as he hadn't acknowledged the control and manipulation Tania had exercised.

However, family relationships consisted of layer upon layer of complexity and emotion, and he remembered how his father would play with him when he was small. There had been a wooden fort and a toy cannon that fired spent matchsticks. They would spend ages lying on the living room floor, taking turns trying to knock over the plastic soldiers that had been lined up on the fort's parapet. Perhaps there had been some good times, all mixed up with the other.

His father had still not commented since he had finished telling the story of his recent escape, and the two of them sat in silence for a while.

'I'm going to help Mum,' said Gordon standing up and, risking that his father might feel 'slighted' at being left alone, he went to the kitchen.

As he walked along the corridor Gordon wondered if the older man recognised anything of himself in the description he had just given of Tania. He suspected not.

Chapter Thirty-Nine

Gemma had thought long and hard about this day, as she had done concerning everything that had occurred over the last few years. She had decided it would be good for the three of them to have a nice time together, particularly after the trauma of the previous months.

This drawn-out, messy situation with Tom had been exacerbated by his strong personality and code of conduct, which had presented a much greater challenge than if he had been any sort of weaker man. In order to dominate and control her husband she had to break him, but there was a lot about his character that she liked — or at least that was useful to her — and it would be no good if she broke him completely or he was sent to prison, which would have had the same effect.

It had been such a delicate road to tread; manipulating events on a daily basis, pushing the boundaries, picking the exact moments to use just the right amount of abuse to wear him down, but without going too far. He was human, after all, and she didn't relish the idea of him losing control, though she had been certain he would never hit her.

His phobia of small spaces had been particularly helpful and even those few hours in the police cell had altered him, albeit minutely. From that night onwards she had sensed a wariness within him that had further edged aside some of his confidence. There was an unspoken acknowledgement that she could get him sent back, which had made him more frightened of her. That was good, although this was almost an aside because Tom's real Achilles heel was his precious daughter. Amy was the weapon that he had no defence against. The threat of separating the two of them had been so terrifying that he would do and say anything to prevent it.

However, it wasn't sufficient that he simply carried out what she wanted. That would be like living with an actor who was merely playing a part, which would make their whole existence superficial and false. Who would want that? The key to her happiness lay in Tom understanding, in the very core of his being, that he had to place her needs and desires above all else. It had to be so instinctive that she never needed to tell him again. Only then would it be enough.

Despite everything that had taken place Gemma loved her husband. She felt it in her heart and would tell him so on occasions so it had to be true. Part of her longed for the fun they used to have, before Amy had become too important. She missed the regular sex they once had and hoped Tom had not been beaten down so much that he couldn't perform the way he used to. It was time to wean him around again.

So she had decided they should have a lovely day out. Tom had taken time off work and they had arranged to meet Jessica and her mother, Eileen, for lunch before the five of them went to the theatre. It was pantomime season and they had tickets for the matinee performance of *Cinderella*. Amy was then going to spend the night with her friend, which meant that Gemma and Tom could have a romantic evening alone.

They met at a restaurant near to the theatre. The two girls sat next to each other and were soon in a conversation, and world, of their own, leaving the three adults to position themselves on the other side of the table. Amy looked lovely, completely overshadowing the other girl. Gemma was happy to show off her daughter, but as soon as Amy started to develop into a young woman she would ensure that there were only the dullest of clothes to wear. No offspring was competing in her house.

Gemma considered Eileen, who was divorced, to be a rather

stupid, ugly woman and had no interest in her friendship whatsoever, but she always acted courteously because it was convenient to offload Amy. In the early days Gemma had been forced to allow Jessica to also stay with them, but it had been easy to put the girl off from wanting to repeat this by ensuring her bedroom was always uncomfortably hot or cold, there were constant interruptions during the night, and breakfast was inedible. Gracious offers for her daughter to stay at any time could be made in the knowledge that Jessica wouldn't want to.

Gemma's outfit had been chosen carefully so that she didn't appear overdressed yet could still show off her figure and demonstrate how beautiful she was. Eileen made suitable compliments and Tom's wife smiled, saying that it was just the first thing she happened to pull out of the wardrobe that morning, even though she had spent nearly two hours getting ready. Her outfits were almost catalogued in the way they were stored. No item was ever pulled out by chance.

Had it been possible, Gemma would have catalogued everything about their lives: what they ate; where they went; who they saw; the things they did. She organised as much as she could and was always frustrated when events occurred that weren't in her master plan. Even people calling at the house unexpectedly were a potential problem. It was partly because of this that she was always 'on display'. Only an experienced eye would discern that she must have spent a considerable amount of effort to achieve the effect that she looked exquisite without trying.

However, the meal was pleasant enough and Gemma liked the way other men in the restaurant stared at her while ignoring Eileen. Even the waiters were not immune to her charms. She was extremely good at being charming. By keeping almost everyone she came into contact with at a certain distance, very few people ever got to know her well enough to realise how much this was an act.

She didn't find the pantomime enjoyable mainly because no one in the audience paid her any attention, but she consoled herself with the idea that it consisted almost entirely of children or frumpy housewives, so who cared what they thought? She was glad when it ended and Eileen took the two children away.

Tom and Gemma went home to shower and change before going out for dinner at a rather expensive restaurant that neither of them had been to before. She had bought him a new jacket, because he had lost weight and his other one looked baggy, but although he perhaps wasn't the imposing figure he used to be Tom could still turn many a head when he was spruced up.

'Wow, you look stunning,' he said when she walked into the lounge.

Gemma knew she was beautiful, but she would accept 'stunning' as being sufficient praise.

'You look alright yourself. Does your new jacket feel comfortable?'

'It's great. Thanks for getting it.'

A taxi took them to the restaurant where they were shown, as pre-arranged, to a candlelit table in the window.

'I want this to be such a special evening,' she said, when they had been served aperitifs, 'a new beginning for all of us.'

'I'll drink to that,' said Tom.

'I know it's been tough, darling, but I think we've come through the fire pretty well, and we'll all be the stronger for it in the future, an even better family unit.'

They raised their glasses. Not sure how to reply Tom simply smiled. Inside, he felt he had been treading on burning coals for months while Gemma hadn't been suffering alongside him, but rather on the sidelines chucking petrol. However, he pushed the image away immediately because that sort of thinking was dangerous. As part of his new regime he had to banish negative thoughts about his wife as soon as they popped up.

'It's been a lovely day,' he said, feeling that this was safe ground. 'The girls certainly enjoyed themselves and it was nice to talk to Eileen. I've never had such a long conversation with her. Thanks for arranging everything so well,' he added as an afterthought before taking another sip.

'Yes, it has been good.'

The waiter brought them menus, but while they studied the various options Gemma stole secret glances across the table. She wished he hadn't turned his head just as she was about to hit him with the pan on the day the social worker called. That was stupid of him. She always took great care to ensure any scars were hidden by his thick brown hair and it was a shame about the thin white line above his eyebrow.

Appearances were everything and Gemma certainly didn't want him disfigured in any way. This was why she had resisted the temptation to use boiling liquids or something like the steam iron as a weapon, even though as a shock tactic such actions would have been extremely effective.

There was no hiding the fact that her husband had aged considerably over the last year. His hair was greyer and there were many more lines around his eyes. His face had lost the firmness it used to have, much like the rest of him.

The regular training he used to do in order to remain on the rugby team had irritated her, so it had to be stopped, but the side-effect was that he wasn't as muscular and fit, which was a pity as she liked his body to be in good shape. Perhaps she would have to devise a training plan for him that suited her requirements.

'Have you decided?'

Gemma was a little startled, as she didn't know what Tom was referring to.

'About what?'

'Your meal. What you want to eat.'

'Oh no, not yet.'

277

'You were miles away.'

'I was just thinking how lucky we all are, you, Amy and me,' she said.

Tom smiled and ordered another drink.

Their love-making that night was wild and exciting, tender and safe. She had cried and he had cried and she had held him, cradled him against her breast, for a long while after the first time, until they both once more felt a stirring of passions that had been held at bay for so long. Tom had drunk too much during the meal, which was very out of character, but she forgave him and it didn't affect his performance. The night just seemed to go on and on and Gemma was almost happy.

While Tom snored softly a silent battle raged within his wife, scaring away any chance of sleep. It was as if there were two people inside her head, with one voice arguing that enough had been done to achieve her aims and she deserved a period of respite, while the other voice ranted that Tom should not be allowed to get away with anything. Gemma tried to fuse the figures into one person, so that she could more easily control what was said. It was all about control.

As rationally as possible, she analysed the events of the previous months, indeed of the last couple of years. When she considered the hurdles that had been climbed, the great many obstacles knocked down and the sheer determination required to maintain her programme of daily domination, she had done extremely well. It was almost frustrating that she couldn't reveal just how clever and resourceful she had been, as this was surely worthy of admiration.

But winning had taken its toll and no one realised how much she had suffered during this entire process. The degree of mental effort required to continuously implement her plans, to constantly charm and manipulate people, had been enormous. Often, she had to force herself to stay awake at night so that she could work out the most effective course of action for the following days.

It had been tedious having to keep Amanda in a constant 'boiling point' of outrage, so that she was forever eager for Gemma to alert the police about Tom's abuse, while never being wound up so much that she might contact them herself. Gemma didn't even like the woman, who was so extraordinarily boring, and in the early years she had only kept the relationship going because it had been amusing to have such a guaranteed ardent admirer. But for her long-term plan to work it had been necessary to have someone who was ready at any point to step forward as a 'witness' on her behalf, to satisfy her obsession to cover all possibilities.

In truth, Gemma didn't really like people. Tom would just about be alright once she had moulded him some more into the character required. With her looks and charm she picked up acquaintances with the ease of picking up a lipstick, but they were kept only for as long as they were useful. Their purpose in life was merely to satisfy the needs of the moment, whether this was flattery, help with a career move, or someone to blame.

It was important that there was always another person to blame. Gemma was perfection, so it was inconceivable that she could ever be at fault or should feel remorse. Over the years she had developed great skill at making others appear to be in the wrong if she had carried out a task incorrectly or badly, or had even forgotten to do something that she should have. It went hand in hand with her talent for making people feel inferior, which, of course, they always were.

Perhaps there should now be a period of calm. Gemma felt exhausted and wanted some peace, a reconnection with the relationship she used to have with Tom in the earlier days. She deserved it after everything she had been put through.

But the other voice in her head hadn't been silenced, and it shouted that her husband didn't appreciate how much she had suffered. It was alright for him to go rushing off into his sister's arms, spewing out stories about his wife, how she had been so horrible to poor, dear big brother. There was no one to comfort Gemma, certainly not her parents. When had they ever cared?

No, Tom had been so full of his own hurt and how he was missing his darling little daughter that he hadn't once considered Gemma, never thought how she needed some attention, even a hug. The only person she had was stupid, fucking Amanda. Well, Amanda had served her purpose and there was no way that relationship was continuing.

But she would be careful not to burn the bridge between them completely. This new lack of communication must be blamed on someone; Tom. Yes, he was forbidding his wife from seeing her dear old school friend because she had acted as a witness against him. Gemma would display great sorrow, but she obviously had no choice in the matter, and Amanda would understand because she *always* agreed so gushingly.

And exactly what had Tom said to his sister? Hadn't he been told not to speak to outsiders about what happened in the house? In fact, just how many people had he talked to about their private life? Hardly private now, was it? Fuck him. Nobody had the right to make comments about her that she didn't like. She hadn't gone through all of this for him not to fully realise how much she was hurting inside. She was special, sensitive. No one felt pain like her. Tom had annoyed her ... REALLY annoyed her.

Quietly, Gemma slipped out of bed. With no neighbours on that side of the house the curtains were rarely closed and moonlight filtered into the bedroom, illuminating her naked body. It was gorgeous. She couldn't resist pausing to take pleasure in studying herself briefly in the full-length mirror, marvelling at how the soft light seemed to caress her breasts and buttocks, as though even the moon bowed to her beauty.

Tom simply couldn't be allowed to get away with not

acknowledging that he had done things she didn't like. She felt under the bed, her hands quickly finding the cricket bat that had been hidden there earlier that morning.

Covering all options.

She stood motionless for several minutes, watching the gentle rise and fall of the duvet covering her husband, sleeping peacefully. The cricket bat hung loosely in one hand. Like a cat stalking its prey Gemma moved stealthily to the other side of the bed as if barely touching the molecules of surrounding air. Then she wrapped both hands around the handle, tightened her grip and raised the bat.

Moonlight illuminated almost the whole of her body, which she could see in the mirror across the room. Gemma thought she looked like a goddess; a goddess about to wreck vengeance upon the minions who hadn't worshipped her properly, who hadn't shown the respect, love and fear that all subjects should give to one so superior.

The ranting voice had been right after all ... and the wood made a gentle 'whooshing' sound in the otherwise silent night.

Chapter Forty

You can tell a lot about a man by his hair: young men making a comment about their views on life like in the old days of mods and rockers, skinheads and hippies; those with expensive styles trying to make everything appear natural when it was obvious they'd spent a great deal; bald men trying to deny the years by sweeping long strands across their crowns, their parting getting ever lower and the overall effect drawing attention to what they so desperately tried to hide; those with severe, almost military cuts revealing a stance against fashion, that they rose above such trivial matters or simply that they didn't care what people thought.

The stranger who walked into the little shop that morning presented quite a challenge to Alfred's powers of deduction. Here was a comment that was complex. The long, almost wild hair covered a large part of the man's face and it was awful, in complete disharmony to the slight build of his body and the shape of his head.

An odd-looking chap, thought Alfred, though he was far too long in the tooth to be fooled into thinking you could tell much about a person by their appearance, or that you could automatically assume someone hasn't experienced much of life because they were young. He had learnt that knowledge and wisdom often had nothing to do with age. Some of the most intelligent people he had ever met had come shambling into his shop, smelly and unkempt, hands shaking after a night of heavy drinking. Then it came to him.

A barrier. He uses his hair as a barrier between himself and others.

Despite everything that had happened to him recently, he

reverted automatically into the 'caricature' that had played such a large part of his life.

'Good morning, sir. Come in, sir. Come in. Let me shut the door and keep out the cold. My crumbling bones don't like it, sir. I think we're in for another long winter. Let me take your coat, sir. I'll just hang it up here on the peg behind you. Now let's get you comfortable in the chair, sir. I'll just move the fire around ...'

The customer hadn't spoken, but sat in the chair as requested while the barber fussed about and tucked in the gown.

'Now is it just a suggestion, sir? Just a suggestion?'

The man looked at Alfred in the mirror and seemed puzzled at what he meant.

'My old boss used to say that if you can tell someone has had a cut then you've taken too much off. He was never pleased at that, sir.'

The man didn't answer for quite a while as if he was considering the point. Alfred waited patiently, something holding back his normally eager scissor hand.

'No. Not a suggestion ... a statement.'

'A statement, sir?'

'Yes. I've hidden behind this for too long. Can you give me a style that is short and neat? Whatever you think suits my face best.'

A complex character indeed.

'Right you are, sir! A statement it is.'

He set to work and the shop was filled with the *click click* of the scissors, as long strands of black hair fell to the floor.

'I don't believe I've had you in my little shop before, sir. I do get quite a few passers-by, though more in the summer months when there are tourists around.'

'I'm been visiting my parents who live nearby.'

'Oh, it's always nice to see the folks. A special occasion, sir?'

Again the man paused. Alfred carried on, but he noticed that the customer never looked at himself in the mirror. Most men watched intently while he worked, but this one either looked at the sink or at his feet, resting on the wooden step underneath it.

'No. I'm starting a new life.'

'A new life, sir? Exciting times. Going abroad, sir?'

'Cornwall.'

'Ah, Cornwall. A lovely place, sir. I used to have an uncle down there. He was very keen on ballroom dancing was my Uncle George. This was many years ago now. But I remember him telling me once how he had gone to a dance and part way through the evening he decided to ask someone sitting on the other side of the hall for the next number. So, he set off across the floor and ended up standing in front of this woman and her friends. "May I have this dance?" he said to her politely.

'Well, she was a hoity-toity sort and she said in a loud voice, "No you can't. I'm very particular about who I dance with". My uncle — hee hee — wasn't about to be put down like that. Lots of people nearby heard her say it. So he replied in an even louder voice: "I'm not particular at all about who I dance with ... that's why I asked you".

'Hee hee hee. I'm not particular ... hee hee. Oh she had a face like thunder as my uncle walked away to ask someone else. Hee hee hee.'

He had stopped cutting during the middle of the story as he was completely incapable once he started laughing. Then the customer joined in, slowly at first as if the sound was water escaping through a hole in a dam, and every passing moment the pressure made the hole larger so that more could get through, until the entire structure was breaking up and being washed away.

Alfred stood transfixed. He had never seen someone's face so altered by a change in expression. You couldn't say the man had miraculously become handsome, but as he sat in the barber's chair, he was ...

What would Enid say?

... lovingly appealing. That's exactly what she would say. Lovingly appealing. Without really thinking, Alfred said:

'That's the ticket, sir. That's the ticket. Let's give you a neat haircut and let the world see that beautiful smile of yours.'

For the first time the man looked at himself in the mirror and the laughter died within the space of half a heartbeat, while his face froze as if he couldn't quite fathom out the image staring back at him. Slowly, as if he feared a sudden movement would destroy the scene, he put a hand up to his cheek.

It struck Alfred that here was a person who had never before seen their reflection while they were laughing or smiling, perhaps not even in a photograph. Both men were motionless, studying the same image yet viewing it with a totally different understanding.

A single tear ran down the man's cheek, losing its shape when it touched the tip of one of his fingers. After a while, Alfred laid a hand gently on the man's shoulder.

'Well, sir, shall we give you that nice neat haircut?' he said kindly.

Alfred, for once, was stuck for conversation while he worked. No, that wasn't completely true. It wasn't so much that he was lost for words, but rather that he felt anything he said would be wrong, insensitive. Then the task was done and both of them remained quite still for some time at the transformation.

'Thank you,' said the customer.

Alfred removed the gown and when the man stood up he brushed his jacket for him, some of his usual self resurfacing.

'There we are, sir, there we are. A new style to start a new life in Cornwall. Now let me get your coat, sir.'

'What do I owe you?'

Alfred retrieved the coat from the peg. He replied with an answer that, in the whole of his long career, he had never given before.

285

'Nothing, sir. Nothing at all.'

'Nothing? But why?'

The old barber knew why. During sixty years he reckoned he had met every conceivable character, cut every type of hair for every possible occasion, but he had never given a haircut that had meant so much to someone. Alfred knew in his heart that he had just helped a fellow human being in a way he had never done before. He didn't understand everything that had taken place in his little shop that morning, most likely he never would, but he knew that to charge for the job would have destroyed something precious.

'Let's just say, sir, that we're both beginning a new life and this is my gift to you for the start of yours.'

They looked at each other. The young man appeared so different with the mess on his head gone, but the change was more than physical. He held out his hand.

'Thank you ... for everything.'

When Alfred was alone again he stood for a long time, leaning against the barber's chair. He thought about the man, walking into the street with his head erect, as if it was not his hair that had been removed, but some great invisible weight that was no longer dragging him down.

What an extraordinary encounter.

Eventually, he decided to tidy up so fetched his brush. It was rare indeed for there to be such long hairs and he swept them carefully into a pile before pushing the whole lot along the floor and into the walk-in cupboard, adding them to the mound at the back wall. He always found this difficult to gather, but the heap had become too large even for him to ignore so he pulled a bin liner from the roll and opened it. However, he hadn't even scooped one handful when the front door opened.

Busy today.

'Just coming, sir, just coming,' he shouted, laying down the empty bag and walking back into the shop. 'David!'

'Hello, Mr Alfred.'

The two men shook hands warmly.

'David, lad. I've wondered so many times how you were, how you both were.'

'I never imagined I could know such grief. I'm sorry I never came to see you.'

'Oh, don't you worry about that. I knew you would come when the time was right and that was the important thing.'

Alfred had assumed it was simply too painful for him to visit and had decided to leave the couple alone. His trained eye couldn't help noticing the state of David's hair and he wondered if Jessica had been cutting it.

'I hope you're going to let me tidy your hair. I'll do it for free. Goodness, that'll be the second time today!'

'I've got some news to tell you first.'

'What's that, lad?'

'It's Jessica.'

'Jessica?'

'She's pregnant ... and it's twins!'

Alfred put a hand to his mouth, but the cry escaped anyway; delight and despair competing with each other in the sound. It was just over a year since he had cut Ben's hair, while the boy had sat in his bed surrounded by tractors ... the day Enid had punched him in the face ... the day he knew, but refused to acknowledge, that he was about to lose the woman he loved.

He was helpless to prevent the memories of the previous twelve months washing over him in suffocating waves. How he had watched Enid slip so quickly away from him, how the person he cherished most in the world had slapped and punched him, how she had broken his heart along with many thrown objects.

The enormous guilt he had felt when she had gone into the nursing home, not appreciating this was her home for the rest of her life, was like something crushing him physically. He relived the unbearable sadness at deciding never to go back. Tears cascaded down his face at the loss, fear and desperation he had endured. She was gone. It was worse than if she had died because they both continued to suffer. There was no closure to the misery.

David knew nothing of this other tragedy and was greatly moved and puzzled by the reaction to his news. Alfred was crying uncontrollably, one hand still in David's and the other, a fist, pushed fiercely against his mouth in a futile effort to hold back the sobs that racked his thin body.

Never in his adult life had David hugged another man, but the barber had been a friend of his father's, had known him since he was born and had been kind to his son, so he took a step forward and held him, patting his bony shoulder as he wept.

But amongst the tears and anguish that had surfaced so uncontrollably, so unexpectedly, Alfred made a decision. He would return to visit Enid. Once a week until one of them died he would go to the nursing home in search of a flicker of memory or recognition. It was worth the heartache and rejection, because without those visits then he had given up. There would be no hope ... and there was always hope.

Author's Notes

The UK Government defines domestic abuse as:

> *... any incident of threatening behaviour, violence or abuse (psychological, physical, sexual, financial or emotional) between adults who are or have been intimate partners or are family members, regardless of gender or sexuality.*[1]

In 1977 I had the idea of writing a stage play about domestic abuse, where the man was the victim. I don't know where the thought came from. This was an era when you didn't read about such matters, when the plight of women was only just beginning to be understood and when the authorities generally turned a blind eye to 'a domestic'. Someone suggesting that a man could be the victim would probably have been laughed out of sight.

I've still got the letter sent to me in 1984 by the BBC rejecting a script for a television drama I had submitted called *Battered Women: Battered Men*. It wasn't until early in 2011 that I decided to use this storyline in the form of a novel.

Although a work of fiction, *Men Cry Alone* reflects the types of abuse and the situations that occur every day in real life. Like Gordon, many people simply don't realise they are involved in an abusive relationship because being screamed at, ridiculed, put down etc. is what they are familiar with.

Jennifer is drawn so gradually into an abusive relationship with her husband that by the time she realises the horror that is now her life, she barely has the confidence to escape. Dear old Alfred might not consider that he is on the receiving end of domestic abuse, while Tom would indeed have to travel from Scotland to Yorkshire to reach the nearest potential bed in a safe house that accommodates men.

A great deal has been achieved in raising the profile of domestic abuse, but much more needs to be done to support men, women and children. In terms of profile and resources, men today are roughly where women were decades ago. However, the subject remains a highly controversial one and it would take a brave politician to stand up and fly the male flag, although this is starting to happen.

The figures shown in the introduction pages of *Men Cry Alone* are quoted fairly often within the field of domestic abuse. The Home Office British Crime Survey 2010/11[2] (page 87) states that 30 per cent of women and 17 per cent of men reported having experienced domestic abuse since the age of sixteen.

This means that for every three victims of domestic abuse, two will be female and one will be male. But the issues surrounding this subject are desperately complex and the British Crime Survey represents only a snapshot.

According to the charity ManKind Initiative there are 72 bed spaces in UK refuges/safe houses available for male victims of domestic abuse. Of these, 24 spaces are available for hetero-sexual men (although gay men can also use them), 18 are dedicated to gay men and 41 are available to either gender. The charity estimates that there are around 4,000 spaces available to women.

By raising the plight of men and their children, I am in no way trying to attack or undermine the excellent and very necessary work that is carried out to help women and their children, in what are often tragic and terrible circumstances, nor for an instant am I suggesting that any funding should be moved across.

Domestic abuse is a heinous crime and I hope that *Men Cry Alone* may, in a small way, help those faced with an abusive relationship, regardless of their gender, sexuality, age, religion or race.

[1]During 2013, the Government will alter its definition of domestic abuse to include 16 and 17 year olds, plus the phrase 'coercive control' (a systematic pattern of abuse and control).

[2](http://tinyurl.com/7slnnom)

There are many organisations and charities that can provide information and/or advice to people experiencing domestic abuse. In addition, your local police station will be able to put you in touch with the nearest domestic abuse liaison officer. Citizen's Advice can provide useful guidance on the problems that accompany domestic abuse such as housing, benefits, legal advice and child support.

The following list represents only a selection of organisations connected with dementia or domestic abuse.

Help with Dementia

Alzheimer's Society
Tel: 0845 3000336   www.alzheimers.org.uk
Alzheimer Scotland
Tel: 0808 8083000   www.alzscot.org
The Alzheimer Society of Ireland
Tel: 1800 341341   www.alzheimer.ie

Help for Men and Women

National Centre for Domestic Violence
Tel: 0844 8044999   www.ncdv.org.uk
Montgomeryshire Family Crisis Centre (Wales)
Tel: 01686 629114   www.familycrisis.co.uk

Help for Men

ManKind Initiative
Tel: 01823 334244   www.mankind.org.uk
Abused Men In Scotland
Tel: 0808 8000024   www.amis.org.uk
Esteem (Cornwall)
Tel: 01209 202688   www.esteemmen.co.uk
Men's Advice Line
Tel: 0808 8010327   www.mensadviceline.org.uk
Amen (Ireland)
Tel: 0469 023 718   www.amen.ie
Dyn Project (Wales)
Tel: 0808 8010321   www.dynwales.org
Men's Advisory Project (Belfast)
Tel: 028 90241929   www.mapni.co.uk

Help for Women

Refuge
Tel: 0808 2000247   www.refuge.org.uk
Women's Aid
Tel: 0808 2000247   www.womensaid.org.uk
Welsh Women's Aid
Tel: 0808 8010800   www.welshwomensaid.org
Jewish Women's Aid
Tel: 0808 8010500   www.jwa.org.uk
Scottish Women's Aid
Tel: 0800 0271234   www.scottishwomensaid.org.uk
Women's Aid Federation Northern Ireland
Tel: 0800 9171414   www.womensaidni.org

Help for Lesbian, Gay, Bisexual and Trans Community

Broken Rainbow

Tel: 0300 9995428   www.broken-rainbow.org.uk

Help for Perpetrators

Respect

Tel: 0808 8024040   www.respect.uk.net

Respect supports men and women concerned about their own abusive behaviour. (It also runs the Men's Advice Line – details above).